UNFORESEEABLE

Books by Nancy Mehl

Inescapable
Unbreakable
Unforeseeable

UNFORESEEABLE

NANCY MEHL

BETHANY HOUSE PUBLISHERS

a division of Baker Publishing Group
Minneapolis, Minnesota

© 2013 by Nancy Mehl

Published by Bethany House Publishers
11400 Hampshire Avenue South
Bloomington, Minnesota 55438
www.bethanyhouse.com

Bethany House Publishers is a division of
Baker Publishing Group, Grand Rapids, Michigan

Printed in the United States of America

Library of Congress Cataloging-in-Publication Data
Mehl, Nancy.
    Unforeseeable / Nancy Mehl.
        pages cm. — (Road to kingdom ; Book Three)
    Summary: "When Kingdom falls prey to a serial killer, Callie needs to uncover the truth before she becomes the next victim"—Provided by publisher.
        ISBN 978-0-7642-0929-1 (pbk.)
        1. Serial murderers—Fiction. 2. Young women—Fiction. 3. Mennonites—Fiction. 4. Violent crimes—Fiction. 5. Nonviolence—Fiction. 6. Ambivalence—Fiction. 7. Kansas—Fiction. I. Title.
PS3613.E4254U54 2013
813'.6—dc23   2013016379

Scripture references are from the King James Bible unless otherwise indicated.

This is a work of fiction. Names, characters, incidents, and dialogues are products of the author's imagination and are not to be construed as real. Any resemblance to actual events or persons, living or dead, is entirely coincidental.

Cover design by Paul Higdon
Cover photography by Mike Habermann Photography, LLC

Author represented by Benrey Literary, LLC

12   13   14   15   16   17   18   7   6   5   4   3   2   1

To my beloved daughter-in-law, Shaen

A wife of noble character who can find? She is worth far more than rubies. Her husband has full confidence in her and lacks nothing of value. She brings him good, not harm, all the days of her life.

Proverbs 31:10–12 NIV

This was my prayer. You were my answer.

CHAPTER 1

"Murder and meat loaf just don't go together," Lizzie grumbled. "Why did the elders agree to let the new sheriff come here? To my restaurant? No one asked my permission."

"It's absurd to think a serial killer could possibly be hiding out in Kingdom," I replied. "I don't see why the sheriff needs to bother us with this."

Lizzie chopped a large onion with a little too much gusto. "Well, your fiancé is the one who suggested it, Callie. Maybe you need to ask him what's behind it."

I set a tray of dirty dishes on the counter and sighed. "Levi says they're bringing Sheriff Timmons here after his meeting with the elders so they can properly introduce him. After that, he plans to speak to us." After washing my hands, I leaned against the sink and frowned at Lizzie. "Levi says the sheriff feels it's important to warn us about these . . . murders."

"'Levi says. Levi says.'" Lizzie shook her head. "You're so funny. I can't remember the last time I saw anyone so much in love."

I pointed my finger at her. "Besides you and Noah, you mean?"

A quick smile flitted across her face and then disappeared.

"After everything this town has been through, to be honest, the idea of more bad news . . ."

"I know. I feel the same way. Why can't the sheriff meet with just the elders and let them decide what to tell us?"

Lizzie sighed. "Women have been killed, Callie. I guess the sheriff is trying to warn us. To keep us safe." She plopped the onions into a big pot of chili sitting on the stove and pushed a lock of curly black hair out of her eyes. "I still wish they'd picked someplace besides my restaurant. Murder doesn't really stimulate the appetite, does it?"

Lizzie had worked hard to make Cora's Corner Café a spot where families felt comfortable. It had taken Cora Menlo, the original owner, a long time to get Kingdom's Mennonite citizens to accept the restaurant. When she'd opened it, over fifteen years ago, most families were convinced meals should be served at home. But over time, Cora's Café had been received by a majority of our citizens. In fact, it had become a popular meeting place for friends to gather and socialize. I was grateful to work there and even more thankful that Lizzie and I had become good friends. During the past several years, I hadn't had much time for socializing. Papa's illness took up almost all of my time. Since he passed four months ago, I really leaned on my relationship with Lizzie.

"I think Levi chose the restaurant because the topic is . . . well, not one easily discussed in church," I said. "This is the only other place in town big enough to accommodate a crowd."

Lizzie grunted. "He's right, I guess. But I still don't have to like it."

"Levi would never do anything to hurt you, Lizzie."

"I know that. I'm not upset with him. Frankly, I'm still trying to get used to Levi's being our pastor. It feels so strange, Pastor Mendenhall's leaving and Levi being elected to take his place. I used to love to tease him, but now it feels . . . I don't know, sacrilegious or something."

Even though our conversation was a serious one, I couldn't hold back a giggle. "Try being engaged to marry your pastor. That's really confusing."

Lizzie frowned at me. "Does it bother him that a few folks in the church think he's too young for the position?"

I shrugged. "He acts like it doesn't, but you know Levi. It's hard to know what he's really thinking."

Lizzie nodded. "I don't like the way he's changed in the last few months. I mean, he's always had a serious side, but we were always able to tease him out of it. Lately he's been different. Almost glum. I'm worried about him."

"I don't think he's unhappy. He just wants to do a good job."

"Well, he's a little too somber for me. Since accepting the pastorate, he doesn't laugh much. Or joke with Noah the way he used to."

I knew exactly what Lizzie was talking about, but for some reason her words made me feel defensive. Levi should be happy because of our engagement, but what Lizzie said was true. Day by day he seemed to grow more solemn.

"I wish people would leave him alone and let him do his job," I said tersely. "Why does everyone have to have an opinion about everything? No wonder he's changed."

Lizzie grunted. "This is Kingdom, Callie. Folks think poking their nose into other people's business is their right. Their responsibility. It's always been that way. Hopefully, the uneasiness about Levi will fade away after a while."

"I guess there were already some concerns because we had three younger elders on the board."

"The blame for that should be directed toward the older elders who quit. My father, John Lapp, and Elmer Wittenbauer." She shook her head. "Seems ridiculous to worry about good men like Levi, Noah, and Ebbie Miller when the church voted for someone like Elmer Wittenbauer. He's old, but that sure didn't make him the right choice."

I nodded my agreement. Elmer Wittenbauer, who'd stepped down over a dispute with Pastor Mendenhall, didn't have a good reputation in Kingdom. When he was first elected, no one knew about all the problems in his home. But after he began serving as an elder, his laziness toward his family and the mistreatment of his wife and daughter slowly became common knowledge. Before Pastor Mendenhall and the other elders were faced with having him removed, he'd quit, citing health reasons. At least the church had learned an important lesson about being more careful in selecting men for positions of authority.

Lizzie grabbed a large spoon and began stirring the chili. "Levi's one of the wisest men I've ever known. Even if he is only thirty." She stopped and turned toward me. "What about you? Do you ever worry about your age? Twenty-two is pretty young for a pastor's wife."

"I try not to think about it too much, but I do pray I won't let him down."

Even though I tried to sound undaunted, I was very concerned about my age and lack of experience. How could I possibly live up to the job? Besides taking care of a husband, a home, and any future children, I was expected to visit those in our church who were sick, as well as coordinate assistance to families who needed help with food, clothing, and other needs. Along with those duties, several of the women had asked that the ladies' Bible study begin again. It had disbanded after Bethany, Pastor Mendenhall's wife, left town. The idea terrified me. I'd spent a lot of time reading the Bible, but as a new bride, how in the world was I supposed to teach married women in the church about being godly wives? It was ridiculous.

I wanted to confess my fears to Lizzie, but I was afraid. Afraid that she'd see me for the fraud I really was. For the failure I felt like. I'd been in love with Levi for a long time, but I'd never considered that one day he might become the pastor of Kingdom Mennonite Church. Now I had no choice but to try to find a way to live up to the role of a pastor's wife. If I couldn't, I risked losing the only man I wanted to spend the rest of my life with.

"Oh, Callie," Lizzie said. "You'll be wonderful. We all loved Bethany, but this last year she was so restless and unhappy that she didn't do much for the church. You don't have a tough act to follow. Everything will work out."

"I hope you're right. I think everyone's in shock because of Pastor and his family moving away."

"Bethany was convinced that living here was keeping them from fulfilling the Lord's admonition to 'Go ye into all the world, and preach the gospel to every creature.' Then when Pastor was almost killed in the church fire last summer, she put her foot down and insisted they leave. It was hard to argue with her when she truly believed it was wrong for them to stay."

"Do you think she was right?"

Lizzie shrugged. "I have no idea. All I know is that I miss

11

them. Of course, I'm thrilled to have Levi as our pastor," she added quickly, "but Pastor Mendenhall was such a blessing to this town. He tried so hard to move us toward grace and away from judgment."

I knew exactly what she meant, but some church members, including Lizzie's father and John Lapp, seemed to believe that Pastor Mendenhall's stand for grace had led to his downfall. No amount of reasoning would sway them or their companions. In the past year, Matthew Engel's attitudes had softened in many ways, especially toward his daughter, Lizzie, and granddaughter, Charity, but his views about keeping the leaven of the world out of Kingdom remained strong—much to Lizzie's dismay. And John, who had recently lost his wife to cancer, stood with Matthew every step of the way.

"Well, I pray the Mendenhalls are happy in Nebraska," I said, "and I hope Levi will be given the chance to fill pastor's shoes without undue pressure."

Lizzie sighed deeply. "The whole church should support him. He was brave enough to accept the position."

"I hope so too. It would hurt Levi to think his appointment might bring strife." I straightened my apron and adjusted my prayer covering. As usual, several curls had escaped my bun. No matter how hard I tried to attain the sleek look most of the women in Kingdom achieved, my stubborn hair refused to stay in place. I finally gave up.

"I hate that you and Levi had to push back your wedding date," Lizzie said.

I sighed. "I understand why it was necessary, but I hope we don't have to wait much longer. We've been engaged for three months now and moved the wedding twice."

"What's the new date?"

"We haven't picked a date, but we're planning for March. Levi feels things should be going more smoothly by then."

Lizzie grunted. "Two more months. I know you're getting impatient."

"I'm trying not to be, but it's hard."

She nodded and turned her attention back to her chili.

I grabbed two clean coffee carafes and carried them over to one of the new electric coffee makers Lizzie had purchased for the restaurant. Now, instead of trying to brew coffee on the stove in large tin coffeepots, we just filled these huge metal containers with water and coffee grounds, flipped a switch, and let them sizzle and pop until the red lights came on, telling us the coffee was brewed and ready to drink. At first the chrome monsters intimidated me, but now I found the convenience wonderful—even though I still felt a little guilty about using electricity.

As I prepared to fill the carafes, I noticed that the red light was lit on only one of the coffee makers. Putting my hand against the other one, I was dismayed to find it was still cold. I checked the plug and jiggled it, but nothing happened.

"This pot's not working," I told Lizzie.

"Oh, Callie," she said, "I forgot to tell you about that receptacle. It's not functioning. You'll have to move the pot over here." She pointed to an empty receptacle near the dishwasher. "Bud Gruber will be back tomorrow to fix it."

I unplugged the heavy container and carried it to the spot Lizzie indicated. "But he was just here this morning," I said. "Why didn't he fix it then?"

"He needed some part he didn't have with him." She shook her head. "He's been working really hard to put in our additional receptacles and help us switch over from our generator

13

to electricity. I feel guilty allowing him to give us so much of his time for the pittance he charges."

"Isn't he the same man who helped Cora get the restaurant up and running when it first opened?"

Lizzie nodded. "Yes. And don't think he didn't catch some flak from the elders back then."

"I'm surprised he was willing to help us again."

"Well, Cora said he was the only one she trusted to get everything up and running. I felt bad about calling him so soon after his wife died, but according to Cora, having something to do is just what he needs."

I laughed. "You certainly have been filling that requirement. He's starting to become a fixture around here."

The addition of electricity to our town was met with joy by some residents and with suspicion by others. At first, those wanting service had to ask for approval from the elders. Some of our downtown businesses received permission, along with a lot of our farmers. But after a while, spurred on by Levi and most of our younger elders, the church lifted its ban. Everyone had to decide for themselves if electricity was something they really needed. Interestingly enough, most folks concluded they liked life the way it was and didn't want to alter their plain existence. Most of us lived in Kingdom because we loved simplicity, so change wasn't always looked upon as progress. A few people, like Matthew, were convinced that the addition of "evil" things like electricity would ruin the soul of our town. In truth, there wasn't much of a difference.

"Well, this coffee maker is full," I said. "The other one should be ready in plenty of time. I'll make the rounds again, but to be honest, most folks aren't ordering much. Except pie, of course. I'm glad you made extra."

Lizzie shrugged. "It's two o'clock. People in Kingdom like to eat their meals at the proper time. They won't start ordering supper until at least five or five-thirty."

I grinned. "But pie is acceptable anytime?"

She laughed. "You've got that right."

I headed out into the crowded dining room. The usual cheery atmosphere was noticeably subdued. I loved the restaurant with its gleaming oak floors, chrome tables, and wooden booths. Oak paneling halfway up the walls turned into red-and-white-checked wallpaper, although not much of the wallpaper was actually visible. Quilts, painted plates, and a few rare pictures from the early days of Kingdom covered almost every available space. A hearty fire crackled in the large brick fireplace, adding an additional impression of coziness. Usually I felt safe and secure inside the inviting room, but today there was a chill that even a roaring fire couldn't quench. Death hung in the air, and though I tried to ignore uneasy feelings of dread, they refused to be banished.

After warming up everyone's coffee and refilling a few water glasses, I took orders for five more pieces of Lizzie's Dutch apple pie. I'd just delivered the last one when I noticed three buggies pull up in front of the restaurant, one right after the other. Behind them, a Washington County sheriff's car drove up slowly and parked a few spots away. I watched as the new sheriff got out. The sudden silence in the dining room was an indication I wasn't the only person interested in what was happening outside.

I almost gasped when I got a clear look at the sheriff. He looked young. Really young. As he and the elders entered the restaurant, it got so quiet I could almost hear people breathing. The men paused to wipe snow off their shoes and boots.

We had almost three inches on the ground, and it had started snowing again early this morning. It was still coming down outside, and I wondered when we'd get a break. I loved the snow, but it made life harder on those who relied solely on a horse and buggy to get around.

I hurried to the kitchen to let Lizzie know the elders and the sheriff had arrived. She followed me back to the dining room. As we entered, Levi had just begun to address the crowd. His eyes sought mine, and he gave me a shy smile. I felt a sudden deep rush of emotion. Levi looked a lot like his younger brother Noah, but was a little taller. In the summer his brown hair became streaked with blond. In winter, however, his hair darkened and was almost exactly the same shade as Noah's. Even though the brothers were similar in appearance, they were very different in personality. Noah was gregarious and friendly, but Levi was more quiet and introspective. Levi had a deep and abiding faith and loved to encourage people to put their trust in God, no matter what the circumstance. Sometimes he would chide me for not trusting enough. I had to admit that my faith needed encouragement. Caring for my father had weakened me physically, emotionally, and spiritually. Levi firmly believed that God would meet every need, answer every prayer, and touch every broken place. In truth, his support and prayers lifted my spirits, and his love gave me hope for the future. Something I'd misplaced during Papa's illness.

Levi's convictions usually kept him upbeat and calm, so the recent transformation in his demeanor worried me, just as it did Lizzie. I not only loved Levi with every fiber of my being, but I respected him more than anyone I'd ever known. If he was struggling, I wanted to help. But so far he wouldn't admit that anything was wrong. Down deep inside me dwelt a nagging fear that he was sorry he'd asked me to marry him. His proposal had been so heartfelt and romantic. Yet now, sometimes, he seemed to be so far away. Could his feelings have changed?

"May I have your attention?" Levi said, although it wasn't necessary, since all eyes were already glued on him. "This is our new sheriff, Brodie Timmons. He has something important to say to you."

Levi stepped back and left the sheriff standing alone. Sheriff Timmons took off his hat and smiled at us. He had short dark hair, light-blue eyes, and deep dimples that made him look even younger than my first impression.

"First of all, folks, I'm glad to meet you. I understand you didn't have a very good relationship with the previous sheriff. I'm real sorry about that, and I want you to know that I'm going to work hard to make things better."

I don't know if he expected his words to make an impact on the conservative Mennonite crowd that stared back at him, but the response wasn't encouraging. We'd been through a lot with his predecessor—a man who disliked us because of our choice to live a simple, set-apart lifestyle. It would take some time for Timmons to build a bridge of trust with the citizens of Kingdom. For the most part, even before our problems with the previous sheriff, we tended to solve our own troubles. Calling on help from the world was certainly a last resort.

Sheriff Timmons blinked several times and took another run at it. "I have a strong faith background too, so I have a lot of respect for your community. Anything you need, anything at all, just ask."

He cleared his throat, and for the first time, his dimples disappeared. "We have a very serious situation right now in our area, and I felt you should know about it. In the past few months, three women have lost their lives due to what we believe is one particular suspect. The Kansas Bureau of Investigation is heavily involved in searching for this killer, and our department has been pulled into the case. The bureau believes the man who committed these murders was involved in similar crimes twenty years ago—also in Washington County." He folded his arms across his chest, still holding his hat, and frowned at us. "It's highly unusual for a suspect to stop killing for twenty years and then take it up again, but it's been known to happen. Take BTK in Wichita."

Levi cleared his throat, and Sheriff Timmons looked at him.

"I'm sorry to interrupt, Sheriff, but I don't know what a BTK is."

Timmons face went slack in surprise. His eyes traveled around the room. "You folks don't know about BTK?"

"I know who he is," Lizzie said. "He murdered several women but then disappeared. After many years he came back and killed again. The police finally caught him." She shook her head. "I lived in Kansas City for several years, but most of these people have no idea what's going on in the world, Sheriff. You'll have to explain things a little more carefully in Kingdom."

"Sorry," Timmons said sheepishly. "I forget that you folks don't get much news from the outside. I apologize." He cleared his throat again, a sign he was nervous. "I brought up that particular case because it helps us to profile our guy a little better. We're looking for someone who's been away and recently returned to the area. Or someone who's been here the whole time but may have had a change in his life. Something unusual happened that's set him off. He may act differently than he used to. Although I doubt seriously he comes from Kingdom, I would appreciate it if you folks would keep your eyes and ears open. If you think of anyone who makes you feel uncomfortable . . . someone who might fit the pattern I'm suggesting, would you please contact me? We'll keep your information confidential. I know you'd hate to cast aspersions toward a friend or neighbor and turn out to be wrong."

He gazed down at his shoes for a moment as if gathering his thoughts. "One other thing. Since the original killings happened in another part of the county, it's possible our perpetrator might be fairly new to the area, although we can't be sure of that. Maybe he just chose another place to kill." He took a deep breath, raised his head, and gazed around at the silent crowd. "Your elders have assured me that your women don't go out alone at night, and that's good. Please don't change that under any circumstances. It's especially important now. It would also be best if no woman wandered around alone at any time—even during the day. And it's especially important they don't leave town without an escort."

I glanced over at Hope. She loved driving her buggy to nearby Washington for supplies, but since it had been an especially cold January, I suspected it wouldn't bother her to forgo those trips for now. As I figured, she didn't seem the least bit bothered by the pronouncement.

Sheriff Timmons' eyes swept the room. "Are there any questions?"

After several moments of silence, Jonathon Wiese, one of

the young single men who lived in Kingdom, raised his hand. The sheriff nodded at him.

"So we're looking for someone who used to live here and moved away, or someone new, or someone who's been here the whole time?" He shook his head. "Um, doesn't that pretty much describe everyone?"

The sheriff colored. "I know it sounds like that. I guess the most important thing is that all of you remain especially vigilant. If someone you know is acting . . . odd, let us know. If you see a stranger hanging around, it's particularly important that you notify us right away."

"There aren't any strangers in Kingdom, Sheriff," Jonathon said. "We all know each other."

Timmons nodded. "That should actually help to keep you safe. Unless . . ."

"Unless the murderer lives here?" Noah said. "I can assure you that there aren't any serial killers in Kingdom, Sheriff."

A small spate of nervous laughter filtered through the room. Although the topic was certainly serious, I also found the notion rather comical—and impossible.

"I heard these recent killings were all north of us, Sheriff," Jonathon said, frowning. "Is there any reason you think Kingdom residents could be in danger?"

He shook his head. "Nothing specific, but Washington is a small county. Anything that happens in one part of the county affects all of us. Besides, it's better to be safe than sorry."

Luke Pressley, a local farmer, raised his hand. "Sheriff, I have lived here all my life, and I do not remember any murders twenty years ago."

"I'm glad you brought that up. Although the deaths were reported, they weren't tied to a serial killer until about two years back. In fact, in two of the cases, there was a suspect, but not enough evidence to charge him. All of the cases went cold. Stayed unsolved. But they were finally linked through state-of-the-art investigative techniques, including DNA tests."

Luke frowned at him. "DNA? I do not know the term."

The sheriff flushed again. "Of course you don't. Sorry. DNA is something found in the nucleolus of a human cell. It's almost like fingerprints, but even more accurate. By looking at DNA, we can tell who might have touched a victim before they died. If the same DNA is discovered at more than one crime scene, we're able to conclude that one specific person is tied to all the murders. That's what happened in this case. Unfortunately, we haven't been able to link the DNA to any known suspect."

Although no one said anything, I was sure most of us were still confused. Lizzie nodded as if she understood, but she'd been exposed to many things when she lived in Kansas City.

I was certain there were more details that could be shared about the murders, but further questions wouldn't be asked in a mixed group like this one. It would be inappropriate. After a few more moments of silence, Levi stepped up next to the sheriff.

"I'm not sure how many of you have heard, but Roger Carson, Mary Yoder's husband, is working for the sheriff's department now." He caught Timmons's eye. "If some of our people feel more comfortable talking to Roger, would that be all right with you?"

The sheriff nodded. "Roger completed his training a couple of weeks ago and is officially my deputy. Anyone who would rather contact him is welcome to do so." He paused for a moment and slowly looked around the room. "I do hope you'll give me a chance though. It may seem that law enforcement isn't on your side, but it's not true."

"I encourage you to take Sheriff Timmons at his word," Levi said. "He's a good man. I don't believe we have anything to worry about under his watch." He waited a moment, studying the crowd while allowing his words to sink in. "If there are no further questions, we'll let the sheriff go on his way. I hope you will all be vigilant and contact him if you see or hear anything that concerns you. And, of course, if anyone wants to talk to me or one of the elders, that's fine too. We'll pass your information along. The most important thing is that you don't dismiss information that could be useful. Lives may be at stake."

With that, the meeting was over. Sheriff Timmons spoke briefly to Levi and then took off. As soon as the door closed behind him, conversation broke out all over the room. It was clear Kingdom residents had a lot to say about the sheriff's visit. Several people rushed up to the elders who stood together near the front door. One of the first was John Lapp, and he didn't look happy. I wondered what kind of trouble he was trying to stir up. After a few minutes, Levi left them and came over to me.

"What do you think?" he asked quietly.

"I think the sheriff's visit will be the number-one topic in town for quite some time."

He nodded. "I suspect you're right. I have to admit that at first I was against his coming here. I felt it would be best if he brought his information to me and the elders and allowed us to inform the community."

I frowned at him. "I've been thinking the same thing. Subjects like this make me very uncomfortable."

His blue eyes locked on mine. "Kingdom is a special place, Callie. I don't want to see us lose our innocence either, but I truly believe Brodie Timmons has our best interests at heart. I know he's an outsider, but he's a good man. I trust him."

I shrugged. "I hope you're right." I shivered, even though the room was warm. "At least I'm certain there aren't any serial killers living in Kingdom. And a stranger would never be able to make his way into town without being spotted." As soon as I said the words, I remembered that a stranger *had* made his way into Kingdom last summer. The consequences from that situation had almost ended in tragedy.

Levi was quiet, and I wondered if he was thinking the same thing. He turned away from me and looked out at the people gathered together in the dining room. His parishioners. His friends. I knew he felt protective of them.

I put my arm through his. "I hate that something so evil has come this close to us. It makes me feel vulnerable."

"Maybe it's just wedding nerves," he said with a smile. "You're not getting cold feet, are you?"

I laughed in spite of the seriousness of our previous conversation. "Nothing could stop me from marrying you." I looked up at him. "How about you?"

He shook his head and sighed. "I may be unsure about a lot of things, but marrying you isn't one of them." He let go of my arm. "We'll talk more about this later. Right now, I've got to get back to the church. I'll return for supper, but I might be a little late."

"Okay." I wanted to kiss him good-bye, but that's something a Mennonite pastor doesn't usually do in public.

I watched as he made his way across the room. Several people stopped him to talk. When he finally got to the door he looked back at me one last time. For some reason, I felt like running after him, begging him not to leave. Something my father used to say echoed in my mind. *"The devil is stirrin', Callie. Can you feel it?"*

I never understood what he meant until that very moment.

CHAPTER/2

After Levi left I went back in the kitchen, trying to shake the strange feeling that had come over me. I was probably just reacting to the sheriff's visit, and I tried to tell myself that the topic was upsetting enough to distress anyone. I was in the kitchen only a few seconds before Lizzie and Noah walked in. Noah looked disturbed.

"So what do you think of the new sheriff?" I asked him.

He shook his head and slumped down into a chair by a small table Lizzie kept in the kitchen for the nights her daughter, Charity, ate dinner at the restaurant.

"I like him, I really do. But this whole serial-killer thing chaps my hide. In the past year we've had two murders and two attempted murders." He looked at Lizzie. "Our church was burned to the ground, and the previous sheriff shot his son not far from where we're sitting. Now we're on the lookout for a serial killer. What in the world is going on? As an elder, I have to wonder if the church leadership is failing in its duty to keep this town safe. I've tried to talk to Levi about it, but you know my brother. He just keeps telling me to 'have faith.'"

Lizzie went over and stood behind her husband, putting

her hands on his shoulders. "I know it sounds like we're no better off than anyone else, but it's not true. The difference between Kingdom and Kansas City is . . ." She paused for a moment. "It . . . it's hard to describe. But here I feel the love of God protecting us, watching over us. Outside of Kingdom, there were so many voices, so much violence, and so much fear. It was hard to feel God anywhere and almost impossible to hear His Spirit speak to my heart. I think Levi's right. We just need to trust God. Believe He's watching over us." She shook her head slowly. "Kingdom may not be impenetrable, but it is definitely a refuge. A place of peace and love." She leaned over and kissed Noah on the head. "And love, my dearest husband, is stronger than any evil the world sends our way. Even the devil himself can't stand in its presence."

Noah reached up and grabbed her hand. Then he pulled her around and onto his lap. Lizzie giggled like a schoolgirl.

"That's nice," I said with a grin. "What a great example for an elder of Kingdom Mennonite Church to set in front of one of his parishioners."

"You're worried about this?" he said. "Just wait." With that, he kissed Lizzie right on the lips.

I couldn't help but laugh. "You two are incorrigible."

Lizzie pushed herself away from Noah and stood up. "You're a mess, Noah Housler. I'm going to tell your brother."

He put his hands up in mock surrender. "Go ahead. He'll think it's funny."

"I'm not so sure about that," Lizzie said. "He hasn't been much fun lately."

Noah sat up straighter. "Well, you're right about that." He rubbed his stubbly chin, a concession to the Mennonite tradition of growing a beard after marriage. Lizzie's abhorrence of full beards had thrust Noah into an uncomfortable place between Mennonite tradition and the favor of his wife. Thankfully, his compromise seemed to satisfy all concerned parties. "I think all the unpleasant incidents that have happened in this town are weighing heavily on him. I have to wonder if he's experiencing a crisis of faith. Of course, he won't talk about it." Noah shrugged. "The Bible talks about how evil the world will become before the Lord returns. That darkness may be reaching past the borders of Kingdom, and it may be impossible to stop. Even for someone like Levi."

I didn't respond. Noah's words disturbed me. Just a few months earlier, churches and people of faith had been attacked by a group of angry young men bent on causing destruction. We'd lost one of our dearest citizens to their wrath. Now, once again, we would have to face the reality of a fallen world trying to breach our boundaries. The realization stoked a sensation of underlying panic that had been stirring up my emotions for almost a month. I couldn't understand it, nor could I banish it. It upset me that I couldn't name the source of my alarm and deal with it. I wanted to talk to Levi about it, but with everything else going on in his life right now, I didn't want to add to his burdens.

Lizzie turned down the fire on the chili and then leaned against the counter. "Well, I still say we're better off here than anywhere else. I have a child to consider, and I can't think of a better place to raise her than in Kingdom."

Noah rubbed an invisible spot on the table with his finger. "I lived in the world for two years, and I couldn't wait to come home. But it wasn't because I felt safer here. I just felt . . . called. I love farming, and I love this town." His forehead wrinkled in thought. "But I worry sometimes that by being so isolated we're not fulfilling Christ's commission to reach the world."

"That's what Bethany believed," I said.

Lizzie sighed. "I totally understood why she felt that way, but sometimes the *world* we're called to is right where we are." She waved her hand around the room. "We have a town of almost three hundred souls to minister to. That's enough world for me."

"Yes, but almost all of them already know God," Noah said. "That's why they're here."

"Jesus also admonished us to feed His sheep, Noah. I just took it literally."

Noah and I burst out laughing.

"And she does too," Noah said. "There will never be an empty stomach in Kingdom, thanks to my wife."

"You're right about that," Lizzie said. "This is exactly where I belong. Maybe Bethany felt the need to leave, but not me."

"I understand," Noah said. "I'm perfectly content here too. But at the same time, not everyone is called to live in Kingdom." He smiled at me. "I think the key is to find the place God wants you to be. He puts the people in your life He wants you to touch, and He leads you to your point of blessing."

"What if one day Charity feels called to leave?" I asked. "Then what?"

"Then she'll have to leave," Noah said matter-of-factly. "What God wants must come first if we're ever to fulfill our destiny. Anyway, that's what I believe."

Lizzie grunted. "Since Charity's only eight, I don't think I'll make plans to pack her up and send her out anytime soon, if you don't mind."

"Well, we weren't suggesting she was going to grab her

bags and head out tomorrow," Noah said, grinning. "She should wait until she's at least ten."

Lizzie picked up a nearby dish towel and snapped him on the leg with it.

"Ouch," he yelled. "I'm being abused. Call the sheriff."

I laughed again, rather embarrassed to be having so much fun right after the sheriff's serious announcement.

"Brodie Timmons won't help you," Lizzie teased. "He'd be on my side."

"I think she's got you there, Noah," I said.

"Changing the subject for a moment," Lizzie said to her husband when he settled down, "can you tell us more about what the sheriff said in your private meeting? I felt like we weren't getting the whole story. Were the women . . . defiled?"

I felt myself blush. Sex wasn't really talked about much in our community, although Lizzie had said more than once it should be. She'd gotten pregnant as a teenager, partially because she'd been unaware of the consequences of her actions. She'd had a long talk with me after Levi and I became engaged. My father had never spoken to me about such things, and since my mother was gone, I'd had no one to fill me in on what Lizzie referred to as "the facts of life." Our conversation was a real eye-opener. Although I'd figured out a lot on my own, having spent many years around farm animals, there were a few details I wasn't aware of. Thinking about it now made my ears burn. Even though it had been a rather embarrassing conversation, I was very grateful Lizzie cared enough to tell me what I needed to know before my wedding night.

Noah shook his head. "No. They weren't harmed in that way. When they were found, they'd been strangled, their hands folded on their chests, and their bodies wrapped in plastic.

Except for the marks on their necks, there were no other injuries." He sighed. "Brodie said the KBI is stumped."

I frowned at him. "But I thought Sheriff Timmons said they'd found D . . . DN . . ."

"DNA," Noah said. "Yes, they did. Most of it came from the victims' necks when he strangled them. They also have some skin and hair samples that were probably left behind when the women fought for their lives."

I felt my stomach turn over. "Oh my."

"Are you okay?" Lizzie asked, looking at me with concern. "You just turned really pale."

I nodded, trying to compose myself. "Yes, but that's so . . . so—"

"Shocking?" Noah said. "Yes, it is. Here's something really strange. Brodie said that wrapping the women in plastic shows the killer had some remorse for what he was doing. In some strange way he was trying to care for the women." He stared at me. "I know. It doesn't make any sense. It's demonic, Callie. Demons seek to kill, steal, and destroy. They're agents of destruction. You can't figure them out."

"But the man must have some reason to kill. What is it?"

"I asked Brodie that same question. He said many times they never find a motive. It could be a deep-seated hatred for all women. Or something happened to him when he was young. But understanding the motive isn't always possible." He shook his head. "Our new sheriff repeated the same thing I just told you—that the devil doesn't make sense."

Lizzie's eyebrows arched. "He said that? Wow, that's a switch. A sheriff who knows God."

Noah nodded. "I think he's going to be an asset to Kingdom. We could actually end up being friends."

"That would certainly be a change over the previous sheriff," Lizzie said.

"By the way," Noah said, "don't repeat that information about the plastic. The KBI is trying to keep some information quiet."

"Well, I won't be telling anyone," I said. "It's not something I want to talk about anyway."

"Thanks," Noah said. "I probably shouldn't have told you and Lizzie, but I know you can keep a secret. And I'm fairly sure neither one of you is a serial killer."

"Thanks, honey," Lizzie said wryly. "That's the nicest thing you ever said to me."

Noah laughed.

I straightened my apron. "Well, I think I'm ready to concentrate on the dinner crowd. No more serial killers or demons for me for a while."

Lizzie grunted. "I agree. The chili's simmering, and I've got to start getting the steaks ready. Why don't you go out and see if we have any real customers or if everyone went home after the meeting?"

I nodded and pushed open the kitchen door. The people who had remained in the restaurant were deep in conversation and didn't seem the least bit interested in ordering food. After checking with everyone, I went back into the kitchen to help Lizzie prepare for supper. Noah offered to keep an eye on the dining room since we weren't busy. Lizzie and I spent the next hour preparing that night's menu items. Neither one of us brought up the murders again. After a while, I started to feel almost normal again. Serial killers and Kingdom didn't go together, of that much I was certain.

A little after four, I was bringing a carafe of coffee out to the dining room when Ruby, Elmer and Dorcas Wittenbauer's niece, walked in the front door. Dorcas's sister in Arkansas had passed away several months earlier, and Ruby's father had abandoned her. Lizzie and I worried that Ruby would be mistreated like Sophie, the Wittenbauers' daughter who had fled Kingdom last summer, had been. Fortunately, Leah, who leads our small Kingdom school, took Ruby under her wing, promising to keep a close eye on her. And Lizzie's daughter, Charity, had befriended the girl as well. Even though Charity was much younger, the girls seemed to have bonded like sisters. As their pastor, Levi checked in regularly with the Wittenbauers, making certain they knew the church would not take kindly to any abuse. I especially felt drawn to the young girl, trying to reach out to her when I helped Leah at the school. But so far, Ruby wasn't responding much to anyone except Charity.

Ruby stood near the door, looking around the room, her expression full of anxiety. I put the carafe on a nearby table and went over to her.

"If you're looking for Charity, she's not here," I said gently. "She goes to her grandparents' house after school on Wednesdays."

Ruby stared back at me. Her large green eyes held a shadow of fear that tore at my heart. No child should be so afraid. I felt protective of her, and my anger at the Wittenbauers began to bubble.

"I know she's not here," Ruby said softly. "But Uncle Elmer was supposed to pick me up after school, and he never showed up. I tried to wait, but it got too cold."

"Ruby, where's your coat?" I noticed for the first time that she was wearing just a thin dress and an apron. Both too large for her. Probably Sophie's old clothes. I could see her tremble.

"Aunt Dorcas said I didn't need one today."

"Take my hand, Ruby," I said, trying to control my rage. "Let's get you warmed up. How about some hot chocolate and a piece of pie?" She was so thin I wondered if the Wittenbauers bothered to feed her at all. By the time we reached the kitchen, I was beyond furious.

"Oh, my goodness," Lizzie said when she saw me. "What's wrong?"

I took a deep, shaky breath, trying to calm myself. The last thing I wanted to do was upset the child more than she was. "Elmer forgot to pick Ruby up from school. She's been waiting outside all this time—without a coat. I thought maybe a cup of hot chocolate and a piece of pie would help to warm her up."

Lizzie pulled out a chair from the small table. "Absolutely. You have a seat here, Ruby."

The child looked back and forth between us, as if unsure of our motives.

"It's okay, Ruby," I said softly. "You like pie, don't you?"

She nodded and sat down at the table. I was trying desperately not to cry. It wouldn't help her to see me upset, but at that moment, Mennonite or not, I wanted to thrash Elmer and Dorcas Wittenbauer to within an inch of their lives.

Lizzie pulled out a large pan and started the hot chocolate. I opened the refrigerator door. "What kind of pie do you like?" I asked Ruby.

At first I wasn't sure she was going to answer, but finally she said, "Do you have chocolate?" Her voice was so soft, I almost didn't hear her.

I smiled. "There just happens to be an entire chocolate cream pie in here. How about—"

Before I could finish, the door to the kitchen swung open and a red-faced Elmer Wittenbauer stomped inside, trailing melting snow behind him.

"What are you doin' hidin' in here, girl?" he said loudly when he spotted Ruby. "I been lookin' all over for you. You get outta here and in the buggy. Now."

Lizzie put down the spoon she was stirring the chocolate with and started to say something. But before she had a chance, the anger inside me boiled over. I slammed the door to the refrigerator and went over to Elmer, grabbing his arm.

"I'd like to speak to you, Brother Wittenbauer," I said between clenched teeth. "Will you please step outside a moment?" Before he had a chance to argue, I pulled him out the door and into the small hall that led to the dining room. No small feat, since he was huge, and I didn't even tip the scales at one hundred pounds.

"How dare you manhandle me," he sputtered. "I will make sure your ungodly behavior is reported to the elders. If you think—"

"Now you listen to me, Elmer Wittenbauer," I said, trying to keep my voice low enough so as not to garner attention from our customers, "you are not going to haul that girl out of here right now. She's having pie and hot chocolate. What you *will* do is sit down out here until she's ready to go."

Elmer pulled his fat arm out of my grasp. "Look here, little girl, you ain't gonna tell me nothin'. I'll take what's mine now and ain't no one gonna stop me. 'Specially you. Yes sir, the elders is gonna get an earful." His greasy smile sent a shiver running through me. "Your boyfriend won't be marryin' you if he wants to stay pastor."

He started to move toward the kitchen door, but I stepped

in front of him. My body shook so hard I felt as if I might fall down.

"You're not going to say anything to anybody," I choked out. "Because if you do, I'll make sure the elders know about the way you've been treating that child." I stuck my small face up as close to his round one as I could. His expression told me I'd hit my mark. "I'm not stupid, Elmer. This is your last chance. If I see even one sign that you've been mistreating Ruby, I'm going to make sure you lose any help the church is giving you and Dorcas. And one more thing"—I stuck my finger just inches from his nose—"I'm going to be watching you. Closely. If that child isn't picked up on time from school, if I see her out in cold weather without a coat, or if I see one thing that concerns me, *you* will be hauled before Levi and the elders for discipline. And don't think for one moment I can't make that happen. They're going to believe me a lot sooner than they'll trust a word that comes out of your mouth." I glared at him. Whatever he saw in my face made the blood drain from his. "Do you totally and completely understand me?"

Elmer didn't say anything, just nodded.

"You go sit down at a table and be quiet. Ruby will come out when she's good and ready. Then you'll take her home, and things will be different. Or else."

I whirled around and ran right into Lizzie, who stood in the doorway, her eyes wide and her mouth hanging open. She stared at Elmer, who seemed transfixed by what had just happened. She quickly pulled the door closed behind her.

"You heard Callie," Lizzie said firmly. "Now get going."

Elmer scampered off like his britches were on fire. Lizzie grabbed me by the shoulders and shook me a couple of times. "Callie!" The expression on her face frightened me.

35

I twisted away from her. "I'm okay. Let me go." My voice trembled like an old woman's, and I felt faint. Lizzie put her arm around my shoulders. This time I didn't pull away.

"Are you okay?" she asked quietly. "I-I've never seen you act like that before." She gazed into my eyes. "You don't look well. I think you need to sit down."

"Wait a minute," I said. "I can't go in there right now. I'm too upset." I was surprised to feel tears running down my cheeks. "I . . . I don't know what came over me."

Lizzie hugged me. "I think I do, but we'll talk about it later. When you're not so upset." She took my chin in her hand. "You put the fear of God into old Elmer. He'll think twice about how he treats Ruby from now on."

I wasn't proud of how I'd acted, but I felt confident my tirade would help the child. Abusing Ruby could cause the Wittenbauers serious trouble with the church. They were dependent on the congregation's assistance. Financial help had increased since Ruby had come to live with them. If the church decided to discipline them, all that free food and monetary aid would disappear. For Elmer and Dorcas anyway. They might actually have to work, and that was something they dreaded more than anything else. I hoped Lizzie was right, that they would change their ways, but I wasn't confident that would happen. More than anything, I wanted to see Ruby in a home where she would be loved and cherished.

I wiped my face with my apron. "I'm all right now, Lizzie. Thank you." I smiled at her. "I have an extra cloak upstairs in my closet that I think would fit Ruby. Will you watch her while I fetch it?"

Lizzie nodded. "Go get it. But for pity's sake, please don't say anything else to Elmer for a while. I thought he was going to have a heart attack right here in the restaurant."

Even though I was appalled by my loss of control, the look on Lizzie's face made me giggle. Lizzie joined in and we cackled like two old hens.

"I have no idea what I'm laughing about," I said, once I regained my composure. "That was hardly ladylike behavior. My father would have been horrified by that ungracious display of temper."

Lizzie looked at me oddly. "Well, maybe he would have been, Callie, but I'm not. I'm proud of you. You stood up to Elmer, and you did it for a child who couldn't defend herself." She leaned over and kissed my cheek. "I'm very, very proud of you," she said again.

My face grew warm with embarrassment, but down deep inside, I was tickled by Lizzie's praise.

"I-I'd better get going."

"Okay. I'll get some food inside Ruby before we send her out in the cold again. I think a nice bowl of chili would help. Looking at Elmer and Dorcas, I can see where most of the food the church gives them is going. Ruby certainly isn't getting enough." Lizzie got a look on her face I'd seen before. "I know she's being fed at school because I take food over there every day. Maybe I can come up with a way to do a little more."

I turned to go, a smile on my face. Ruby wouldn't need to worry about food from this day forward. Lizzie would see to that.

As I made my way into the dining room, I noticed Elmer sitting at a table, talking to John Lapp. When Elmer saw me, his face went slack and he clamped his mouth shut. John looked my way, a scowl on his thin face. I ignored them both and hurried up the stairs. Going through my closet, I found both my cloaks. I took out the nicest one and grabbed a couple of warm dresses as well. For once, being small was helpful, although realizing I was the same size as a fourteen-year-old girl didn't make me feel very mature. I'd also noticed that Ruby's shoes were coming apart and not appropriate for winter. I took a pair of black lace-up boots from my closet and added them to the other clothes.

The entire time, my body continued to tremble, as if it had a mind of its own. I'd never lost my temper before the way I'd just done with Elmer. I had concerns about Ruby, but so did Lizzie, and she hadn't seen fit to verbally assault anyone.

After praying for God's forgiveness and asking for His help, I tried to compose myself by breathing deeply and repeating the Scripture verse about the peace of God that passes understanding. Little by little, I felt the calming influence of God's Spirit wash through me.

Once I was ready, I headed downstairs. I could only hope that news of my insolence wouldn't get back to Levi. What would he think? How could I possibly be the wife of a pastor if I acted so unpleasantly toward a member of our church?

When I reached the dining room, I refused to look at Elmer and Brother Lapp, keeping my eyes trained straight ahead. In the kitchen I found Noah, Lizzie, and Ruby all together. Lizzie stood at the stove, and Noah sat at the table with Ruby, who welcomed me with a big smile on her face.

"This is the best chili I ever tasted," she said. "Mama used to make chili, but it wasn't nearly this good."

"Lizzie's a great cook," I said. "She makes lots of wonderful things."

Ruby gazed around the kitchen as if it were the most wonderful place she'd ever seen. "I wish I could cook. Good food makes people so . . . happy."

Lizzie cleared her throat, obviously moved by Ruby's statement. "We've been talking," she said, looking over at me, "and Ruby will be coming here after school from now on. Elmer will pick her up after supper. She and Charity can work on their homework together until it's time to eat."

"Except on Wednesdays," Ruby said, "'cause Charity goes to her grandparents' house. Then I get to study with you."

"I didn't think you'd mind if I volunteered you," Lizzie said with a smile. "Noah and I will take care of the dining room until five. It's not very busy in the afternoons anyway."

"That sounds great," I said hesitantly, "but does Brother Wittenbauer know he's picking Ruby up here in the evenings?"

Noah grinned. "He's been informed. Oddly enough, he didn't seem to have any objections."

"Good." I took a plastic sack out of the cupboard. "Ruby, here are some clothes I don't need. You take these home. But for now, let's go ahead and change your shoes. These are the right kind for snow. Is that all right?"

Ruby nodded. "My feet get so cold." She frowned as I slipped off her tattered old shoes. "My socks have holes in them."

"Those socks have more holes than material," Lizzie said, watching from the stove. "Noah, you go downstairs and get some socks out of the dryer. Grab about three pairs." She smiled at Ruby. "My socks will be a little big for you, but at least they don't have holes."

Noah jumped up from the table and hurried down the stairs.

Ruby's eyes shone with tears. "Thank you. You're being so nice to me."

"People should be nice to you, Ruby," I said as I peeled the ragged socks off her feet. "If they're not, you must come and tell us." I cast a quick look at Lizzie, who nodded her approval. "Will you do that? Will you let us know if the Wittenbauers are mean to you?"

Ruby looked down at the floor. "If they get mad at me, I won't have any place to live. They told me they would send me to an orphanage."

Lizzie's face flushed. "They will *not* send you to an orphanage, Ruby. Don't you worry about that. If we need to, we'll find you another place to live. Okay?"

The young girl nodded as a tear splashed down on her thin dress.

I wasn't worried about Lizzie's promise. People in Kingdom took care of one another. If Ruby couldn't get along at the Wittenbauers', someone would surely open their home to her. The look on Lizzie's face made me wonder if that new home might be with her and Noah. What a blessing that would be for the young girl.

I got a warm washcloth and washed Ruby's dirty feet. It was obvious she wasn't getting regular baths. It was getting too late to do anything about it tonight, but I'd make sure she got a nice hot shower after school tomorrow. Noah came back with the socks, and I pulled a warm pair onto Ruby's feet.

"That feels really good. Thank you," she said softly. "Thank you for everything." She stood to her feet. "I'd better leave. I don't want Uncle Elmer to get any madder at me."

I held out the bag of dresses and the extra socks. "Here, take this." I picked up the cloak I'd carried downstairs. "This should keep you warm." I looked over at Noah. "Would you make sure Ruby's uncle understands that she is to wear this every day when it's cold?"

"Oh, I'll make absolutely certain he understands that," Noah said firmly. "Come on, Ruby. I'll walk out with you. There are a couple more things I want to tell your uncle."

Ruby started toward the door, but suddenly she whirled around and ran to me, wrapping her thin arms around me. "Thank you, Miss Callie."

"You're very welcome." I tried to keep the emotion out of my voice, but I failed.

When she let go of me, Ruby went to Lizzie and hugged her too. "Thank you," she whispered. Without looking back at us, she ran out the door, Noah behind her. Lizzie and I looked at each other with tears in our eyes.

"She'll be all right, Callie," Lizzie said. "We'll keep a close eye on her."

All I could do was nod. Without any further discussion, we got back to work, preparing for our supper crowd.

When it was almost time to serve the evening meal, I grabbed my order pad and went out into the dining room. I'd just approached Jonathon Wiese's table when the front door flew open. Mercy Eberly, the daughter of the man who runs our hardware store, stumbled in. Her eyes were wild, and she was as white as a sheet. Everyone stopped talking and stared at her.

"A . . . a woman," she said. "There's a woman. She's . . . she's dead!" With that she fainted and fell to the floor.

CHAPTER 3

Someone screamed and I jumped, almost dropping the plates in my hands. I quickly put them down on the table next to me. Then I ran over to where Mercy lay motionless. As I knelt down to make sure she was all right, voices exploded behind me. Noah hurried over and sank to his knees beside me.

"What did she say? Did she say someone was dead?"

I brushed back a couple of dark-red curls that had escaped from under Mercy's prayer covering. Her forehead was damp with sweat, yet it was freezing cold outside. "Help me get her cloak off," I said to Noah. "She's too hot." Together we held her up while we removed her heavy cape. I pulled her into my lap. "Can someone get me a cool damp rag?" I asked loudly. Noah started to get up, but then I heard Lizzie's voice from behind us.

"I'll get it."

I turned my head and watched her jog toward the kitchen.

"Mercy?" I said softly, turning my attention back to the unconscious teenager, "are you all right? Can you hear me?"

Her eyelids fluttered several times and then slowly opened. The confusion on her face was also reflected in her eyes. "What . . . what happened?"

As I helped her sit up, she gazed around, obviously frightened by the crowd gathered around her.

"You said you found a dead woman on the road?" I tried to say it delicately, but there really wasn't any way to sugarcoat it.

She nodded, her eyes wide with shock and fear. "Yes."

"On the road to Kingdom?" Noah asked.

"Yes, Elder." Tears slipped down her cheeks.

"What were you doing out there?" I asked. Normally children went straight home after school. Mercy was supposed to go to her father's hardware store. For her to be out on the road was highly unusual.

"Max, our cat, didn't come home last night. I was trying to find him." Her voice broke. "Where is my papa?"

"He was here a little while ago," Noah said. "He must have gone back to the store." He searched the room until he caught sight of Jonathon, who stood nearby. "Jonathon, can you go to the hardware store and fetch Harold? And find my brother. He should be at the church."

Jonathon didn't take time to answer, just hurried out the front door.

Noah stood to his feet. "This woman," he said to Mercy in a somber voice, "how far away is she?"

Mercy wiped her wet face with her sleeve. "About halfway between here and the main road outside of town."

"Okay." Noah looked around the room. "Ebbie, will you come with me? We need to—"

"I don't know what you're planning to do," Lizzie interjected, as she came back into the room, "but don't touch anything and don't get too near the body." She handed me a damp rag. "The sheriff will want the scene to stay undisturbed, in case her death wasn't an accident. You know, for clues." She turned around and quickly headed back to the kitchen.

"It's not an accident," Mercy said to me, her voice shaking with emotion. "Someone . . . someone put her there." Her sky-blue eyes sought mine, and she leaned in close to me. "She's wrapped up in plastic," she whispered.

Had the serial killer the sheriff was looking for come to Kingdom? The possibility made me catch my breath, and I felt sick to my stomach. I tried to comfort Mercy the best I could while we waited for her father.

A few minutes later Harold Eberly rushed into the dining room. "Mercy!" he cried. Jonathon and Levi trailed behind him.

I helped the young girl to her feet, and her father took her from me, holding her up as she leaned against him. Together they walked slowly toward the front door. Several people started to follow them.

"Wait a minute," Levi called out. His face was so pale it frightened me. Obviously Jonathon had told him what had happened. Everyone stopped in their tracks and looked back at their pastor.

"You all must stay in town. The last thing we need is a bunch of people gawking at this unfortunate woman. It's not . . . decent. Let's show some respect."

Although no one acknowledged that they were headed to check out the place Mercy had described, a few of them looked decidedly guilty. But everyone seemed to agree with Levi's warning. The idea of people staring at the woman's body seemed so invasive. A shudder of something cold and ghastly slithered down my spine. This is Kingdom. How could something like this happen? I started to tell Levi what Mercy had whispered to me, but I remembered that Noah said it was a detail the authorities were keeping to themselves. If I told him now, it was possible someone in the room might hear. I decided to wait until we were alone.

"Let's get going," Levi said to Ebbie and Jonathon. "I'm fairly certain Mercy saw what she said she did, but before we call the sheriff, I think we need to make absolutely sure. What if she's wrong?"

I felt pretty confident that Lizzie had already notified Sheriff Timmons, but not wanting to cause any further disturbance, I kept quiet.

"I understand," Ebbie said, his dark-brown eyes troubled, "but I have to admit this is something I really don't want to see."

"Don't you think I feel the same way?" Jonathon asked sharply. "But Levi's right. Let's make sure before we stir up trouble we don't need."

"I'm going," Noah said.

Levi shook his head. "Why don't you stay here, Brother? I don't want people wandering out onto the road out of curiosity. You can keep an eye on those here and offer reassurance as needed."

I could tell Noah was torn between wanting to go with Levi and his friends, and his obligation to those of us who were terrified by Mercy's revelation. But he nodded slowly, ready to support Levi's decision.

Ebbie stood to his feet, still holding Hope's hand. "I'll be back soon," he told her gently. "Pray for us."

Her eyes filled with tears. "I will. Take care, Husband."

Levi glanced over at me. At this point, all he knew was that there was probably a body lying on the road to Kingdom. Even though no one had said the woman's death was

46

the result of a serial killer, everyone who had listened to the sheriff earlier in the day surely suspected it. I was probably the only person who was almost certain of it.

The look in Levi's eyes made it clear that he dreaded what awaited him. I wanted to hug him. Tell him everything would be all right. But to be honest, I wasn't sure it was the truth. Right now, all I could do was pray it was someone we didn't know. That sounded awful. Shallow and selfish. This was someone's daughter, sister, maybe even a wife and mother. But the idea that she could be a stranger somehow made the situation easier to endure. We'd had to say good-bye to so many friends and family lately. Besides Papa, we'd lost Avery Menninger and Frances Lapp. Although Pastor Mendenhall hadn't died, his leaving had almost felt like a death. And then there was Sophie Wittenbauer. No one really talked about her departure because of her harmful actions toward our town, but I felt sorry for her and kept her in my daily prayers. Her absence still hurt.

Who could the dead woman be? Unbidden, names and faces flooded my mind. Who hadn't I seen this morning? Who was missing? Suddenly one face floated into my thoughts. "Leah," I whispered, cold fear seizing my body. She usually came in for a cup of coffee after school let out, but she hadn't been in today. "Where is Leah?" I asked loudly, my voice trembling.

The silence in the empty room came back to me like an echo of terror. Then a voice from behind me made me jump. Lizzie had come back into the room.

"It's not Leah, Callie. I took food over to the school at lunchtime. She told me she had to stay late with one of the children and wouldn't be by today. I'm sure she's still there. Besides, Mercy would have recognized Leah."

Relief flowed through me. "You're right. I didn't think of that. Thank you, God."

Lizzie looked around the room, frowning. "Where did everyone go?"

"Levi, Ebbie, and Jonathon went out to make sure Mercy actually saw what she says she did," Noah replied. "I think a lot of people are hanging out in town to wait for the news they bring back. If Mercy's right, Levi will call the sheriff when he returns."

Lizzie folded her arms across her chest. "Well, it's too late for that."

"Lizzie!" Noah exclaimed. "Why didn't you check with Levi before you made that call?"

She scowled at him. "Well, let me see. Possibly because I still have my own mind and can make a few of my own decisions."

The look Noah gave her seemed to reduce some of her bluster, and she dropped her arms to her side. "Sorry, but it was the right thing to do. The sheriff needs to get to the scene as quickly as possible. I hope no one touches anything they shouldn't."

"We shouldn't jump to the conclusion that this woman's death is connected to the man the sheriff talked about this morning," Noah said.

I motioned to both of them to follow me over to the corner of the room. I couldn't take a chance that anyone could hear me.

"Mercy told me . . ." A wave of nausea hit me, and I balked.

"Told you what, Callie?" Lizzie said, frowning.

I took a deep breath and tried again. "Mercy told me that the woman was wrapped in plastic."

Noah and Lizzie were silent for several moments.

"Oh no," Noah said finally. "God help us."

"Then it's even more important that the men don't disturb the scene," Lizzie said firmly.

"I can guarantee you no one will touch anything," I said. "They took your advice to heart. Besides, they were all very upset, and no one really wanted to go. I'm sure none of them plan to get any closer than they have to."

Lizzie nodded. "I don't blame them." She cocked her head to the side and stared at her husband. "Why are you still here?"

He raised his voice to a more normal level. "According to my brother, I'm supposed to keep everyone corralled in town and off the road. Oh, and to provide counsel to anyone who might need it."

Lizzie grunted as she gazed around the room. The only people remaining were Noah, Hope, Lizzie, me, and John Lapp. John shook his head and stood up. John was a tall, thin man with dark hair, dark eyes, and an even darker expression. I couldn't actually remember ever seeing him smile.

"You do not need to counsel me," he said, staring at Noah. His deep voice always made me uncomfortable. No matter what John said, a note of menace seemed to creep into each word. "This is just one more sign of the evil that has been allowed to permeate this town. When the door is opened, the devil will dance in."

"Brother John," Noah said firmly, "this isn't the time for you to air your grievances with the direction the church is taking. Whatever happened to this poor woman had nothing to do with us."

John's expression turned toxic. "If the church was doing what was right, violence wouldn't hover so close to our doors."

Noah shook his head. "Kingdom is fine, John. Except for some residents who judge everyone but themselves. A woman may be dead. Why don't you spend your time praying for her family instead of spewing poison?"

John's pale face grew red. "I do not spew poison, *Elder* Housler." He winced as if the use of the title caused him physical pain. "What I give you is truth. It is up to you as to whether or not you accept it. God will judge between us."

Noah kept quiet as John put on his coat and left, but I could see the muscles in his jaws work in frustration.

"Ever since Frances died, that man has gotten more judgmental," Lizzie said. "They both rejected me when I got pregnant with Charity, but after coming back to Kingdom, we'd actually become civil with each other. Then Frances died. Now John barely acknowledges my presence."

"I'm sure he's grieving," I said. "He and Frances were together almost twenty years."

"Frances wasn't much nicer than John," Noah said with a sigh. "But she seemed to keep him in check. God help us all now that her steadying hand is gone."

Lizzie frowned at the front window and watched as John walked past. "John lives out of town," she said slowly. "He has to use the main road."

Noah stood to his feet. "I didn't think of that. Surely he'll wait until Levi comes back. He was right here when Levi told everyone to stay put."

"Are you kidding?" Lizzie said. "John Lapp doesn't listen to anyone."

"Maybe you should go after him, Noah," I said. "If you can catch him . . ."

Noah hurried over to the window. "He's already on his way.

I think it might be better if I just make sure no one decides to follow him."

He grabbed his coat off the rack and walked out the front door. I looked outside to see what was happening. Hope got up and joined me at the window. Snow was still falling, but it was a little lighter.

"I wouldn't worry, Callie," Hope said gently. "Levi, Ebbie, and Jonathon will turn anyone back who tries to get past them."

"Not John. Telling him what to do only makes him angry. Especially if it's coming from Levi. John hates him."

"Oh, Callie. John doesn't *hate* Levi. Maybe he thinks Levi's too young to be our pastor, but everyone respects him. It's impossible not to. Levi is one of the best men I've ever known. We couldn't have a better pastor."

I looked into her almost violet eyes. Maybe outer beauty wasn't important, but Hope was certainly blessed with it. Her hair was so blond it was nearly white, and her skin was flawless. I found myself involuntarily reaching up and trying to push my wayward curls back where they belonged.

"I believe that too, Hope," I said. "But not everyone in town feels the way we do. Obviously John Lapp is one who doesn't."

"That's just John's way. He never listened to Pastor Mendenhall either. You can't judge him by the way he acts. It's his nature to be cantankerous."

We watched Noah talking to a group of people standing outside. They all seemed to be looking in the same direction—the way John had gone. A couple of them pointed toward the road. I couldn't hear Noah, but after a couple of minutes, their heads began to nod, and the entire group turned and began to walk toward the restaurant.

"Looks like we'll need some coffee," I said. I reached out and touched Hope's shoulder. "Thank you. You've made me feel better. I'm so glad Levi has your support."

Hope put her hand on mine. "You have my support as well, Callie. Never forget that. We're family, and we always will be."

The events of the day had stirred up my emotions and tears filled my eyes. "Thank you. That's the way I see it, but sometimes I'm not sure everyone else does."

Hope started to reply, but suddenly the front door opened and people began to file in. I left Hope and hurried to the kitchen to get coffee cups and coffee. There was no reason to ask if anyone wanted it. Chapped red faces told the story. I came back with two pots of steaming hot coffee. Hope took one of the pots and served one half of the room while I took care of the rest. The coffee was gratefully accepted by everyone.

After every person had been served, I joined Noah at a table in the corner near the fireplace. "I . . . I can hardly believe what's happened today," I said, collapsing into a chair. I felt as if my legs couldn't hold me up any longer even though I wasn't physically tired. "Why is it every time I think life has finally straightened out in this town, something happens to stir the pot?"

Noah snorted. "Because the devil doesn't sleep, Callie. Unfortunately, we're in a fight with an enemy who won't admit he's already defeated."

John's words came back to me: *When the door is opened, the devil will dance in.*

Lizzie came over and sat down next to me. "The important thing to remember is that we have God on our side," she said gently. "When you understand how much He loves us, and that He'll never leave us or forsake us, we can face anything with confidence."

Lizzie's words brought me a measure of reassurance. God had never let us down, even in the face of an unforeseeable enemy. Although we couldn't always predict the devil's attacks, God was never unprepared to help us.

After giving me a hug, Lizzie stood to her feet and stared toward the window. "I wonder how long they'll be."

"I don't know," Noah answered. "It depends on whether or not the sheriff gets there before they leave. It could take a lot longer if he questions them."

Lizzie sighed and went over to talk to Hope, who was looking out the window too.

"Why would he question them?" I asked Noah. "None of them know anything about this."

"The sheriff doesn't know that, Callie. If the dead woman was murdered, Sheriff Timmons will want to talk to almost everyone in Kingdom."

"No one who lives here killed that woman," I said, unable to keep my voice steady. "There are no murderers here."

Noah sighed and shook his head. "As an elder I've heard things in counseling that shocked me. The devil is the same all over the world. Maybe we've limited the ways he can attack us by removing some of his favorite tools, but temptation and sin will find other ways inside if a heart is open to them."

His grave pronouncement made me shiver. "Maybe so, but no one in Kingdom would do something like this."

Noah smiled. "I didn't mean to upset you, Callie. Most of the people in Kingdom are good people."

I wanted to feel assured by his words, but I didn't. What kind of stories was he hearing in counseling? With a shock I realized that Levi had to be privy to the same information, but he'd never mentioned anything he heard during his personal sessions with church members. "Levi hasn't told me anything troubling about our friends and neighbors."

"And he won't. Whatever is said during counseling is private. Not to be repeated to anyone. You know that."

I started to reply when Lizzie came back to the table. "I wonder how the KBI will react to us. I doubt they have much interaction with towns like ours."

"The KBI?" I repeated. "I remember Sheriff Timmons mentioning them, but I don't remember who they are."

"The Kansas Bureau of Investigation," Lizzie said. "Like the FBI, only in our state."

I was too embarrassed to ask what the initials FBI stood for, so I just nodded. There certainly had been a lot of initials thrown around today. KBI, FBI, DNA. Seemed to me that living in the world came with its own odd language. One I didn't know how to interpret. Lizzie's time away from Kingdom had obviously afforded her knowledge of things I had no way to understand.

"Well, I can't sit around all day," Lizzie said. "I've got to start frying some steaks and chicken for supper. It's almost five."

"I wouldn't count on a big crowd," Noah said. "I doubt many people will be in the mood to stay in town tonight. Once they get the answers they want, they'll probably head home and lock their doors."

Lizzie shrugged. "Maybe. But they're just as likely to gather here and talk about it. I want to be ready in case they do."

She whirled around and hurried toward the kitchen. I nodded at Noah and followed behind her. She pushed the door open and went over to the refrigerator, pulling out meat that would soon be turned into her famous chicken-fried steaks. I loved the huge refrigerator. Although I doubted Levi would agree to add electricity to our home after we married, secretly I wanted an electric refrigerator like Lizzie's. Maybe not quite so large. Our small refrigerator at home had run on propane, which meant we had to keep our propane tank filled all the time. It wasn't always easy. Sometimes in the winter, after a big snow, it was difficult to get to town to have our tank replenished. After Papa got sick, men from the church helped us, but they had to take care of their own families first. Many times it took a while for assistance to arrive, so we'd store our food in an outside shed. Since it was so cold, the food was just as safe as if it was in our refrigerator. Except for one winter when a group of wild dogs burrowed their way under the shed and carried away all of our meat.

Kingdom was full of animals. Although most of our older citizens weren't raised to think of animals as pets, things had changed over the years. Many thoughtless people dropped off unwanted dogs and cats in the country, and a lot of them, just like the dogs who took our meat, found their way to our town. Those that hadn't turned wild ended up as beloved members of Kingdom families. Even elderly residents who had never had pets when they were young became loving owners. Lizzie had adopted two abandoned cats that lived at the restaurant. The Houslers also had a darling dog, a white cairn terrier mix they'd named Muffin. The dog, dropped off and abandoned on the road to Kingdom, quickly won the hearts of the entire Housler family. Charity and Muffin bonded immediately, so there was never any question that he'd found his forever home. Now the dog slept on Charity's bed and followed her everywhere she went. Muffin got his name not long after moving in. Lizzie discovered him standing on her kitchen table, eating some of the muffins she'd set out for breakfast. The small dog had already eaten two of them before his thievery was discovered.

Since I lived at the restaurant, the cats and I had become friends. After a while, Lizzie seemed to think they belonged to me. I didn't mind. They were very sweet, and I'd grown fond of them.

One of the cats, Prince, a small calico, lay under the table in the kitchen. He looked completely relaxed. I wondered where the other cat, Dora, a Siamese, had gone to. She was probably upstairs sleeping on my bed.

"Are you okay?" Lizzie had stopped her supper preparations and was studying me.

I sighed. "I don't know. So much has happened today, I'm having a hard time sorting out my feelings. I don't remember ever getting as upset as I did earlier." I paused and considered what I'd just said. "You know, Lizzie, except for today, I don't recall ever getting really angry. I guess I'm just not that type of person."

Lizzie looked at me strangely. "Everyone gets mad, you know. It's not a sin, Callie. We just need to deal with it and not allow it to fester."

"I guess. But I don't seem to be able to let go of this. Maybe it's everything else that's going on." I shook my head. "I honestly don't know, but I don't like this sensation. It makes me feel . . ." I struggled for the right word but couldn't seem to find it.

"Human?" Lizzie said.

"I hope not. Experiencing this all the time would be terrible. I've already been out of sorts for the past month or so. Dealing with bouts of uncontrolled anger would be too much."

"Callie," Lizzie said softly, "didn't you ever get mad at your father?"

I stared at her in amazement. "Papa? Of course not. I loved him, and he loved me. Why would I ever be angry with him?"

Lizzie crossed her arms and leaned against the counter. "Why would you be angry with him? Because it's normal, Callie. We all get upset with our parents sometimes. Even if we love them. Surely there were difficult times when you were a child."

"No, not really. When I was young, life seemed so peaceful. Some days I actually wish I could go back to the way things used to be."

Lizzie frowned. "What are you thinking? Your childhood wasn't ideal. I mean, with your mother leaving and all."

"Goodness. You're right. Guess I just kind of blocked that out. Papa always did his best to keep our lives on an even keel."

Lizzie didn't say anything, but her measured silence spoke volumes.

"I know you too well, Lizzie. When you get quiet, something's wrong."

She turned to look at me, biting her bottom lip. Finally, she said, "I remember our childhood. Even though you were younger, we spent a lot of time together. You lived just down the street from us. I also remember when your mother left. Your father . . ." Lizzie looked away for a moment, as if turning something over in her mind. She murmured something under her breath, but I couldn't make it out. Then her eyes met mine. "Your father treated you like it was your fault your mother ran away. I can't get some of the things he said to you out of my mind. I recall one day in particular when he and my father were talking in front of us. Your father said . . ." She hesitated again.

I wanted to tell her to stop, but for some reason I couldn't seem to find my voice.

She took a deep breath. "Your father said that he planned to do the Christian thing and take care of you, but he wished your mother would have taken you with her."

Lizzie's words felt like knife wounds in my heart, and I stared at her in disbelief. "Lizzie Housler! My father never said any such thing! Why would you say something so awful?"

She walked over to where I stood, stopped only a few inches away from me, her dark eyes peering into mine. "Callie, he said it. How could you not remember? There is a part of your soul that you refuse to acknowledge. Look, I know you loved your father, and you took good care of him. But you've forgotten the way he treated you. I see how insecure you are. He's the one who put it there. Sometimes I wonder if you really believe anyone loves you. Even Levi. And he adores you."

I stepped back from her. "I'm sure you mean well, but you don't know what you're talking about. My father loved me. And Levi loves me. I know he does." Even as I said the words, I knew they weren't completely true. Hadn't I just been wondering if he was sorry we'd gotten engaged?

"I wish you really believed that," she said with a sigh. "You've pushed a lot of hurt and anger into a closet in your soul. You think you've locked the door and thrown away the key. Dismissed the past. But I think your reaction to Elmer shows that your closet is too full. It could burst open, and I'm worried about that. Worried about what will happen when it does." She reached out and touched my arm. "The past is not so easily forgotten, Callie."

An emotion I couldn't understand coursed through my body. For some reason, I wanted to lash out at Lizzie. But she was my best friend. How could I?

"You're . . . you're wrong, Lizzie. Dead wrong. Please, I can't talk about this right now. Not with everything that's happening. It's just too much to bear."

She gazed at me for a few seconds longer and then turned away. "Okay. I'm sorry. Maybe you're right. Knowing there's a body right outside of town has my nerves on edge too. Let's just forget it." She pulled a huge pan out of the oven, put it on a nearby counter, and lifted the lid. The aroma of meat loaf filled the room.

I was still upset, but I knew I'd have to deal with my feelings. I had no intention of allowing anything to come between Lizzie and me. In my heart, she was the sister I'd never had. Obviously, she was confused. Maybe she'd overheard something as a child and mistakenly related it to Papa. I knew beyond a shadow of a doubt that she would never try to purposely hurt me. After deciding to ignore her insensitive comments, I forced myself to say, "That smells wonderful. I know what I'm having for dinner."

As if nothing had happened, she smiled at me. "You may be eating all of it if no one shows up." She poked a fork into the large loaf and looked it over carefully. When she was satisfied, she took the fork out, re-covered the pan, and put it back in the oven to keep it warm. "Did you check the salt and pepper shakers?" she asked. "They were looking a little light."

I sighed. "I started to, but with everything going on, I completely forgot. I'll take care of it now."

I spun around and hurried out to the dining room. Hope and Noah stood near the front door. Hope smiled when she saw me.

"Callie, will you tell Lizzie I'm going back to the shop for a while? I have a couple of things I want to do, and I know Beau needs to go out. I'll be back in about an hour."

"You can tell her yourself if you want. She's not that busy right now."

"That's okay. I don't want to bother her." Hope wrapped herself up in her cloak. "Maybe when I come back there will be some news."

"Are you bringing Beau with you?"

Hope and Ebbie's dog, Beau, had been adopted by the entire town. He'd once belonged to Avery Menninger. When Avery died, Hope's father took him in. After Ebbie and Hope got married last summer, Samuel gave him to the newlyweds. Lizzie had welcomed Beau into the restaurant without hesitation. He was a very clean dog and never begged food or acted obnoxious with the customers.

Hope laughed. "Yes, I'll bring him with me. He would hate to miss the evening crowd."

Noah held the door open and Hope slipped out. The cold air swept in, as if desperate to find warmth. He started to shut the door but pulled it open again when someone walked up to the entrance. Margaret Harper, one of Kingdom's newest residents, stepped inside. Four months ago, Margaret had petitioned the elders to move to Kingdom after her husband was killed in a farm accident. Claiming to be second cousin to a resident who passed away many years ago, the elders felt an obligation to help her. She was very shy and for the most part kept to herself. For some reason, however, she seemed to gravitate toward me, always wanting to talk. I tried to be friendly, but there was something about her that made me uncomfortable. Unfortunately, Margaret and I had a tie that wouldn't be broken anytime soon. The church purchased my home for her after I decided to move, wanting to distance myself from the memories of my father's illness. My eyes drifted longingly toward the stairs that led to my apartment. More than anything in the world, I wanted to escape from this day and take a nice, long, leisurely nap, but there wasn't any way I could desert Lizzie. Besides, I needed to be here for Levi when he returned.

"Hello, Margaret," I said. "Can I get you something?"

Her eyes darted back and forth, taking in all the empty tables. "Are . . . are you closed? I thought you usually served dinner about now."

"We do, but there's been an unfortunate situation. A woman has been killed."

Her dark-blue eyes grew wide. "Killed? Who? Someone from our church?"

I shook my head. "We don't know. Levi and some of the men have gone to find out who it is. We're waiting for their return."

"Oh. I saw lots of townspeople gathered in the hardware store and inside the market. That must be why."

"I wondered where they went. Got tired of waiting in here, I suppose."

She granted me a rare smile. "I suspect it's because Lizzie doesn't cotton much to gossip. Harold Eberly's usually at the center of it, and Aaron Metcalf's too busy working at the general store to listen to folks blathering."

"I'm sure you're right. What can I get for you?"

She rubbed her hands together. "Just a cup of coffee, please. It's so cold out."

She sat down at a nearby table and removed her cloak. All her clothing looked old. It wasn't tattered, just faded. She was always dressed in black or dark blue, although most of the women in town had transitioned to other colors and patterns. We still dressed modestly, but at least now there were choices—something that wasn't allowed before the recent transformation in our church. Not everyone in Kingdom welcomed change, however. I wondered if Margaret dressed the way she did because of her beliefs, or if she didn't have anything else besides the two or three dresses she wore over and over. With her work-worn fingers, she pushed a strand of brown hair, streaked with gray, behind her ear. Her bun was always messy, as if she wasn't used to fashioning it. However, her most noticeable characteristic was a terrible scar that started over her left eye and ran down her cheek, twisting her features. I tried not to stare at it, but it was hard to miss. I wondered how it had happened. Although I didn't like the woman much, I did feel sorry for her.

"Lizzie has some Dutch apple pie that would go very well with that coffee," I said, feeling guilty about my aversion to Margaret. "It looks like she made way too much. If you'd like a slice—"

"Oh yes. That would be wonderful. Thank you."

I nodded and went back to the kitchen, where I relayed to Lizzie what I'd said. "I'll be happy to pay for it."

"Don't be silly. You know I'm happy to give anyone what they need. Besides, you were telling the truth. I really don't want this pie to go to waste." She grinned at me. "You're getting to be as bad as I am." She cut a large piece of pie and handed it to me. "And put some ice cream on it."

I got the vanilla ice cream out of the freezer and added a

big scoop to the plate with the pie. Then I poured a cup of coffee and carried them both out to Margaret's table. When I set the pie and ice cream down in front of her, the weariness in her face seemed to ease a bit. I'd noticed that she always looked tired, and whenever she could manage a smile, it never reached her eyes. There was a deep sadness about Margaret that seemed to have seeped into every part of her body. Losing a husband had to be very difficult, and being so badly scarred was probably a heavy burden for a woman to bear.

"Do you have time to sit a bit?" she asked.

I shook my head. "I've got to refill the salt and pepper shakers before supper, but we can visit while I do it."

What little animation there was in her face melted. She was obviously lonely. As her sister in Christ, it was my obligation to treat her with kindness. Why was it so hard for me? I went back to the kitchen to get the large containers of salt and pepper. Taking a moment to send up a prayer for patience, I went back into the dining room, determined to show Christian love. Margaret looked up from her pie as I neared her table. The abject unhappiness in her expression made me instantly ashamed of my selfish attitude.

"So how are you adjusting to the house?" I asked as I filled the shakers on her table.

She grasped her coffee cup with both hands, and I noticed they shook slightly. "I'm so grateful for all the work being done by the church to fix it up. With a little effort, it will be quite comfortable."

"I'm glad. When Papa was well he took good care of it. But after he got sick, I'm afraid it fell into disrepair. I tried to keep it up, but I was so busy caring for him and working that after a while I just gave up." I was concentrating on filling the salt shaker, and when I looked up, I saw her grimace, the way someone might when they're in pain.

"Are you all right? Is something wrong?"

She shook her head and put her hand on her stomach. "I'm a little sensitive to milk. Ice cream upsets my stomach some."

I frowned at her. "I'm so sorry. If I'd known . . ."

She waved her hand at me. "It's okay. Some things are worth the pain."

I grinned at her. "I'm exactly the same way with dairy products. But I have no plans to give up ice cream. Life without ice cream? Can't imagine it."

Margaret nodded. "I agree."

"I do stay away from milk though. Never did care much for it. Even when I was a little girl. Of course, most of that probably comes from the way it affects me."

"My mother tried to make me drink milk when I was young, thinking it was good for me. She didn't realize how uncomfortable it made me."

"The same thing happened to me," I said. "It made my mother feel bad when she realized I was allergic."

Margaret didn't respond, she just looked at me in an odd way. That prickly feeling returned, and before I realized it, I'd filled the shaker too full, and salt ran over the side. I tore my gaze away from the strange woman and concentrated on cleaning up the mess I'd made. My stomach turned over, and it had nothing to do with milk.

"I-I'm sorry I stare at you so much," Margaret stuttered, noticing my reaction. "It's just that you remind me of someone. A woman I knew in Missouri."

"Really? I hope she was a friend."

"I guess she was a friend once. In a manner of speaking."

Not knowing what to say, I just smiled and moved on to the next table. Although my back was to her, I heard her clear her throat.

"She had red curly hair, just like yours. And her eyes were blue. Bluer than yours. Your eyes are more grayish-blue, I guess. She was a beautiful woman, but she didn't value herself very much. She had a sad life full of wrong choices."

"I'm sorry."

"You're a very attractive young woman. Are you aware of that, Callie?"

I turned to look at her, startled by her declaration. "Me? Attractive?" I shook my head. "I don't see myself like that." I found her words odd, since Mennonites are raised not to think about outer beauty. In fact, in our community, even looking in a mirror is discouraged. Papa and I didn't have any mirrors in our house. Whether it was because of our Mennonite beliefs or because of my mother, I was never sure. Papa told me once that Mama was very proud of her looks, and that her lack of humility drove her from us.

Margaret shook her head slowly. "You're wrong, Callie. You're not only beautiful on the inside, kind and compassionate, but you're physically beautiful as well." There was a hint of sadness in her voice. "Beauty isn't anything to be ashamed of, as long as you don't let it become your identity."

I had to wonder why she'd said that. With that awful scar, it was impossible to tell if she'd ever been attractive. Even without it, her eyes were sunken, shadowed underneath by dark rings, and there was almost no color in her cheeks. I tried to imagine her much younger, and without the scar, but I just couldn't.

"Excuse me a moment, will you?" I left to finish filling the shakers on the other tables. It took several minutes. When I turned back to check on Margaret, I saw that Ruth Fisher was sitting with her. They seemed to be engaged in a very animated conversation. I breathed a sigh of relief, grateful to have been given a way out of our awkward conversation.

I was getting ready to carry the salt and pepper containers back to the kitchen when I heard the sound of an automobile engine outside the restaurant. I glanced toward the window and saw the sheriff's car stop just outside the door. I hurried back to the kitchen.

"They're here," I told Lizzie.

We stared at each other, neither one of us making a move toward the door.

"Whatever they say, we'll get through this, Callie," Lizzie said. "We'll be okay."

She put down the piece of steak she'd been breading and hastily washed her hands. As I waited for her, I wondered if her words would prove to be true. Or if what was waiting for us would change Kingdom forever.

CHAPTER 4

Lizzie and I rushed into the dining room and watched out the window as Levi's buggy pulled up to the railing in front of the restaurant. He jumped out and tied up his horse, Stormy, while the other men climbed out and waited for the sheriff to join them. Two men got out of the car, the sheriff and Roger Carson. Everyone in the dining room was unusually quiet as the men walked single file up the steps and entered the room. I was alarmed at the expression on Levi's face. Although his cheeks were ruddy from the cold, beneath them, his skin was ashen. The look in his eyes made my breath catch in my throat.

Lizzie and I stood there as if our feet were glued to the floor. There wasn't a sound from those gathered in the room. Before the sheriff had the chance to speak, the front door opened and another group of people shuffled inside. Most likely the folks who'd been waiting at Harold's or Aaron's. Some of them quickly found a seat. The rest stood expectantly near the back of the room.

I wanted to hear about the woman on the road—yet I didn't. At that moment, I wished I were somewhere else. Anywhere else. I wondered if Lizzie felt the same way. I snuck a look at her. Her face was set like flint, and I couldn't tell what she was thinking.

"Well?" she said finally.

Sheriff Timmons removed his hat. Roger stepped up next to him, almost as if he were trying to offer support. He cast a quick glance around the room, looking rather uncomfortable until he saw Noah. Having a friend nearby appeared to relax him a little.

"She was definitely murdered," the sheriff said slowly. "It's too early to conclude that this is the work of the serial killer I told you about, but I certainly can't rule it out. The KBI has taken over the case and will make that official determination." He spoke without hesitation, but it was obvious there was something else on his mind. I tried to catch Levi's eye, but he wouldn't meet my gaze.

"You're not telling us everything," Lizzie said bluntly. "What is it? Is she one of us?"

Their silence alarmed me. The men looked back and forth at each other. Sheriff Timmons began to say something when the door to the restaurant opened, and Harold Eberly rushed in.

"John Lapp said he was turned away on the road out of town. Some men, official types, told him he couldn't use the road, Sheriff," Harold said in a loud, angry voice. "Many of us need to get to our homes. Why are we being forced to stay in town?"

The young sheriff frowned at Harold. "I'm sorry, but the KBI has closed the road until they finish gathering evidence. Shouldn't be too long."

"My little girl has been through enough," Harold insisted. "She needs to go home."

I heard Lizzie grunt. "Harold Eberly, you hush up. A

woman has died. I don't think asking you to hang around for a while is out of line."

Harold's mouth dropped open, but instead of arguing with Lizzie, he turned and stomped out the door. He probably realized that trying to win an argument with Lizzie was an almost impossible task.

When the door closed behind him, she hurried over and locked it. Then she gazed slowly around the room. "I'm not planning to kick anyone out," she said, "but if you came here out of some kind of morbid curiosity, I'd like you to leave. People of faith should be showing respect, not acting like the world."

A few people hung their heads, and I marveled at her boldness. After several seconds, she pointed at the sheriff, who was staring at her in surprise. "Okay, so what are you keeping back? Do we know her?"

Noah, who had been watching this scene unfold from a corner table stood to his feet and came over to stand near his brother and Roger.

"It's not anyone from Kingdom," Levi said in a low, strained tone. "She's a stranger." Even though I was thankful for the good news, his solemn manner frightened me.

"Levi, what's going on?" Noah asked.

Although it seemed to take great effort, Levi lifted his eyes to his brother's. "Do . . . do you remember the book of martyrs I lost a few weeks ago?"

"Yes," Noah said slowly, looking confused. "What about it?"

Levi seemed incapable of continuing. Finally Noah looked over at the sheriff. "What's he talking about?"

Sheriff Timmons took a deep breath and let it out. "The dead woman— Levi's book was clutched in her hands."

No one said a word for what seemed like hours but was surely only a few seconds. For some reason all I could do was stare at the young sheriff. His eyes were locked on mine, and I couldn't break my gaze away. When Lizzie spoke, it finally shook me out of the strange stupor that had overtaken me.

"Are you saying you think Levi killed someone?" The incredulity in her voice triggered a reaction inside me.

"That's ridiculous," I sputtered, finally finding my voice. "Are you insane? How could you—"

"Callie!"

Levi's harsh tone startled me. "But this man—"

Roger took a step forward. His normally ruddy complexion was redder than normal. "The sheriff isn't saying Levi killed that girl," he said in a soothing tone. "He's simply trying to find out what happened. Of course Levi had nothing to do with this. But we do need to figure out why the book was found at the crime scene."

"How can you be sure it was your book, Levi?" Lizzie asked. "I know the book you mean. There are quite a few copies in Kingdom."

Levi sighed. "It's mine, Lizzie. It has my name written on it."

I started to say something, but Sheriff Timmons raised his hand. "Please, everyone, calm down. If your pastor had anything to do with this, he'd have to be the stupidest man alive. The book wasn't accidentally left at the scene of the crime. It was purposely put into the dead woman's hands. Unless he wanted to be caught, no murderer would do something that dumb."

"Of course he wouldn't," I said. "But why would anyone put Levi's book there?"

70

"That's the question we're asking," Timmons said. "I wish I had the answer, but I don't. Not yet."

He glanced around at our obviously concerned expressions. "Try not to worry. I don't believe anyone thinks Levi is a viable suspect. If this is the work of the serial killer, twenty years ago Levi was only a child. He couldn't have been running around the county killing women. One of the KBI agents said that, in his opinion, the book was an afterthought. Like the killer decided at the last minute to put it there." He frowned at Levi. "But I have to warn you, Pastor, the authorities will question you. They're going to want to know how the killer got that book and why he felt the need to leave it at the scene. Right now, your book might be the strongest piece of evidence they have. Finding out how it got there could lead them to their suspect."

Levi nodded but stayed silent. I wanted to forget decorum, run over, and wrap my arms around him. But propriety kept me from following my emotions. It hurt that I couldn't offer him any consolation.

"I'll do whatever I can to help them catch the man who did this," Levi said in an even tone. "I doubt there's any information I have that will help, but I'll certainly try."

"I know you will," the sheriff said. He gazed around the packed room. "Most of you will be interviewed too. We need to know who came down that road and when. You might have noticed something that will help our investigation. Even if you don't realize it."

"I don't know, Sheriff," Noah said, frowning. "She would have been hard to see. Anyone driving a buggy—or a truck that sits high like mine—could have easily missed her. And with the snow—"

"I'm aware of that," the sheriff said. "It's possible several people went right past her without realizing she was there. We still need to know everyone who drove down that road between late last night and this morning, before she was discovered." He nodded toward Roger. "My deputy will be interviewing you. Please give him your information—and the names of anyone else that might have been out there during the time in question." He looked out at the crowd. "All we can do is try our best to uncover the truth. Anything you can remember—especially anything unusual—could really help us."

The silence that followed the sheriff's statement made it clear that people were already turning the sheriff's request over in their minds.

"Have you found any clues?" Lizzie asked. "Anything that might point to the killer?"

Timmons shrugged. "There are all kinds of things out on the road near the victim," he said. "We've found scraps of papers and material. A bottle opener, two pencils, and a pen. Some change. We're keeping all of it, but so far, we don't have anything that connects us to any certain suspect."

"Harold said you closed the road outside of town?"

"*I* didn't. The KBI did. No one can travel that way until the KBI decides to open it again."

"It's not just Harold who goes home that way," I said. "Many of our people live outside the town itself. Especially the farmers. How long must they stay here?"

He shook his head. "I don't know. One of the agents promised he'd let me know as soon as the road is clear."

"That means you're stuck too," Lizzie said.

The sheriff nodded. "I hope that won't be a problem."

"Don't be silly," Noah said. "You're welcome here."

"Of course you are."

I jumped at the sound of Jonathon's voice. I'd forgotten he and Ebbie had gone with Levi. Although Jonathon seemed to be handling the situation well, Ebbie was quiet. Too quiet. Sadness was etched into his features. His usual smile had been replaced with something dark and sorrowful. It hurt me to look at him. Ebbie was such a tender man, easily touched by the pain of others. He caught me staring at him and turned toward the door.

"I've got to tell Hope I'm back," he said softly. He tried the door, but it was still locked. After bumbling around with it for a moment, Noah stepped over and turned the lock. He put his hand on Ebbie's shoulder for just a brief moment. It was a sweet gesture of comfort and brought tears to my eyes. We could get through this. As a family. I pulled my shoulders back and tried to sound determined.

"If folks can't get home, they'll probably want something to eat," I pointed out. "Are we ready to serve that many people?"

Lizzie put her hand to her forehead. "It's all prepared, but I'm going to need some help."

"What can I do?" Noah asked.

Lizzie seemed to come to life. "First of all, would you drive over to my parents' house? Tell them to keep Charity until we come for her. Warn them that it might be late. I don't want her anywhere near here right now."

"I'll have to tell them what's going on," Noah said slowly. "Your father will probably run right over, searching for information."

Lizzie shrugged. "If he does, he does. I'll deal with him

if that happens. My mother can watch Charity. She's good with her."

"Okay. I'll take care of it, and I'll be back as soon as I can so I can help you serve." He grabbed Lizzie's hand. "Don't worry. Everything will be fine." He quickly kissed her forehead. Then he grabbed his coat from the rack near the front door and left.

Lizzie blinked several times and looked at me with tears in her eyes. "I hope he's right. I really do." With that, she turned around and headed for the kitchen.

I realized Sheriff Timmons was still standing in the middle of the room with Roger. He looked decidedly uncomfortable. Before I had a chance to say anything, Levi walked up to him.

"Why don't you and Roger have dinner with us, Sheriff?" he said. "Lizzie's a great cook."

Timmons looked relieved. "Thank you, Pastor. I'd appreciate that. Didn't have time for lunch today, so I must admit to being a little hungry."

"Thanks, Levi," Roger said. "One of Lizzie's amazing meals is just the ticket. While I'm waiting, I'll start taking statements."

Levi pointed toward an empty table. The sheriff walked over and sat down while Roger began circulating through the room with a notebook. I hoped people would talk to him. Right now folks seemed more interested in studying the new sheriff than in listening to anything Roger might have to say. I was proud of Levi for caring about the young lawman's feelings, even in a tense situation like this. I hurried over to the table.

"What can I get you, Sheriff?"

He smiled at me. "What do you recommend, Miss—"

"It's Callie. Just Callie."

He took off his hat and set it on the chair next to him. "Okay, just Callie. What do you recommend?"

I smiled at his joke. Under the circumstances, it was a little hard to feel relaxed, but he'd managed to lighten the atmosphere just a little.

"Some nights, like tonight, Lizzie focuses on a few special dishes. We've got meat loaf, fried chicken, and chicken-fried steak. But if you want a hamburger, a sandwich, or a steak, she can make that for you."

"I recommend the chicken-fried steak," Levi said. "It's incredible. Just thinking about it makes me hungry."

"I love chicken-fried steak," the sheriff said. "Haven't had one for a long time. You two just talked me into it."

"Good choice."

"You might as well order the same thing for Roger," Levi said with a smile. "You know that's what he wants."

I nodded and wrote it down on my note pad. Roger ordered chicken-fried steak whenever it was on the menu. I was on my way to the kitchen when I heard the front door open. The wind had picked up and it blew through the room, knocking napkins off tables and rattling the windows. Snow swept past the entrance and onto the floor, where it quickly melted while the flames in the fireplace danced wildly. Aaron Metcalf closed the door as quickly as he could. I waved at him and then hurried back to the kitchen where Lizzie was busy cooking up a storm.

"Levi's eating with Sheriff Timmons and Roger," I told her. "All three of them want chicken-fried steak."

She nodded absentmindedly but didn't say anything. I knew her well enough to know that she hadn't really heard me.

"Lizzie, did you hear what I said?"

"What?" She stopped breading steak and frowned at me. "Yes, I'm making chicken-fried steak. Can't you tell?"

"Oh, Lizzie." I walked over and put my arm around her. "I'm worried too. But this murder has nothing to do with us. These men from the KBI will figure out who killed that woman, and then we'll all go back to normal. Won't we?"

She looked at me, a strange expression on her face. "I hope so, Callie. I love this town, but I truly wonder if we can continue to weather these storms and stay untouched. Suddenly I'm not so sure."

Her words caused a chill to run through me, and I let her go. "But earlier you said the devil didn't have a chance against us. That God would protect us." Even though her words echoed my own thoughts, for some reason I felt distressed. Lizzie was usually a calming voice when dark clouds gathered. I needed her encouragement, her assurance that everything was going to be okay. What she'd said only brought the darkness closer.

"I need three chicken-fried steak dinners for Levi, Roger, and the sheriff," I said quickly. "We've got a full house. I should get out there and take some orders."

"Okay." She reached out and caught my arm before I could get to the door. "Callie, I'm sorry. Please forgive me. It's just that . . ." She stared past me, a forlorn look on her face. "How am I going to explain this to Charity? I hate telling her about the horror in the world. It tears me up."

"I'm so sorry, Lizzie. It didn't occur to me. Having a child is a huge responsibility. I can't imagine how difficult it must be sometimes."

Lizzie smiled sadly. "Yes, difficult and joyous, all at the

same time. Just ignore me. I'll figure it out. God will give me the right words, I'm sure."

I nodded. "You've raised a wonderful child. She can handle this. I truly believe that." I turned to go but then stopped. "Lizzie, why would someone put Levi's book in that woman's hands? I can't understand it."

"I don't know. Maybe the killer found it somewhere and wanted to draw attention away from himself." She sighed deeply. "Don't think about it, Callie. You know Levi had nothing to do with this. Allowing yourself to consider anything else is useless." She offered me a weak smile. "We really don't have time to discuss it now. Let's get these people fed, okay?"

I tried to nod but couldn't stop the tear that fell down my cheek.

Lizzie put her hands on my shoulders. "I'm sorry, Callie. This is obviously harder on you than I realized. What can I do to help?"

"It's not that. It's—"

"It's what?" she said. I could hear the concern in her voice, but it was colored with impatience.

I looked into her eyes. "It's that book, Lizzie. I'm afraid of what it means."

Lizzie frowned at me. "What are you talking about? What do you think it means?"

I took a deep breath and let it out slowly. "If you weren't distracted, you'd have seen it too." I tried to control my trembling. "Oh, Lizzie. Levi misplaced that book somewhere in town. Probably at the church—or maybe here in the restaurant. That means that only someone who lives in Kingdom could have found it. Doesn't that mean that the killer is almost certainly one of us?"

At first Lizzie only stared at me, but as she considered my words, her face went slack. "I . . . I hadn't considered . . ."

I grabbed her hands with my own and pulled them off my shoulders. "It seems so clear to me. No one from the outside could have taken it. Someone who lives here had to place that book with the body. Someone we know."

"Oh, Callie. I'll bet Levi left the book in his buggy when he went to Washington. Anyone could have taken it when he stepped away. I'm sure it wasn't anyone from Kingdom."

I was so frightened for Levi I hadn't thought of that. People in Kingdom bought a lot of their supplies in Washington. Levi traveled there frequently. I felt a rush of relief. Maybe Lizzie was right.

Before I could respond, the door to the kitchen swung open and Levi walked in. "Sorry to interrupt," he said, "but you have a full dining room, Lizzie. I thought you might need some additional help." His voice trailed off as he noticed the looks on our faces. "What's wrong?"

Lizzie swung away from me and picked up some steaks that had already been floured and seasoned. She tossed them into a large pan of hot grease. The loud pop and sizzle broke the tension that filled the room.

"Nothing," she said brusquely. "We need to get to work before we get so far behind we can't catch up."

Levi nodded. "What can I do?"

Suddenly, the door to the kitchen swung open again. "We're full up out there," Noah said, a concerned look on his face. "What's going on?"

Lizzie quickly explained the situation, and within a few minutes, Levi and Noah were carrying out plates and taking orders. When we finally caught up, they sat down to eat with the sheriff, who still looked uneasy. Given the stares he was receiving, it was understandable. Once Roger had circulated through the room, he joined them.

After toting coffee around, I went back to the kitchen. "Everyone's been served," I told Lizzie.

She smiled at me. "Thank you, Callie. And I'm sorry for how I acted earlier. I want my daughter to grow up in a safe environment. That should be Kingdom. When something like this happens, I take it personally. I didn't mean to pass along my discouragement to you."

"I understand. I really do."

She nodded. "The truth is, even with the challenges we've faced, life *is* better here. I guess I want perfection, and even Kingdom isn't perfect. No matter where you live or what you do, the devil is out there trying to get in."

"Well, we just won't let the devil overtake us," I said. "Ruth told me once that it's actually our reaction to bad things that makes or breaks us."

Lizzie leaned against the cabinet behind her and studied me. "Ruth is a wise woman. She's right, and so are you, as long as we're not ignoring the truth." She was quiet for a moment before saying, "Callie, I also want to apologize for what I said about your father. I didn't mean to poke my nose into your business. Will you forgive me for that too?"

I nodded dumbly, not knowing what to say.

"Thank you. I think I'll shut up for the rest of the night. Seems to be the only way I can keep myself out of trouble."

I couldn't help but laugh at that. "First of all, I doubt you could stay quiet very long. Secondly, I would hate it if you stopped talking to me. Besides, I think I'm the one who's opened her big mouth too much today."

She chuckled. "Well, then I'm in good company." Her eyes narrowed as she studied me. "You haven't eaten, have you?"

"No, there hasn't been a moment."

"Well, there's a moment now. You said you wanted meat loaf?"

I nodded. "I can't think of anything that sounds better. It's hard watching everyone else eat when you're so hungry."

Lizzie busied herself with preparing a plate for me. "Has my father shown up yet?" she asked as she added mashed potatoes and gravy to my dish.

"I haven't seen him. Not sure why."

She shrugged. "Maybe he decided to stay out of the situation for once."

"Maybe."

I found that hard to believe, although I didn't say it. There are some people in life who think they have all the answers, and Matthew Engel was one of them.

Lizzie came over and put the plate down in front of me. "Too late for coffee?"

"Actually, I would love a cup. I'm asleep on my feet."

Lizzie poured two cups of coffee and sat down across from me.

"Have you eaten?" I asked.

She laughed. "You know better than that."

I did. Lizzie was a nibbler. She was always worried about her food, wanting it to be the best it could be. She dished out samples of everything as soon as it was done, checking the flavor. By the time food was ready to be served, she'd actually eaten enough for an entire meal. No matter how much she ate though, being on her feet so much helped her to burn off extra calories. Her slim figure proved it. I, on the other hand, was constantly being urged to eat. I'd always been small. Instead of three large meals, I usually ate four or five times a day. Smaller portions. I'd eaten this way as far back as I could remember. However, today, all the turmoil had kept me from grabbing anything. I was just about to say something when I heard a commotion from the dining room. I jumped up and ran to the kitchen door, flinging it open. Lizzie and I got there just in time to see Sheriff Timmons and Roger following behind three men in dark suits and coats who were leading Levi toward the front door of the restaurant.

"What are you doing?" Lizzie cried.

Noah glared at the men and then turned toward us, his eyes wide with emotion. "They're arresting Levi. They think he murdered that woman!"

CHAPTER 5

Noah's words seemed to echo in my mind. At first I couldn't make sense of them. Slowly a wave of indignation rose up inside me, and I cried out Levi's name.

Sheriff Timmons told the other men to stop and turned to face the stunned crowd. "No one thinks Levi killed anyone. I tried to explain that he is only wanted for questioning. I never said he was under arrest."

"What's the difference?" Noah said angrily. "If you didn't believe he was involved somehow, why would you compel him to go with you?"

Jonathon Wiese rose from the table where he sat with his parents. "I agree. Why can't you question Levi here? Why does he have to go with you?"

Brodie glared at Noah. "I explained this earlier. I told you why the authorities wanted to talk to your brother. I thought you understood."

"I did, but you never said they would spirit him away like some criminal."

Roger turned and walked toward the middle of the room. "Don't worry, folks," he said, his voice calm and even. "The sheriff is telling you the truth. These men are from the KBI, and they need to ask Levi some questions. He may know something important and not even realize it. They're just taking him into town to talk to him. The only reason they can't do that here is because we have resources at our office that aren't available in Kingdom."

Before anyone had a chance to respond, a deep voice rang out from the doorway.

"May I ask just what is going on? Who are these men and what are they doing in our town?"

Matthew Engel, Lizzie's father, pushed past the group of men. Matthew presented an imposing figure dressed in black, from his wide-brimmed hat, long black coat, and dark slacks to his black boots.

The government agent who had addressed us took a step back.

I noticed Charity standing in the doorway, obviously frightened by the scene taking place in front of her. Wanting to protect her, I hurried over, took her by the hand, and told her to go upstairs and stay there until we came to get her. She seemed hesitant to leave her mother, but Lizzie nodded at her, so Charity obeyed and disappeared up the stairs.

As soon as she was out of earshot, Lizzie walked up to the man standing next to Levi. She faced him with her hands on her hips and a challenge in her expression. "Do you have a warrant?"

He raised an eyebrow. "We don't need a warrant to ask questions, Miss. We're not charging Mr. Housler with anything." He frowned at Levi. "I thought you wanted to help us find this person before they kill again, Pastor."

Levi shook his head. "I'm happy to help you in any way I can, but I must say once again that I have no idea how my book ended up where it did. I assure you that I didn't put it there."

Matthew came up next to Levi and put his hand on his shoulder. "I do not approve of having people from the outside world in our town, Pastor. I think it would be best if you go with them. For the sake of Kingdom. Besides, suppressing the truth is not much different than lying."

Levi's mouth dropped open. "Suppressing the truth? I don't know anything about this situation, Brother Matthew. I'm not trying to hide anything."

Matthew scowled at him. "No one is saying you are, but I believe it is your duty to avoid any appearance of evil. Resisting their investigation makes you look . . . untrustworthy."

Noah made a noise and rushed to his brother's side. "Levi is not untrustworthy. How dare you cast doubt on his character? I won't allow you or anyone else—"

"Noah, stop it!"

Levi spoke so forcefully that everyone in the room froze in place. "I'm not resisting anything." He gazed around at the people gathered in the dining room. "I have no culpability in this awful matter. I'm going with these men because it's the right thing to do. If I can shed any light on this heinous act, I intend to do so. The rest of you need to remain calm and try to maintain a quiet and godly attitude. Everything will be all right." I knew his words were meant to comfort us, but they didn't have that effect on me. Even though I knew Levi wasn't a murderer, the idea that someone in Kingdom might have been involved in something so . . . so monstrous made my stomach clench. Was that person in the dining room right now? Was he watching Levi being whisked away like a common criminal? For a moment, I worried about getting sick in front of everyone. However, that feeling disappeared as the agent took Levi by the arm again and began leading him toward the front door.

"Stop!" I called out. I ran over to the coatrack and grabbed Levi's jacket. Then I took it over to him, holding it out. "You're not taking him out in the cold without his coat," I said to the agent. For the second time today, I was filled with anger. I helped Levi into his coat and handed him his hat. As he turned to leave I grabbed his arm and turned him back toward me. "You'll be home soon." My voice was strong, but it quavered with unbridled emotion. For a brief second I wondered if I had embarrassed him. But when I looked into his eyes, I saw something there that confirmed my words had strengthened him. Walking out the door, he stood tall, his shoulders straighter, when only moments before they had been slumped in humiliation.

"How will he get home?" Sheriff Timmons asked.

"We'll drive him back when we're done," one of the men said. "It shouldn't be longer than two or three hours."

"I'll come to see you in the morning," Levi said to me. "Don't worry. God is with me."

Even though I nodded and tried to look unconcerned, the tears on my face gave me away. I watched as the men put him into their car and drove off. For some reason I couldn't find the strength to turn around and face all the eyes I knew were fastened on me. Then I felt a hand on my shoulder.

"Come with me," Lizzie said gently. She led me through the silent crowd and back to the kitchen. When I got there, I collapsed into a chair.

"Oh, Lizzie," I said, sobbing. "How could anyone think Levi would be involved in such a grotesque act? It's preposterous."

She knelt down next to me. "Of course it is," she said softly. "Remember that the man from the KBI said they only wanted to question him about the book, Callie. They don't think he killed anyone."

I took a deep shuddering breath and wiped my wet face with my apron. "I know they said that, but I'm not sure I believe them." My eyes sought hers. "They're from the world, Lizzie. Worldly people lie, don't they? That's what Papa said. We can't trust them."

She put her arm around me. "Not all people who live outside our borders are bad, Callie. I knew many good people when I lived in Kansas City. People I could trust." She gave me a hug and stood to her feet. "We're not that much different here. Kingdom is filled with all kinds of people. Good and bad. It's the same in the outside world."

I shook my head. "I know we're not perfect, but I'd like to believe that for the most part we're different. If we're not, why are we here? Why should we live away from the rest of the world?"

She crossed her arms across her chest. "I do believe we're different, Callie, but I don't think we're perfect. If you expect too much from those of us who live here, I'm afraid you'll end up disappointed. And hurt." She shook her head. "You've built a wall of protection around yourself to keep out painful truths or emotions you can't control. Someday that wall may fail. I'm not sure you're prepared for what's on the other side."

I stared at her, not knowing what to say. Papa used to tell me that I lived in a dream world. Was Lizzie saying the same thing? I started to respond but the phone shrilled, cutting me off. I nearly jumped out of my skin. The phone in the kitchen didn't ring much, but when it did, it was disconcerting, to say the least. Lizzie picked it up and said hello. She listened to whoever was on the other end, thanked them, and hung up.

"That was Roger. The KBI has opened the road. There are still agents out there, and they'll be checking the cars and buggies that go through, but at least people can start heading home."

I sighed. "Well, that's a little good news." I started to ask her if she'd like me to announce the road opening to the crowd in the dining room when the kitchen door opened and Noah came in with Charity. Charity held out her arms to her mother, who hugged her fiercely.

"Sorry I had to send you upstairs for a while, Cherry Bear," Lizzie said.

"That's okay," Charity replied. "I got a lot of my homework done."

"I thought you were going to ask my mother to keep her a little longer," Lizzie said to Noah.

"I did, and she said she would, but your father decided to bring her back because your mother wasn't feeling well."

Lizzie sighed with exasperation and let Charity go. "I wish my mother would just tell us when she's ill. I know she thinks she's being a good soldier, but she could make Charity sick too."

Noah grunted. "You know your mother. She wouldn't complain if her hair was on fire."

Lizzie nodded. "You're probably right."

Noah was clearly upset and didn't acknowledge my presence. His attention was fixed on Lizzie. "I wanted to go with Levi, but the men from the KBI wouldn't let me."

"He'll be all right, Noah," she said soothingly. "They said

they'd only keep him a couple of hours. Don't worry. They know he didn't do anything wrong."

"I've got to call my parents and let them know what's going on. I don't know how I'm going to explain it."

I looked over at Charity, whose large dark-brown eyes were wide with anxiety as she stared at her parents. Lizzie noticed her too.

"Callie, could you take Charity out to the dining room? Maybe you could get her a piece of pie."

I nodded and quickly cut a piece of pie and a grabbed a fork. Then I motioned to Charity. "Let's go, honey."

She followed me into the dining room without argument, and I sat her down at the only empty table in the room. I noticed that Ebbie, Hope, and Beau were just getting ready to leave. I hurried over to them.

"Ebbie, the road is open now, though it's still being patrolled by some of the men from the KBI. Could you let folks know?"

He nodded and walked to the middle of the room. Although it took a couple of tries to get everyone's attention, once he shared the news, people immediately began to leave. I quickly checked out the customers who hadn't paid yet, but within ten minutes, the room was empty except for Charity, Matthew, and me. Charity asked for a glass of milk, so I told her to stay put and headed for the kitchen. As I opened the door to the kitchen, I heard Noah say, "You've got to talk to her. And soon. She needs you to be honest with her."

"I'm sorry," I said quickly. "I need a glass of milk for Charity."

"Oh, sure," Noah said, looking uncomfortable. "I'll go out and tell everyone the road is open."

"Don't worry about it. Ebbie already did." I took the milk out of the refrigerator and got a clean glass out of the dishwasher.

"Thanks, Callie," Lizzie said.

"By the way," Noah said, "the KBI talked to Harold. Told him that he and Mercy weren't to describe what she saw to anyone. Specifically, they're not to mention the plastic around the body or exactly where the woman was found."

Lizzie snorted. "As if Harold can keep a secret."

"I know Harold's a gossip," he said, "but all in all, he's a good man. He won't say anything. He wants this killer caught as much as anyone. Maybe more. Mercy will have to live with that awful image the rest of her life. That's got to be tough on a father."

"Speaking of fathers," I said, "how did your mother and stepfather take the news about Levi?"

Noah shook his head. "That's a call I never want to make again. They were shocked, of course. Marvin's first reaction was to drive over to the jail, but I encouraged him to wait. I doubt he'd get to talk to Levi anyway, and I don't think he needs the distraction. I told him we'd call if we heard from Levi first."

I nodded and poured the milk into a glass. As I put the milk container back into the refrigerator, I could feel their eyes on me. Were they wondering if I'd overheard Noah's comment? Had they been talking about me? I wanted to ask them about it, but I couldn't. What if it had nothing to do with me, and I ended up looking ridiculous? I grabbed the glass and left the room.

I delivered the milk to Charity, who was sitting with her grandfather. "How about a piece of pie, Brother Matthew?" I asked.

"Thank you, Callie, but no," he said. "Anna feeds me too much as it is." He smiled at me, and I was struck by the difference in him over the past several months. He had definitely changed in some ways, although his earlier actions reminded me of the old Matthew.

I was trying to come up with a topic of conversation when I heard the kitchen door open. Lizzie and Noah came into the room.

"Are you hungry, Father?" Lizzie asked. I could hear the weariness in her voice. It had certainly been a tiring day. Emotionally and physically.

Matthew shook his head. "Callie has already offered me food. I am convinced you are all trying to fatten me up."

Lizzie smiled, but Noah didn't.

"Levi is a good man, Matthew," Noah said sharply. "He wasn't trying to avoid going with those men."

Matthew sighed. "I did not mean to make it sound as if he was resisting. Perhaps I was not careful enough with my words. My intent was simply to encourage him not to fight their request."

Lizzie sat down at the table with us. "We should all be praying for Levi—and trying to help officials find the person who committed this horrible crime."

"I agree," Matthew said. "The idea that something like this could come so close to us . . ." He shook his head. "It is hard to accept."

Noah didn't say anything. He just kept frowning at Matthew. His lingering anger with his father-in-law was evident.

"What happened?" Charity asked after swallowing a piece of pie. "What horrible crime is Grandpa talking about? Why is everyone so upset?"

Lizzie reached over and brushed a dark curl out of Charity's face. "Nothing for you to worry about, Cherry Bear. Finish your pie. We're going home." She looked at Noah. "Would you mind warming up the truck? It's freezing out there."

He rose slowly from his chair. "No, I don't mind." He stood there for a moment as though he wanted to say something else to Matthew. However, after getting a warning look from Lizzie, he put on his coat and went outside.

"Charity, why don't you run to the bathroom before we leave?" Lizzie said. When Charity started to argue, Lizzie stopped her. "I'm not asking," she said. "It's a long ride home, and there's nowhere to stop. Just go."

Charity sighed and stuck the last bite of pie into her mouth before getting up and walking toward the bathroom. She gave her mother one last withering look and closed the door. As soon as the lock clicked, Lizzie scowled at her father.

"I know you've been saying things around town about Levi," she said. "And I want you to stop it. Don't you dare use this situation to hurt him. He's a wonderful pastor. His age has nothing to do with his ability to do his job."

Matthew's expression hardened. I'd seen that look on his face before and knew what it meant. Sure enough, what he said next wasn't a surprise.

"God's Word states very clearly that a man in authority in the church should not be a novice. It is not God's way to use young men to oversee His church! I do not say this of my own opinion. It is from God himself."

"Being a novice has nothing to do with age, Father," Lizzie blurted out. "Levi is hardly untrained when it comes to the things of God. He has studied the Word and served the church for many, many years. He knows more about God than almost anyone I've ever known." She quickly glanced toward the bathroom door, obviously worried about Charity overhearing her discussion with her father.

Matthew's solemn expression turned even more venomous. "Age has everything to do with this, Elizabeth. Obviously, the longer a man lives, the more he learns. Levi is not even married yet. I believe the church overstepped clear boundaries when he was elected as our pastor. He should not have been considered for this position. He does not qualify."

"But he is getting married, Father," Lizzie said, trying to keep her voice low. "And soon. All of the Scripture requirements will be fulfilled." She shook her head. "Please don't stir up trouble for him. You know he doesn't deserve it."

Matthew stood to his feet. "Getting betrothed simply so he could be voted in as pastor is not sufficient, Daughter. And now, he has become entangled in this evil situation." He shook his finger at Lizzie. "This is what happens when God's commandments are broken. Mark my word. This situation will get much worse before it gets better."

"I wish you'd explain to me why you waited until after Levi was appointed to the pastorate to begin your objections. Why were you silent when his name was offered as a candidate?"

He shook his head. "I wanted to object, but at the time I was encouraged by several in the church to stay quiet— for the sake of peace. After the vote, I realized I had been wrong to allow myself to be swayed by the opinions of others. Christ did not come to earth to bring peace, but a sword. He said clearly that a man's enemies would be those in his own household."

"Brother Matthew," I said hesitantly, "wasn't Jesus talking about the world's system in that passage? That He wasn't bringing peace to the world and that households would be disrupted because some in a family would choose to follow Him and some wouldn't?"

"Callie's right, Father. Christ is the Prince of Peace in the hearts of His children. And you are trying to bring strife and division into His church. I think the Bible has some pretty strong things to say about that, doesn't it?"

"I will not quarrel about God's Holy Word with you," Matthew snapped. "How dare you try to teach the Word to me?"

Lizzie pounded the table with her fist. "Father, I mean it. If you don't let this drop—"

The door to the bathroom swung open, and Charity came back into the room, halting the vitriolic conversation in its tracks. She walked slowly over to the table and sat down next to her mother, leaning against her shoulder. "I'm tired, Mama. When can we go home?"

Lizzie patted her daughter on the head. "Get your coat and your school bag. Your dad should have the truck warmed up by now."

Charity smiled and jumped up, skipping over to the corner where her coat hung on the coatrack and her bag lay on the floor underneath. While she pulled on her coat, Lizzie pleaded with Matthew.

"Please, Father, I'm begging you to think about this before you cause damage that can't be undone. Your legalistic attitude has created so much harm." Lizzie wiped away a tear that snaked down her cheek. "Don't stir this up."

Matthew stared at her, his jaw working. I expected an angry backlash, but instead he only nodded and buttoned the front of his coat.

"I will carefully consider your words, Lizzie," he said finally.

"And yours as well, Callie. Forgive me for losing my temper. It is a problem I struggle with. But you must realize, Daughter, that sometimes we will disagree. I am not always wrong. You are not always right. However, it is true that God is merciful to His children. He has been merciful to me. Perhaps I am not behaving the same toward others." He fastened the last button and frowned at his daughter. "But remember that God also warns us about certain situations—just as a parent warns a child to stay away from danger. We must listen when He chastises us. Both of these paths lead to our protection and security." He stood to his feet. "I know you have confidence in Levi. I hope you will also have some confidence in me." He smiled at Charity, who had come back over to the table. "Thank you for coming to our house today, Charity. I am always so glad when you visit us. You make your grandmother and me very happy."

She grabbed Matthew in an exuberant hug. "I love you, Grandpa," she said.

"And I love you," he responded. He turned his eyes toward Lizzie, and I was surprised to see tears in them. "And I love you too, Elizabeth."

With that, he left. Lizzie was silent as she watched him get into his buggy and drive away.

When he was out of sight, I turned to her. "I'm worried. He could make things very difficult for Levi."

"I know," she said slowly. "My father is as stubborn as they come. If he believes he's right, he won't back down."

"What's the matter, Mama?" Charity asked in her little-girl voice. "Is Grandpa doing something bad again?"

The innocence displayed on her face hurt me. The last thing I wanted was for division to once again rear its ugly head in Lizzie's family.

"No, honey," Lizzie said. "We just disagree about something. That doesn't mean Grandpa's being bad." She cast a quick look my way.

"Your mama's right, Charity," I said gently. "You and your mother don't always agree, but you still love each other, right?"

Charity's dark eyes narrowed as she thought this over. Then she smiled. "Yes. Mama makes me go to bed too early sometimes, but I still love her." She shook her head and her dark curls bounced. Like her mother, Charity didn't wear a prayer covering except on Sundays in church. "I don't want anything to go wrong with Grandpa." She sighed deeply. "It took a while to straighten him out."

Even though Lizzie and I were both concerned about Levi, we couldn't help but laugh at Charity's statement.

The front door was suddenly pushed open, and I shivered from the chilly air that rushed in.

"Truck's warmed up," Noah said loudly. "Let's get going."

Lizzie stood up. "You get in the car with your father," she said to Charity. "I want to talk to Callie for just a minute."

"Not too long, Lizzie," Noah said. "It's late and it looks like we've got more snow on the way."

"Okay."

Lizzie was silent as she watched Noah and Charity head for the door. They both said good-bye to me and went outside to their truck.

"Listen, Callie," Lizzie said when the door closed, "I don't want you to worry about my father. I'll talk to him."

"I hope he reconsiders," I said. "At least he promised to think about his attitude."

"And that's a step in the right direction," she agreed. "He

needs to understand that stirring up trouble in the church again would put us right back where we were a year ago. I don't think he really wants that."

"I'm sure he doesn't."

"As far as I'm concerned," Lizzie continued, "Ebbie Miller, Noah, and Levi are the best leaders we've ever had. And Levi is a wonderful pastor. They all work so well together. I'm convinced they will bring positive changes to Kingdom."

"Elder Zimmerman, Elder Scherer, and Elder Wittsman are strong men of God too."

She shrugged. "I guess. They certainly don't seem to have the passion of the younger men though."

"Maybe that's the reason younger elders are such a blessing. They bring great enthusiasm to the position." I sighed. "Levi loves being our pastor, Lizzie. He's never cared about anything except serving God."

Lizzie grinned. "And being with you."

I could feel myself blush. "Yes, and being with me." I stared at her silently until she frowned.

"What's wrong, Callie?"

I hesitated a moment, not certain I wanted to open a door I might not be able to close. "It's late, Lizzie, and your family is waiting. Why don't we talk tomorrow?"

"A few minutes won't make any difference. What's on your mind?"

I took a deep breath. "Is it possible Levi became engaged to me just because an elder is supposed to be married?"

"Oh, Callie. Is this because of what my father said?" Lizzie got up and slid into the chair next to me, taking my hands in hers. "I know Levi's not very demonstrative, but if you could see his face when he looks at you . . ."

97

I wrinkled my forehead in confusion. "I see his face all the time, Lizzie. He doesn't look at me in any special way."

Lizzie squeezed my hands and laughed softly. "He hides his emotions around you, sweetie. But when he's sitting in the dining room, watching you work . . ." I was startled to see tears in her eyes. She cleared her throat and smiled at me. "Never doubt his devotion to you, Callie. Trust me. Levi loves you. You really need to believe that. It could be very important in the days ahead."

"I was afraid to bring this up. I was so insistent earlier when I said I knew he loved me."

She nodded. "I've been concerned that you didn't really trust his love. But you should." She gazed earnestly into my eyes. "There may be some things you might doubt, Callie. But Levi's sincere devotion shouldn't be one of them."

I was encouraged by what she said, but I still wondered. Did my father think the same thing about my mother before she left us? Would Levi's feelings for me change when he got to know me better? When he realized how flawed I really was? My fear was that someday I would see disappointment in his face. That he would be sorry he married me.

"I still remember when you came to work here," Lizzie continued. "You told me the very first day that you intended to marry Levi. Of course, poor Levi had no idea you'd set your cap for him."

"It must have seemed silly to you."

She smiled. "I guess it did. But after I got to know you, I realized you were the best thing that could ever happen to him. I'm so glad you two fell in love. You already feel like my sister, but when you marry Levi, we'll be real family. Noah's excited too. His brother's been alone for a long time."

"I know. Even though we both had to wait awhile, it was worth it."

Lizzie chuckled. "You're still young, Callie. You didn't really wait that long."

"Well, it seemed like forever to me."

Lizzie's eyes shone as she smiled at me.

"You know what? I understand exactly what you're saying. I felt the same way about Noah. Like I waited an eternity for him. But now—"

"It feels like he's been in your life forever?"

She nodded. "You're going to make me cry, and if I go outside with tears on my cheeks, they're liable to freeze on my face."

I laughed. "You'd better get going before Noah comes back and drags you out."

She let go of my hands and stood up. "You're right." She took off her apron and started toward the kitchen.

"Leave it here," I said. "I'll take care of it."

She stopped and looked around the room. "I feel awful leaving this mess for you."

"Don't be silly. Cleaning up at the end of the day is my job. Besides, I kind of like being in the restaurant by myself." A small meowing sound came from the stairs. Dora had come down to check on me. "Well, almost by myself." She ran into the dining room, stopped, and slowly stretched. Then she meowed again, this time with more enthusiasm.

"I think she's ready for dinner," Lizzie said.

As if he'd been waiting for his friend, Prince's plaintive mew came from the kitchen. "I guess they're both ready," I said with a chuckle.

Lizzie paused as she put on her outer garments. "This

certainly has been a strange day. Frankly, I'm glad it's almost over."

"It won't be over for me until Levi is home."

"I'm sure he'll be fine, but I'll certainly feel a lot better when I know he's been released."

"Me too."

"How are you doing upstairs?" Lizzie asked suddenly.

It took me a moment to readjust my worried thoughts to something positive. I managed a smile. "I love it, Lizzie. Your apartment is so cozy and relaxing. Thanks for letting me move in."

She nodded. "Do you miss your house at all?"

I shook my head. "No. Selling it was the right thing to do. Papa was sick and sad for so long, I'm afraid it wasn't a very cheerful place. He was never the same after Mama went away."

"I understand," Lizzie said, "and I'm so glad you like our apartment. I loved living here, but I'm much more content in our new house. Lots more room." She snorted. "And a bathroom near the bedroom. A nice luxury."

"Well, the apartment has plenty of room for me, and I don't mind using the restaurant bathroom. To be honest, I think I'll miss living here after Levi and I get married."

Lizzie chuckled. "Trust me. Getting married and moving into your own house is much better."

"I'm sure you're right. We're looking forward to living in Avery's home. It needs some work, but it will be a great place for us to start our lives together. I just wish it was closer to the restaurant. It will take me a lot longer to get here than it does now."

"To be honest, Callie, I'm not sure the elders will want

you to work at the restaurant after you marry Levi. They'll probably expect you to be available for church work."

"I know. And I'll do whatever they decide. But to be honest, I'd really miss coming here. I love my job."

She smiled at me as she wrapped a thick winter scarf around her neck. The sound of an automobile horn spilt the silence.

"Noah's getting antsy. I'd better go." She put her hand on the doorknob. "Lock this door behind me, Callie. I'm sure you'll be perfectly safe, but it's smart to be cautious."

Until that moment, it hadn't occurred to me that I could be in any danger. A wave of doubt washed through me. But my concerns were silly and childish. The woman on the road wasn't from Kingdom, and there was no proof the killer was anywhere within a hundred miles of our small town.

"I will," I said, trying to sound braver than I felt. "And I'll see you in the morning."

"Okay. Good night."

Lizzie stepped outside onto the porch and closed the door, but instead of leaving, she stared at me through the big front window. I got up and hurried to the front door, making a big show of locking it. Lizzie nodded and jogged down the stairs. Then she climbed up into the truck. I watched the truck turn around and drive away from town. I wondered how long the men from the KBI would be guarding the road. The thought that they might still be out there made me feel a little better.

I spent the next two hours feeding the cats and cleaning up. Before I finished, snowflakes began to fall, illuminated by the porch light outside our door. I made a cup of hot tea and took it upstairs to my cozy apartment. Dora and Prince followed behind me, their soft, padded feet silent on the stairs.

I took down my hair and brushed it out. Then I changed into my nightgown and curled up on the couch. Prince found his favorite place on my lap, and his quiet purring brought me the first feeling of peace I'd had all day. I closed my eyes, sipped my tea, and was enjoying the quiet, when suddenly, a noise from downstairs cut through the silence. The previous sensation of serenity fled, and I jumped up, spilling Prince onto the floor. He meowed loudly in an effort to relate his dissatisfaction at being dumped without warning.

I eased toward the top of the stairs, my heart racing. Why did I agree to stay here by myself? The sound of a crash almost brought me to my knees. I was alone, with no way to get help. I turned and ran to the window, staring outside, but there was no one there. The streets of downtown Kingdom looked like a ghost town at night. I hurried back to the stairs and slowly began to close the door. It wasn't much, but at least it would afford some protection. It was almost shut when something brushed against my leg, causing me to shriek. I twirled around and found myself looking at Dora, who was busy licking her paws, her mouth suspiciously white. If I could have found my voice, I would have scolded her. I pulled the door open and walked slowly down the stairs. As I suspected, a pitcher of cream was lying on the floor. I'd accidently missed putting it away when cleaning up. After retrieving it and wiping up the floor, I went back upstairs.

"You're a rotten cat," I said when I returned. Dora didn't look the least bit repentant, and frankly, I was so relieved, I couldn't be mean to her.

I got back on the couch and tried to reclaim the tranquility I'd felt earlier. Everything was fine. I should have felt completely safe, but now an undercurrent of alarm stirred inside me. The silent streets outside my window provided no reassurance. It was as if something dark and sinister lurked in the blackness. As I gazed out on the streets of our small town, I could swear I felt something staring back at me. Something evil.

CHAPTER 6

Even though we'd picked up almost four inches of snow overnight, Tuesday morning started out busy and only got more frantic. The whole town was buzzing over the events of yesterday. I kept watching for Levi to show up, but by nine o'clock he still hadn't come in. I began to worry that he hadn't been released last night as promised.

Around nine-fifteen, Roger walked in the front door. After hanging up his jacket on the coatrack, he motioned to me. I filled Abel Bennett's coffee cup and rushed over to him.

"Do you know anything about Levi?" I asked before greeting him.

"That's why I'm here. I drove him back to the farm late last night. He asked me to tell you that he probably won't be in until lunchtime."

I breathed a sigh of relief. "Thank you, Roger. I haven't been able to think about anything else all morning."

"I was afraid you'd be worrying."

"I was. This situation is so upsetting."

"We need to find out who did this and why they tried to implicate Levi. For the life of me, I can't understand it."

"Me either. Levi's the last person who would be involved in something so horrible."

Roger nodded. "I agree."

"By the way, I've been wanting to tell you how nice I think you look in your uniform. You seem so . . . professional."

He laughed lightly. "Well, it may take some time before I feel that way. Right now, I feel like a kid dressed up for Halloween."

I just smiled. I'd heard a little about Halloween, but it wasn't a holiday celebrated in Kingdom, so my knowledge on the subject was minuscule at best.

"Your pocket's torn," I said. "I'm surprised Mary let you out of the house like that."

Roger glanced down at his uniform shirt. "I didn't even notice."

"She must not have seen it either. She's the best seamstress I've ever known."

"If the department had allowed it, I think she would have made my uniform herself."

"That sounds like her. How is she? I haven't seen her for a while."

"She's fine. Busy, but fine."

"How are things with her parents?"

"All in all, very good," he said. "We've been to their house a few times, and they're scheduled to have dinner with us next week. Mary's very happy to have them back in her life."

"I'm so glad. I know this is something you've both been working on for a while."

He sighed. "That's true. It hasn't been easy. For any of us. The Mennonite church has a way of getting into people's heads and keeping them prisoner to outdated doctrines."

I stared at him in surprise, not sure how to respond.

"I'm sorry, Callie," he said, looking embarrassed. "I shouldn't have said that."

I waved his comment away. "It's okay. I'm sure there's truth in what you say, but the church in Kingdom is changing, Roger. Moving away from some of those teachings you might be thinking about."

He nodded. "I'm sure that's true. Again, I'm sorry. Sometimes I don't think before I speak."

"Don't worry about it." I pointed to his ripped pocket. "Can I mend that for you? It won't take but a minute."

He shook his head. "Thanks, but I'm sure Mary will take care of it tonight." He glanced around the room. "I suppose everyone's pretty upset by what's happened."

I shrugged. "I can't blame them. The situation was already unsettling. But when those men took Levi with them, it only made it worse. For the most part, people in this town respect Levi. Unfortunately, there are a few who don't think he should be our pastor. This just adds fuel to the fire."

"I'm sorry." Roger took off his hat and held it in his hands. "Levi's a good man. I hate seeing him dragged into this thing."

"Me too," I said. "How about some breakfast?"

"That was the plan, but it looks like you're full."

At that very moment, Aaron Metcalf stood up from his table and walked to the cash register.

"Why don't you grab Aaron's table?" I told Roger. "I'll get it cleaned as soon as I check him out."

Roger nodded and hurried quickly toward the empty table before someone else grabbed it. I put the pitcher of coffee I was holding down on a nearby table and went to the cash register where Aaron waited.

"How are you, Callie?" Aaron asked as I stepped behind the counter.

"I've been better, Brother Metcalf. First we were faced with this awful murder, and now Levi has been pulled into it. It's disturbing."

Aaron nodded, his dark-brown eyes reflecting his concern. He ran his fingers through his thick blond hair before putting on his hat.

"I know this trial will pass," he said. "We've weathered many storms in Kingdom. This is just one more. God won't desert us." He smiled reassuringly. "Levi will rise above this, Callie. Everyone knows he had nothing to do with that woman's death."

"Thank you for your words of encouragement," I said, smiling at him. "They are appreciated."

He tipped his hat and handed me his money. "They are sincere, Sister."

As he left the restaurant I wondered if he would ever marry. Frankly, he seemed very content to live alone. Aaron was a very private person, even though he ran the general store. Lizzie told me once that there was something about his past he'd confessed to the previous elder board when he'd come to Kingdom, asking to live here. But whatever he'd said was kept secret. Although I'd been told that some churches required those caught in sin to reveal it before the entire congregation, here in Kingdom, those admitting to transgressions were allowed to do so in private. Our early leaders believed that in a town so small, it would be difficult, if not impossible, for a repentant sinner to feel free of his past if everyone knew about it. So anyone who felt the need to repent sought a meeting with the elders, and it was their job to counsel the convicted church member and pray with him to be released from the power of the devil. Confessed sin was never mentioned again—unless the sin continued or someone might be hurt by the actions of the supposedly repentant soul.

I worked hard all morning, trying not to worry about Levi. Finally, when it was almost noon, he walked in the front door. It took everything in me not to run to him, but I finished taking a lunch order from Harold Eberly and then joined Levi as he stood near the cash register.

"I'm so glad to see you," I said, trying to keep my voice calm. "Are you okay?"

"I'm fine." His words were reassuring, but the look on his face betrayed him.

"Why don't you sit down? I'll get you something to eat."

He nodded absentmindedly, gazing around the room. Several of our customers, all church members, stared back at him. I wanted to yell at them to mind their own business. To leave him alone. But of course I couldn't do that. He was on his way to a table that had just emptied when Noah came out of the kitchen and spotted him.

"Levi!" he called loudly. "Thank God you're back."

As if Noah had opened the floodgates, other people began to react. Several told him they'd been praying for him. Relief washed through me, and I felt ashamed to think I'd believed the worst about my brothers and sisters instead of trusting their ability to love and support their pastor. Maybe everything would turn out all right after all.

When everyone returned to their tables, Noah ordered me to sit down and have lunch with Levi while he finished taking orders for me. Although at first I resisted, I was grateful for his offer.

"What time did you get home last night?" I asked Levi when we were alone.

"I don't know. Sometime after eleven. I was so tired I could barely keep my eyes open. My mother and Marvin were waiting up for me. They'd been worried about me so we talked for a while. It was almost one in the morning before I got to bed."

I reached for his hand. Although Levi is usually very hesitant about showing affection in public, he grasped my fingers and held them tightly.

"So what happened at the sheriff's office?" I asked. "Was it . . . awful?"

He shook his head. "No, not really. They just kept asking me about the book. Where I left it. When I lost it." He took a deep breath and let go of a shaky sigh that seemed to come from somewhere deep inside him. "I just can't remember, Callie. I know I had it at the church, but I wanted to take it home to study so I could use the story of Dirk Willems in one of my sermons. Somehow, between the church and home, it went missing." He sighed again and ran his hand across his face. "Those men just kept hounding me with questions, but no matter how hard I tried, I simply couldn't remember the last time I saw that book."

All Mennonites knew the story of Brother Willems, a martyred Anabaptist. He was captured in 1569 and charged with betraying the beliefs of the official church in Holland. He escaped and could have gotten away, but the man chasing him across a frozen pond fell in when the ice beneath him broke. Brother Willems turned around and went back to save the life of his would-be captor. Because of his compassionate gesture, Brother Willems was rearrested. Though the man he saved begged officials to let Willems go free, church officials burned him at the stake. Even as his body was destroyed by flames, Willems refused to condemn the men who took his life. It's a powerful story of love, forgiveness, and choices.

"Levi, could you have left the book in your buggy? Is it possible someone took it when you were in Washington?"

His eyes narrowed as he considered my question. Finally he shook his head. "I'm not sure. I've had so much on my mind, I just can't remember."

"But it could have happened?"

"Yes, it's possible." He took a deep breath and let it out. "Frankly, it would make me feel better to think someone from outside Kingdom did this. If it was someone I knew . . ."

"I feel the same way. This whole situation is terrible. I feel sorry for that poor woman, sorry for you, sorry for our town."

He looked at me, his eyes shiny with tears. "The whole time they questioned me, I just kept thinking . . . why are we trying so hard to hang on to Kingdom? The idea was to create a safe place where our families could live without fear. Without the evil that is in the world. But I'm not sure anymore if it's even possible."

I grasped his hand tighter. "I know what you're saying. I've wondered the same thing. Even Lizzie has questions, but in the end, she believes in Kingdom. She lived out in the world, and some of the stories I hear frighten me. Surely this place is better. Safer."

"Noah agrees. He still talks about what he saw in college. Young people rejoicing in sin as if they were proud of it, the world trying to push God out of every nook and cranny. In Kingdom, we try to honor Him. To live for Him. Even so, sometimes I wonder if the Mendenhalls were right." He lowered his voice. "To be honest, there are times I've considered leaving Kingdom. There's a world out there that needs to know God loves them."

"But isn't there a point when the world becomes so dangerous—so rebellious against God—that we have no choice but to protect ourselves? Lizzie tells me that children cannot pray in school anymore. She says men and women who don't believe in God work hard to remove any trace of Him from public places. I know we teach that God's kingdom and the world should be separate, but to act as if believing in God is a sin? How can a nation expect God's protection when they push Him away? How can we avoid disaster without His help?" I frowned as I thought about Levi's statement. "I don't want my children to grow up in a world where they're not allowed to pray—and where they are regularly taught things that are in direct rebellion to God's Holy Word."

"For the most part, our school in Washington was fine," Levi said. "There were a few things not in accordance with God's Word. But it didn't happen that often."

"Lizzie says it's changing. Now evil is taught as good and good is taught as evil."

"But if we remove ourselves from a world that so badly needs God, how do we expect to influence them for Him?"

I shook my head. "I don't know the answer to that, Levi. There are times I actually envy Lizzie and Noah for seeing life beyond this town. Maybe that sounds wrong, but how can we judge something we've never experienced? I've never been out of Kansas, have you?"

"No, never."

Before I had a chance to say anything else, Noah brought each of us a big bowl of chili and a large piece of corn bread slathered in butter. I'd been so busy all day, I hadn't realized how hungry I was. Levi and I abandoned our conversation while we ate.

I kept glancing at him. He looked worn and worried. I missed his humorous side. Levi and Noah were both funny, but now Levi rarely joked with his brother.

I could still remember the first time I began to have feelings for him. We were only children, and the church was hosting a picnic. The boys were playing baseball, and Levi was pitching. He was sixteen, and I was only eight. When Noah stepped up to bat, Levi seemed to hesitate before throwing the ball. When he finally pitched, it was almost as if he wanted Noah to get a hit. And he did. But Levi had substituted the ball for an unripe apple. When Noah smacked it, it disintegrated, spraying him with small bits of fruit. It was so unexpected that at first people froze, unsure of what had happened. But then Levi began to laugh, and before long, everyone else joined in. And no one laughed louder than Noah. It was at that moment I began to desperately want what the Houslers had. A family that loved one another. That laughed and had fun. I made a decision that summer afternoon that someday I would have a family like Levi's. Down through the years, my desire changed as my love for Levi grew. Now I didn't just want a family like his, I wanted him and his family as my own. His mother and stepfather had incredible love for each other. And their love for their sons was evident in the way they treated them, the positive words they spoke over them, and their undying belief and loyalty toward them and Marvin's other sons.

Unfortunately, even though Levi and I had known each other since childhood, he'd never paid any attention to me until about six months ago. Right after Papa died. He came to console me, and he preached at Papa's funeral service. After only a couple of months of getting to know each other, we both wanted nothing more than to be together forever. Anyway, that's what I'd believed until recently. Had he simply needed a wife? Maybe I was the easiest choice, since I was already smitten with him.

"I have several appointments this afternoon," he said abruptly. "I'll be at the church for several hours."

I was so wrapped up in my own thoughts, I just stared at him.

He smiled. "You looked so far away."

"Sorry. Sometimes when I'm deep in contemplation, I forget other people are around."

He laughed lightly. "I've never known anyone who can drift so far away when they're thinking. I'll have to learn to tread lightly when you have that look on your face." For just a moment, the concerns that weighted him down seemed to lift. But his improved mood didn't last long. His smile vanished as he pushed his empty bowl away.

"I'd better get going. I can tell it's going to be a long day."

I nodded. "I'll see you tonight. I love you, Levi."

He frowned at me for several seconds. "Thank you, Callie." With that, he left.

I stared down at the table, trying to gather my emotions. Levi rarely said he loved me. Today he'd just thanked me after I expressed my own feelings. Was I being overly sensitive? Or was it time for me to face some hurtful facts? Lizzie was convinced he cared for me, but Lizzie wasn't marrying Levi. I was.

I picked up our dishes and was heading toward the kitchen when the front door opened and Bud Gruber came in. He was bundled up against the cold, and his thick parka strained against his bulk. One button had already popped off. His wife, Thelma, had passed away with cancer a few months ago, and Bud didn't seem to be taking very good care of himself. Thelma's cooking had been replaced by fast-food meals and offerings at a local diner in Washington where Bud lived. Lizzie and I both felt sorry for him. Although he wasn't Mennonite, he'd been a friend to Kingdom for many years.

"Hi, Bud," I called out.

"Why hello, Callie," he said with a smile. "I'm here to fix that outlet you been havin' problems with."

I motioned for him to follow me. "Lizzie will be thrilled to see you. I'm glad you didn't have any trouble with the roads."

"They're not too bad, but there's a big storm on its way. Did you all hear about it?"

"I haven't, but Lizzie stays pretty close to the radio in the winter. It's a long drive back to their house, so she likes to leave early when there's a promise of bad weather."

Bud frowned. "Saw some official-lookin' cars out on the road on my way in. Know anything about that?"

"Yes." There were only about a half dozen people left in the dining room, but rehashing yesterday's events wasn't something I felt like doing in front of them. "Follow me to the kitchen, and I'll tell you all about it."

He nodded and trailed behind me, carrying his heavy toolbox. I could hear the tools rattle as he walked. When we reached the kitchen, Lizzie was cleaning the counters.

"Bud!" she said. "So glad to see you. How about something to eat before you get started?"

"Why, I'd never turn down somethin' from your kitchen, Miss Lizzie," he said with a grin. "My mama didn't raise no dummy."

She laughed. "Why don't you put your toolbox down and go back out into the dining room? What are you in the mood for?"

A wide smile spilt his face. "You know what I like."

Lizzie chuckled. "A plate of fried chicken, mashed potatoes and gravy, and my country green beans coming up!"

"I'll bring it to you when it's ready, Bud," I said. "Looks like you have a button missing on your jacket. Do you still have it?"

He took off his black wool cap and shoved it into his pocket. His shaggy salt-and-pepper hair stood on end. "Nah, I don't know where it popped off." He put his thick fingers on another button and wiggled it. "Couple other buttons are barely hangin' on by a thread." He shook his head, looking slightly embarrassed. "Thelma used to keep my buttons sewed on tight, but I just can't seem to figure out how to do it myself. I can fix anything electrical, but I can't seem to thread a blasted needle." He colored. "Sorry. Didn't mean to say nothin' rude. Thelma used to keep my mouth in check too."

Lizzie chuckled. "You're not the least bit rude. Don't worry about it."

He looked over at me. "You was gonna tell me about them cars out on the road. What's goin' on?"

I quickly filled him in on the gruesome discovery, leaving out the worst details and the things Noah had warned us to keep private.

"So they think it might be some guy who did this before?" he asked. He shook his head. "What is this world comin' to?" His forehead wrinkled with concern. "Are you folks safe?"

"We'll be fine, Bud," Lizzie said. "Don't worry about us."

"Well, I think I'll worry anyway, if you don't mind. You all are so isolated."

"The sheriff and the KBI are looking out for us. And no one can get into town without us knowing about it. Besides, I'm sure it's just a fluke that the body showed up so close to Kingdom. The killer's probably long gone by now."

I frowned at Lizzie. I wasn't the least bit convinced of that, but I could tell she was trying to reassure Bud. If he thought we were in danger, he was the kind of man who would camp out on the road until the murderer was behind bars.

"Why don't you give me your coat?" I said, trying to change the subject. "I'll bet Hope has some buttons at the quilt shop that would work just right. While you eat and fix our outlet problem, I'll get your buttons sewed on tight."

Bud looked down at the floor. "I . . . I can't thank you enough," he said quietly. "You folks are so good to me. Sometimes this town feels more like home than Washington."

Lizzie reached over and patted his arm. "I think that's fine, Bud. You've done a lot for us, and we appreciate it."

He slipped off his large coat and handed it to me. "Don't know who's done more for who, but I thank you for sayin' that."

"You go on and sit down," Lizzie said. "How about some coffee and rolls to get you started?"

Bud smiled. "Sounds like the perfect medicine for a cold day." He placed his toolbox against the wall, out of the way, and then went out to the dining room.

"If you'll get his coffee and some rolls, I'll make up his plate," Lizzie said. "But I'm going to give him only a couple of pieces of chicken and a small serving of potatoes and gravy. He needs more vegetables than fried foods. Good thing he likes my green beans."

"He's sure put on weight since Thelma got sick and died," I said. "I'm concerned about him."

"Me too. I wish he lived here so we could keep a better eye on him."

"You heard him say this place felt like home?"

She nodded. "I wonder if the church would let him move to Kingdom?"

I picked up a carafe of coffee and a basket of rolls and butter. "He's not Mennonite. I've never heard of anyone outside the church getting approval to live here." I shrugged. "Anyway, Bud didn't say he wanted to move. Maybe he's happy in Washington. He and Thelma lived there a long time."

Lizzie sighed. "I know. I just hope someone is looking out for him. Maybe he'll meet a good woman and get married again." She took the coffee and rolls from me. "You go on over to Hope's. I'll serve his food."

"Thanks. I'll take the coat with me so we can match the buttons."

I left the kitchen and went upstairs to my apartment, carrying the large coat. As I put on my cloak, I looked out the window toward the church. I could see the steeple, although the actual building was hidden from view behind the businesses that lined Main Street. Dark clouds moved in from the west and provided an almost black backdrop to the gleaming white steeple. Black and white. Good and evil. A chill ran through me as I tied the string of my cloak. I felt a storm coming. One from the heavens and one from the hearts of men. At that moment, I wasn't sure which one was the most dangerous.

CHAPTER /7

It didn't take long for Hope to find buttons the right size for Bud's coat. We ended up removing all of them and sewing on new ones. We also sewed up a few torn places in the lining. It was almost three o'clock by the time I got back. Bud was just finishing his work on the outlet when I returned.

"Perfect timing," Lizzie said when I handed Bud his coat. She pointed at him. "Now get going. That storm is almost here."

"Thank you so much, Callie," he said as he pulled his coat on. "You ladies sure take good care of me."

With that he grabbed his toolbox and headed toward the front door. Before leaving he turned around to look at us, concern written on his face. "You both gonna be safe? Radio says this storm could be a bad one."

Lizzie nodded. "I'm closing up, and Callie only has to go upstairs to her apartment. We'll be fine."

"Okay." He seemed to hesitate a bit.

"Bud, we'll be okay. Don't worry about us."

He sighed. "All right. But you call me if you need anything."

Lizzie laughed at him. "We will. Now go."

He tossed us a quick smile and headed out the door.

"Just goes to prove that there are really good people who live outside Kingdom," Lizzie said. "In fact, most of the people I deal with in Washington are wonderful. You've met some of them when you've gone to town with me."

"I've been thinking about what you said earlier, and you're right," I said. "Papa's doctor was a very kind man. And the people at the funeral home couldn't have been nicer. I was wrong to judge everyone outside of Kingdom as if they were all the same."

The door opened and Noah came in. "Where's Levi?"

"He said he had some appointments at the church," I answered.

"I've got to clean up," Lizzie said. "I'm closing early so we can get home before the storm moves in."

Noah nodded. "Good idea. It's looking pretty bad out there."

"Callie, you're welcome to come home with us," Lizzie said. "You don't have to ride out this storm alone."

"I really appreciate that," I said with a smile. "But I'll be fine."

"Okay, if you're sure."

"I am. Thanks."

Lizzie and Noah stayed in the kitchen while I went to check out our last customer. Samuel Kauffman, Hope's father, had finished a late lunch and stood waiting at the front counter.

"Everything okay, Samuel?" I asked as I joined him.

He smiled. "Never had a bad meal here," he said. "Decided to eat now so I can just snack on fruit and bread this evening. Not sure now if I'll even need that. Lizzie's portions are plenty big enough."

"How are things at the store? You've been running it awhile now, haven't you?"

Samuel had taken over Menninger's Saddle and Tack Store

after Avery Menninger's death. He and Hope used to run the quilt store together, but now Hope handled it alone. It did my heart good to see another woman manage a business in Kingdom. The first woman to step out was Cora Menlo, who started the restaurant. Now there were two women handling their own establishments. Lizzie and Hope would soon be joined by Priscilla and Belle Martin, who were getting ready to open a bakery in the spring.

"The store is doing very well," Samuel said. "And even though I miss working with my daughter, she is right across the street. I can see her whenever I wish. God is good."

"Yes, He is." I handed him his change. "Are you heading home soon?"

He nodded. "Yes. I think all of our businesses are closing early today."

We heard a noise from outside. The sound of children's voices told us that school was out. I said good-bye to Samuel just as Charity came in, lugging her book bag.

"Where's Mama?" she asked. "Miss Leah said there's a storm on its way. We need to go home."

I came from behind the corner. "Your mama and papa are in the kitchen. They're cleaning up so you can get on the road before it gets too bad."

Before Charity had a chance to fetch her parents, they came out.

"Mama!" Charity cried.

Lizzie wrapped her up in a big hug. "Keep your coat on, Cherry Bear. We're headed home."

"I know," she said, her voice muffled by her mother's shoulder. She pushed away, her little-girl face scrunched up with concern. "Teacher says this storm might be a big one."

"It might," Lizzie said, "but we'll be fine."

"She also said to tell you that Brother Wittenbauer picked up Ruby and was taking her home so you didn't need to worry about her."

Lizzie and I exchanged smiles. Elmer was certainly being careful.

"Thank you for telling us," Lizzie said.

"Callie, you said Levi had some appointments?" Noah asked. "What kind of appointments?"

"Counseling. I'm not sure how long he'll be."

"Levi sure does a lot of counseling," Lizzie said. She was taking her coat down from the coatrack. "I think that's his favorite thing to do."

Noah sighed. "Most people would like some time off after everything he's been through, but not my brother."

"Is the truck still running?" Lizzie asked.

Noah nodded. "Yes. I wanted to keep it warm for the ride home."

"I certainly don't want to detain you," I said hesitantly, "but I wonder if I could talk to the two of you for just a minute before you leave."

"Charity, why don't you go wait in the truck?" Lizzie said, smiling at her daughter. "We'll be there in a couple of minutes."

Charity crossed her arms and frowned. "You guys are gonna talk about something you don't want me to know about, aren't you?"

Lizzie raised an eyebrow and studied her daughter. "I'm not actually *asking* you to get in the truck, Charity."

"I know, I know. You're *tellin'* me. I get it." She put her arms down and gazed at me with a forlorn expression. "Bye, Callie. I gotta go now. Sorry to rush off."

"Bye, Charity. I'll see you soon," I said, trying not to laugh. Charity was nothing if not dramatic.

"Lock the doors after you get in," Noah said in a stern voice.

I couldn't remember him ever giving his daughter that particular instruction. It was just one more chilling reminder that an unforeseen evil lurked somewhere nearby.

After Charity left, I sat down at a table near Lizzie. "Are you both certain the police don't suspect Levi of killing that woman? I'm not so sure they're telling the truth."

Noah shrugged. "We have to take them at their word. Besides, if they're looking for someone who's been doing this for a long time, it couldn't possibly be Levi. And frankly, even if they suspected this recent murder was committed by someone else, there's no foundation for suspicion. Levi's been in town all week. Never left once."

"Well, actually he did drive to Washington with Aaron to help him get supplies," Lizzie said. "That was Monday."

Noah frowned. "I didn't know that."

"Your brother doesn't tell you everything he does, you know," Lizzie said with a smile.

"Well, no one can suspect him of hunting down that woman and killing her while he was with Aaron," I said. "And he was in town before her body was found." I shook my head slowly. "I still can't figure out why the killer would put Levi's book at the scene of the crime. Unless he wanted to misdirect the police."

"Maybe it wasn't the killer," Noah said. "Maybe someone else stumbled across the body and placed the book there."

"That doesn't make sense," Lizzie said. "No one in Kingdom would do such a thing."

"I hope you're right," I replied. "But you know as well as I that there are people opposed to Levi's leadership. This would be a great way to disgrace him."

"You mean like my father?" Lizzie said sharply. "I don't agree with him about everything, but he would never do something like this. He may be harsh and stringent in his beliefs, but to plant false evidence at the scene of a crime? A murder?" She shook her head with gusto. "No way."

"Look," I persisted, "someone purposely put that book there. It wasn't an accident. Either it was the killer, or it was someone else. Whoever it was, we need to figure it out. For Levi's sake. Maybe none of those officials think he's involved now, but what if that changes?"

Noah grunted. "I think you're right, Callie. We need to find out who hates my brother so much he'd actually want to make him look guilty of murder. Whoever it is may do something even worse to incriminate Levi. Our only hope is to bring the truth to light."

Lizzie shook her head. "You two. I'm going to start calling you Holmes and Watson."

I wrinkled my nose. "Who are Holmes and Watson?"

Noah chuckled. "Wonderful detectives created by an author named Arthur Conan Doyle. I'll lend you a book if you want."

"Papa only allowed religious books in our house," I said. "I don't know if I should read something so—"

"Worldly?" Lizzie said. She sighed as she looked at me. "The stories of Holmes and Watson are entertaining. Sherlock Holmes was a character who was dedicated to bringing guilty men—and women—to justice. That's a good thing, isn't it?"

I thought about it for a moment. "Well, yes. I'm aware that

some of our people read outsider fiction. Ruth Fisher has a shelf full of books like that."

"Ruth is very independent minded," Noah said. "Lizzie and I have books we love, and some we read to Charity. We're very careful though."

I frowned at them. "Was Papa wrong to forbid me to read anything not approved by the church?"

"I wouldn't say he was wrong," Lizzie said carefully. "There are still quite a few people in Kingdom who believe the way your father did. But there are even more who have decided that not all books outside of those officially accepted by our church have negative influences."

I turned this over in my mind. "I wonder what Levi believes. We've never talked about it."

Noah grinned. "Next time you see him, ask him about the Narnia books we read as children."

"Narnia?" I repeated.

Noah nodded. "My mother and father were both devout Mennonites," he said. "But they also believed in being led by the Spirit. Not by the rules of men."

"Pastor Linden was much more conservative than Pastor Mendenhall," I said, mentioning the pastor who had ruled the church when we were children. "Your parents were brave to go against his wishes."

Noah came over and sat down next to me. "You and Levi will have to be brave too," he said solemnly. "You'll be looked to for leadership, and I'm afraid there will always be controversy. In the Bible, Paul fought against those who tried to put Christians back under the law. The teachings of the church should bring people closer to God—not push them away."

"Some people believe Mennonites are too strict and legalistic," Lizzie said. "But the choices that set us apart now are there to help us. To keep us safe. It wasn't like that when I left. Pastor Mendenhall started moving us in the right direction. I believe you and Levi will continue to bring us closer to what God really wants for us."

As Lizzie spoke, a shiver of excitement ran through me. Could I really be used in such a wonderful way? The past several years had been full of work as I cared for my father. Sometimes I felt as if God had forgotten about me. But maybe there was something I could do for God—and for Kingdom. The possibility thrilled me.

"I'd like to help Kingdom get closer to God," I said slowly. "But I think someone else has other plans. Before we do anything, we need to find out who is trying to destroy Levi's reputation."

Noah stood up and stretched. Then he looked back and forth between Lizzie and me. "I think there's even more at stake than that. A killer needs to be stopped before someone else dies."

"Oh, Noah," Lizzie said, "don't say anything like that around Charity. I don't want her to be afraid."

"But we want her to be safe," he shot back. "We've got to talk to her about what's happened."

"I know." Lizzie shook her head. "I've been putting it off, but I guess we can't avoid it any longer."

The wind blew hard and rattled the building. "Let's get going," Noah said, "before it gets any worse." He nodded at me. "We'll stop by the church and check on Levi. Make sure he knows about the storm."

"Thank you. If he's still there, would you tell him to run

by here and let me know he's on his way home? That way I won't worry about him."

"Will do."

I hugged Lizzie and said good-bye to my two close friends. I watched as they drove away, glad they were on their way home, but Noah's words weighed heavily on my mind. Suddenly, I wished I'd taken Lizzie up on her offer to go with them. I'd told myself that a killer couldn't possibly be living among us. But could I be wrong?

CHAPTER /8

I waited for another hour, but Levi didn't show up, so I finally headed upstairs. He must have gone straight home after his counseling sessions. I'd just gotten settled when the phone rang downstairs. I hurried down with both cats on my trail. Prince and Dora loved to follow me anytime they thought something exciting was happening. Unfortunately, they were very adept at getting under my feet. I almost fell on the stairs and had to scold them. I hoped whoever was calling wouldn't hang up before I got to the kitchen, but thankfully, the phone continued to ring and I was able to get to it in time.

I grabbed it midring. "Hello?" I said breathlessly.

A woman's voice came through the receiver. "Callie, is that you? It's Dottie Hostettler."

"Yes, Dottie. It's me." I loved Dottie. She was such a gracious, kind woman, and I hoped someday she'd feel like a real mother. That was something I wanted desperately.

"I'm sorry to bother you, but Levi hasn't shown up, and I'm worried. Is he there with you?"

"N-no. Noah and Lizzie left a while ago and said they would stop by the church and check on him. He should have been home by now."

"Oh, dear," Dottie said with a sigh. "I'd have Marvin drive over to the church, but he's out rounding up the animals and putting them in the barn. I guess I can get in the truck—"

"Nonsense," I said, interrupting her. "I'll run down to the church. If Levi's there, I'll send him home. Or if the storm gets into town before he has a chance to leave, I'll tell him to stay put. Either way, I'll call you when I get back."

Dottie hesitated. "Are you sure, Callie? I don't want to cause you any trouble."

"Don't be silly. It's only four short blocks. I'll be there and back before you know it. Long before the storm reaches us."

The wind shook the building again. I didn't feel as confident as I sounded, but I knew Dottie was worried. Frankly, so was I. Maybe I got lost in my thoughts sometimes, but Levi was worse. Noah teased his brother about being an "absent-minded professor." Deep thinkers like Levi were prone to losing themselves in thought and not being aware of present serious consequences.

"Well, if you're certain . . ." I could hear the concern in Dottie's voice. It only made me more determined.

"It's fine. I'll call you back in a little while."

Dottie thanked me, and I hung up the phone. I ran back upstairs, changed my clothes, and put on my cloak. The cats seemed interested in my every move and once again followed me down the stairs, weaving in and out between my feet. When I stepped outside, they planted themselves on the window ledge and watched me as if I was the most interesting thing they'd ever seen.

It wasn't a long walk, but after going only a block, the wind began to increase. The temperature seemed to plummet from freezing to bone-chilling. If I got to the church and found that Levi had already left, I would have to hurry back to the restaurant. If I wasn't fast enough, I'd be caught in the ferocity of the storm.

The streets were completely deserted. Everyone had obviously gone home. Except for the light from the restaurant, and the streetlight outside the general store, the remainder of the town was hidden in shadows. I'd hoped Aaron might still be at the store, since some nights he slept there, but all his windows were dark. The flashlight I carried lit the way for me, but just barely. All of a sudden, the sheriff's words about not being out alone jumped into my mind. Once again, I chastised myself for not taking Lizzie up on her offer to ride out the storm with them. What had I been thinking? A wave of panic rushed through me. By the time I reached the church, panic had turned to near hysteria.

As I approached the front of the church, I spotted Levi's buggy. Stormy, his horse, was tied up to the post outside the church. Parked a few spaces away was a white van. I ran to the front door, fighting the wind, and pushed it open. Thankfully, it was unlocked. Once the door closed behind me, I felt incredible relief. Every sound had made me wonder if I was being chased. I locked the door and went looking for Levi. When I entered his office, I found him sitting behind his desk, someone else in the chair that faced him. Levi's eyes widened when he saw me.

"Callie, what are you doing here?" There was a tone of annoyance in his voice.

"Your mother asked me to check on you," I said. "There's a storm on its way. You should have gone home hours ago."

"It's my fault." The man in the chair turned around, and I

saw that it was Aaron Metcalf. "I've kept him too long." He turned back to Levi. "Forgive me, Pastor. I've been selfish."

"It's fine," Levi said. "Are you staying at the store tonight?"

Aaron shook his head. "No, I don't want to get snowed in. I'm headed home now. I hope you'll do the same. And again, I'm sorry I've delayed you."

"I'm here for you whenever you need to talk, Brother," Levi said. "I must apologize for the interruption. Counseling sessions are supposed to be private."

Indignation rose inside me, and I wanted to defend myself. Instead, I kept quiet. Aaron got up, said good-bye to both of us, and left. I waited until I heard the front door close.

"I came here because your mother was worried about you," I said, my voice shaking. "I ignored the sheriff's warning about being out alone because I care about you. Chastising me in front of Aaron was extremely inappropriate."

Levi flushed, and for a moment, I thought he was angry. Instead, he covered his face with his hands. I immediately went to his side and dropped to my knees.

"Levi, I-I'm sorry. Forgive me. It was insensitive of me to say that."

He shook his head and visibly gathered himself together. When he removed his hands, he looked upset. "I'm sorry, Callie. I really am. Forgive me. You didn't do anything wrong. It's my fault."

"Of course I forgive you," I said, taking his hand. "What's the matter? Is it the murder or has something else happened?"

He was silent, but I could see the conflict in his expression.

"Levi, I'm going to be your wife. There isn't anything you can't tell me."

He took my hands and pulled me to my feet as he rose

from his chair. "No, there are some things I can never share with you."

"I don't understand."

He let go of me and walked to the window. Snow had begun to fall, and the force of the wind carried it sideways. "As long as I hold this office, anything said in confidence can't go beyond these walls."

"Obviously someone has shared information that's upset you. Surely it has nothing to do with the murder."

Levi didn't respond. He kept his eyes focused out the window, not even turning to look at me. A cold tickle of fear ran down my back.

"Levi, has someone confessed to the murder of that young woman? Do you know who did this awful thing?"

Still no response.

I could feel my legs lose strength, and I grabbed the edge of Levi's chair with both hands, lowering myself into it before I collapsed.

"Levi, if you know something, you've got to tell the sheriff."

He whirled around and glared at me. "You're jumping to conclusions. I didn't say anyone had admitted to murder."

"And you didn't say they hadn't."

He turned from me and grabbed his hat and coat. "We don't have time to talk about this now, Callie. If I have any chance of getting home before it gets worse, we have to leave now."

I pulled myself to my feet. "You don't need to bother with me," I said stiffly. "I'll walk back to the restaurant. You get going. I'll call your mother when I get back and let her know you're on your way."

"Don't be ridiculous," he snapped. "I'm not going to let you wander around in a snowstorm even if it is only a few blocks. I'll take you back to the restaurant, and then I'll go home."

After blowing out the oil lamp on his desk, he grabbed my hand and pulled me out of his office and partway down the hall. I jerked my hand from his.

"It's too dark to see." I switched on the flashlight so we could find our way in the thick blackness that surrounded us.

Levi didn't argue. I trembled with emotion but wasn't certain what I was more upset about—the idea he was hiding something that could lead to the capture of a serial killer, or the discovery that he didn't trust me. I realized that confessions revealed in counseling were considered a sacred trust, but I was about to become his wife. Surely this edict didn't apply to spouses. How could we share the sanctity and privacy of a marriage with secrets locked in our hearts?

We finally reached the front entrance, and I grabbed the door handle, since I was walking slightly ahead of him. Before I yanked it open, he grabbed me from behind and pulled me to him. Wrapping his arms around me, he spoke into my ear, his voice breaking.

"Please, Callie. I didn't mean to speak harshly to you. I'm just worried—and confused. If you could just give me some grace until I figure out what to do. And don't ask me any questions. Until I have clear direction, I can't answer them." His arms tightened as he held me. "I don't ever want to do anything to hurt you. You're so important to me."

"I'll try to be patient," I said, returning his embrace. "But you've got to learn to trust me, Levi. How will we ever have a successful marriage unless we have faith in each other? I would never repeat anything you say to me in confidence." I pulled my head back and gazed into his eyes. "We're going to be one person. How can a human being keep a secret from himself?"

Levi's eyes narrowed as he stared at me. "I hadn't thought of it that way," he answered slowly and kissed the top of my head. "I'll think about it, Callie, I promise. But right now let's get you home."

He released me and pulled the door open. Wind and snow blew inside with such ferocity, I almost lost my footing. I heard Stormy whinny loudly, obviously frightened.

Fighting against incredibly strong gusts, we pushed against the wind, trying to make it to Levi's buggy. His hat flew off his head and blew away in the darkness.

"I should have brought Marvin's truck," he yelled. "I'm sorry."

I climbed into the buggy as Levi untied Stormy's reins from the post. Then he struggled toward the buggy, finally pulling himself up into the seat next to me.

"I don't know if we can make it," I cried out, trying to be heard over the shrieking wind. "Maybe we should stay here."

Levi shook his head. "We've got to try. I need to let my mother know I'm okay. She's just stubborn enough to get out in this if she thinks I'm in trouble."

He spurred Stormy ahead, but for a moment, I wasn't sure the beautiful black horse would move. After a high-pitched whinny that sounded full of fear, he jumped forward. The snow was so thick we couldn't see more than a few feet in front of us. I tried to use the flashlight to aid us in our progress, but it was like holding a match up in the middle of a tornado. The weak light was useless against the gale.

Levi kept urging Stormy on, and finally a light cut through the darkness. It was the streetlight in front of the general store.

At least we were headed in the right direction. More than once, Stormy stumbled, and I was afraid he'd hurt himself. After what must have been just a few minutes but seemed like an eternity, I could finally make out the glow from the restaurant on our right.

I grabbed Levi's coat sleeve. "There it is!" I yelled.

He nodded and directed Stormy toward the light. When we stopped, Levi jumped out and came around to my side of the buggy. He held out his arms, and I fell into them. He held on to me as we fought against the wind, trying to get up the stairs. The snow was blowing so hard, it stung my face like thousands of little needles. Frankly, I was surprised I could feel anything at all. My fingers and toes had grown numb in the frigid air. We'd barely gotten to the top of the stairs when a frightening sound split through the roar of the storm. We turned to see the buggy flip over, Stormy still harnessed to it. The horse shrieked with terror. The weight of the buggy was pulling him over, but afraid to fall, he was scrambling to stay on his feet. I grabbed the porch railing and tore myself out of Levi's grasp.

"Help him," I screamed. "Get him loose before he breaks a leg."

Levi struggled down the stairs and approached the panicking horse. Within seconds he'd released him from the harness.

I pulled myself down the steps, holding on to the railing with every bit of strength I possessed.

"Put him in Matthew's stable," I shouted. "There's no way you can make it home. The stable's unlocked, and Stormy will be safe there."

"Get inside and wait," Levi yelled. "I'll be back as soon as I can." He pointed a finger at me. "Do not leave the restaurant, no matter what. Do you understand?"

Although I didn't want to let him go, I had no choice, so I nodded my agreement. We were all in danger in this blizzard, and unless the three of us found shelter fast, our lives were at risk. I watched as Levi disappeared into the storm. Then I fought my way toward the front door of the restaurant. It took great effort to get it open, but finally I did, falling into the dining room, exhausted, covered with snow, and shaking from the frigid temperatures. It took several attempts to get to my feet, and several failed efforts to close the door. When it finally latched, I stood there for a moment, totally drained. I wasn't sure I could even make it to a chair without collapsing. Prince and Dora came running down the stairs to greet me but stopped a few feet away. They both eyed me suspiciously, not sure if this drenched, trembling, windblown creature could possibly be the person they lived with.

I wrenched off my cloak, made heavier by the quickly melting snow and pulled it over to the corner. Then I went to the window and stared out toward the street. It was impossible to see anything. Was Levi all right? Should I go after him or should I stay inside as I'd promised? I prayed out loud as I tried to make up my mind.

"Heavenly Father," I said, my voice quivering from the chill that held me in its icy grip, "please take care of Levi . . . and Stormy." I could feel salty tears on my face. They stung my frozen cheeks. "Give Levi the strength to get Stormy into shelter. And bring him back safely. Thank you for your loving protection."

After what seemed like hours, I saw Levi fighting his way toward the restaurant. He fell to his knees twice but finally made it up the stairs. I forced the door open, almost losing it to gusts that threatened to pull it off its hinges. When he finally crossed the threshold, we both pushed hard against the door until it latched again. I threw my arms around him.

"Oh, Levi. I was so frightened. If you'd taken any longer, I would have come out to find you."

After taking a few moments to catch his breath, I was surprised to hear him laugh. "A little slip of a girl like you? You would have been carried away in the wind. Then what would I have done?"

I looked up to find him smiling. I wanted to chastise him for his lack of seriousness, but as I gazed at him, I caught a quick glimpse of the young rambunctious boy I'd fallen in love with all those years ago. My fear and concern seemed to melt along with the snow that was causing puddles on the floor.

"Very funny," I said. "But neither one of us will be laughing when the snow melts and our clothes are soaked." I pulled myself away from him and collapsed into a nearby chair. "Noah keeps some clothes here in case he needs them. I'll get something dry for you. Why don't you go in the bathroom and get out of those wet things?" I looked down at my own dress which was beginning to cling to me, and I shivered. "And maybe you could add some wood to the fire? It's going to be a cold night."

Levi hadn't moved, and I frowned at him. The humor he'd shown only seconds before was gone and his expression had changed.

"What's wrong?" I asked.

"I can't possibly stay here," he said.

I stood up, holding on to the chair to calm my shaking body. "What are you talking about? Surely you're not concerned with decorum! We just barely survived a blizzard. No one, not even Matthew Engel, would think anything untoward about us."

"You're wrong," he retorted, waving his arm around the room. "They will know that I allowed myself to get into a compromising position. They'll think we spent the night inappropriately. They'll think . . ."

I threw my shoulders back, anger shoving away my fear. "*They'll think, they'll think?* What is happening to you? *You* know the truth. And so do I. Are you really so worried about what everyone else thinks?" I felt a fire rise inside me. "Do you really believe God is condemning us for finding shelter? For reaching safety? Is that who you think God is?" I was quivering again, but this time it wasn't because of the cold.

Levi just stared at me, his eyes wide. And I stared back, wondering where that burst of emotion had come from.

Without warning, he began to laugh. Then he grabbed me and kissed me with a fervor he'd never shown before. At first I was stunned, but stirrings of love replaced feelings of anger, and I wrapped my arms around him. When he finally let me go, my head was spinning. Too many feelings at one time had made me giddy.

Levi gazed down into my face. "Do you know when I first noticed you?"

I shook my head.

"We were kids," he said smiling. "It was at a church picnic. You probably don't recall this, but some of the boys were playing baseball. As a joke, I substituted an apple for the baseball and pitched it to Noah. He hit it and it made a huge mess."

Levi brushed some hair from my face, and I realized that my prayer covering was gone. Blown away in the wind.

"No one laughed harder than you," he said softly. "You giggled so hard you squirted cider out your nose. Do you remember that?"

I nodded as tears filled my eyes. It was the same day I held in my heart. I had no idea that Levi even knew I was alive back then.

"Then when you were a teenager, I fell desperately in love with you. I've loved you every day since then," he said softly. "But after your mother left and your father got sick, you began to act differently. I wondered if you'd ever again be the girl who got my attention that summer on the baseball field."

"So you asked me to marry you? Even though I wasn't the girl you fell in love with?"

He blinked away tears. "Because I believed I could find you again. But instead of loving you the way I should have, I've kept you at arm's length. I've been trying so hard to be a pastor, I forgot to just be a man."

"But why didn't you let me know how you felt? I had no idea. Except for polite exchanges at church or in public, you never showed any interest in me. Not until a few months ago."

"You were taking care of your father, helping at the school, and working at the restaurant. I didn't want to be a distraction."

"A distraction?" I sighed. "Oh, Levi. Losing my father would have been so much easier with you by my side."

"I'm sorry, Callie. You're right. That was about the time I was elected pastor. I let that sidetrack me. If I could go back in time, I'd do it differently. You wouldn't have had to face a single moment alone. Can you forgive me?"

I nodded. "As long as you spend the rest of your life loving me, I can forgive anything."

His arms tightened around me. "You'll never get rid of me. Ever."

I involuntarily shivered. The fire in the fireplace was dying, and all the snow had melted into icy water. Levi let me go.

"You go upstairs and change your clothes. I'll get the fire going and then take these things off in the bathroom. After you're dressed, bring me a set of Noah's clothes."

"But what about staying here? Are you still worried about what people will think?"

He sighed. "I'm still concerned about being in a situation that looks wrong. But you and I know there's nothing inappropriate about our being here together. At this point I don't know what else we can do. We don't seem to have any other choice."

A huge gust of wind screamed past the building, rattling the windows.

Levi shook his head. "Anyone who would want me to venture out in this storm has no regard for my safety. The people who love us will respect our decision and trust us."

"Oh, Levi. I just remembered. We've got to call your mother and let her know you're all right."

"I'll do that. You get going."

"Okay. I'll be right back. After I change I'll cook us a dinner you won't soon forget."

I turned to go, but he grabbed my hand before I had the chance to get away. I looked back at him.

"This *is* a night I'll always remember, but it won't be because of the food. It will be because we're together."

I smiled at him and then ran upstairs to change. As I picked out a different dress, I thought over what Levi had said. With the blizzard still raging, there was nothing he could do but stay the night here. Even so, I worried that when this storm passed, we would be left with consequences more damaging and long lasting than anything caused by the tempest that churned outside our door.

CHAPTER 9

After getting into dry clothing, Levi and I sat in front of the fire until our frozen limbs thawed. With the force of the wind beating against the building, I kept expecting the electricity to go out, but so far it hadn't. If it did, we still had the generator that had been used to power the restaurant for years. To get it going, someone would have to brave the elements, because it was housed in a shed next to the building. Unfortunately, the thing we needed the most, the phone, was dead as a doornail.

"My mother must be crazy with worry," Levi said. He'd followed me into the kitchen to watch me prepare dinner.

"I know," I said, "but she knew I was on my way to the church to check on you. I hope she realizes you're not alone."

"I pray she doesn't send Marvin out in this mess."

"I'm not convinced his truck could make it through this much snow."

"Yes, but his tractor might. If she knew I was safe, she'd keep him inside. But if she thinks for a moment that I might be in trouble . . ."

"She loves you, Levi. Most mothers will do anything for their children."

"I know. But she worries about me way too much."

"I like your mother." I hesitated before asking, "Is she glad we're getting married?"

"No, she pleaded with me not to marry you."

I almost dropped the spoon in my hand. "What? Why doesn't she—" I stopped when I noticed his mischievous grin. "Levi Housler! Why would you tease me about something like that? I thought you were serious."

He stood up and came over to me. "You've got to have more confidence, Callie. My mother adores you. There's no one else she's ever wanted me to be with but you. Can't you tell when people care about you?" He took the spoon from my hand and put it down on the cabinet. Then he took both my hands in his and gazed into my eyes. "What happened to you when you were young? Why did you stop seeing yourself as lovable? Can you tell me what it was?"

I shook my head slowly. "I don't know for sure. My mother left, and I began to wonder why. Was I the reason? Didn't she love me enough to stay?"

"But the real change came later."

I put my hands on his chest and pushed him away. "If you want something to eat, you need to sit down and get out of my hair."

"You're avoiding the subject."

"No, I'm not. I just don't know the answer."

"Then we'll search for the truth together, Callie. We need to get everything out of the way that might interfere with our relationship. I intend to spend the rest of my life making you happy. If there's anything that might hinder those plans, I want to deal with it now."

I sighed and shook my head. "You think something that happened to me as a child, something I can't even remember, is important to our future? Yet you can't tell me what upset you in one of your counseling sessions? That doesn't make any sense, Levi."

He didn't respond, just stared at me.

"If you can't confide in me, at least talk to the sheriff." I met his gaze head on. "If someone else dies, will you still believe you've done the right thing? Is this commitment worth another life?"

"Callie, you're just going to have to trust me. If I had information that would stop the killings, I'd scream it from the housetops. But I don't."

I wanted to argue with him, try to push him to share the truth with me. Surely I could help him make the right decision. But the look in his eyes told me he'd drawn a line that I shouldn't step over.

"All right, I trust you," I said slowly. "Just make sure you're not putting some rule laid down by the elders above what's right."

"I understand." He folded his arms across his chest and studied me. "Now, answer my earlier question and quit changing the subject. Did something happen when you were young? Something that hurt you?"

I sighed. "I wish you'd let this go. I have no idea what you're talking about. The only thing bad that ever happened to me was my mother leaving and my father getting sick." I shook my head. "Maybe I just started growing up."

Levi grunted. "Maybe, but it was like the happiness drained out of you. All these years I've waited to see that spark come back."

I gaped at him. "You don't think I have a spark?"

He smiled. "Don't misunderstand me. I love the person

you are. You're kind and generous. Intelligent and amazing. But sometimes I'm not sure you're really happy."

I shook my head and went back to stirring the stew. "Happy, happy, happy. What does that mean? You may be asking too much, Levi. People can't simply decide to be happy, can they?"

"Yes, Callie, that's exactly what they can do. No matter what happens around us, we can rest in the joy inside our hearts. The fruit of the Spirit is alive in us. We just need to allow it to overpower our circumstances." With that he grabbed the basket of bread I'd prepared, along with the butter dish, and left the kitchen.

As I stood there, waiting for the stew to get hot, I thought about what he'd said. Was I supposed to be cheerful about my mother leaving? About my father getting sick and dying? That didn't make sense. Suddenly a Scripture popped into my head. *For as he thinketh in his heart, so is he.* Is that what Levi was talking about? Another beloved Scripture came to me. It was in Isaiah. *To appoint unto them that mourn in Zion, to give unto them beauty for ashes, the oil of joy for mourning, the garment of praise for the spirit of heaviness; that they might be called trees of righteousness, the planting of the Lord, that he might be glorified.* Was it really up to me to put on a garment of praise when it seemed life was handing me something too hard to bear? These thoughts kept turning over in my head as I spooned stew into bowls and carried them out to the table where Levi waited for me.

"The storm doesn't seem to be letting up," he said as I set the bowls down on the table. "We may be trapped here for longer than one night."

"What are we going to do?"

Levi shrugged. "I have no idea. I can't worry about it."

"My plan was to help you be a wonderful pastor, not ruin your reputation."

"I'm concerned just as much about your reputation, Callie. The last thing I want to do is bring your character into question. But what choices do we have?" He held his hands up in an expression of surrender. "Don't get me wrong. I know I have a responsibility to the people in this town, but neither one of us should have to die to protect our honor." He reached over and took my hand. "Look, more than anything I want to be the person God has called me to be. The next most important calling in my life is to be your husband. A good husband. I can't do either one by being someone I'm not." He raised an eyebrow as he gazed at me. "And the same applies to you."

I sighed. "Well, apparently I don't know who I am."

Levi started to say something, but I held up my hand to stop him. "Before you say anything else, you might as well know that Lizzie has been saying the very same things to me. To be honest, I'm not sure who Callie Hoffman is anymore. If you'd seen me yesterday afternoon . . ."

He frowned. "What happened yesterday afternoon?"

As I related the story of my actions toward Elmer Wittenbauer, I expected Levi to scold me for my uncharitable behavior. But he didn't. At one point he covered his mouth with his hand, and by the time I finished relaying the details, we were both laughing.

"I don't know what's so funny," I said, wiping tears of laughter from my face. "I certainly wasn't walking in love. Nor was I turning the other cheek."

Levi grinned. "How about I chastise you later? Right this moment, I'm enjoying this side of you. And as far as finding out who Callie Hoffman is, how about this? I'll help you find yourself if you'll help me in the same way. According to my brother, I've changed too." The smile slid from his face, and he stared off in the distance. "Maybe we've both lost our way." He swung his gaze back to me. "But my heart tells me that together we can find the right path. The one God has for us."

I nodded my agreement as I felt tears prick my eyelids. "I had almost convinced myself that you got engaged to me because the church insists that pastors must be married."

Levi's eyebrows shot up in surprise. "How could you possibly think that?" Before I had a chance to answer, he said, "Wait a minute. Now that I think about it, I can totally understand why you'd come to that conclusion. It's the way I've been acting. I'm sorry, Callie."

I smiled at him. "It's all right. I'm just so grateful we're finally talking. To be honest, I'm indebted to this storm. Who knows how long it would have taken us to open up to each other if the blizzard hadn't forced us to?"

He laughed. "Now *that's* the Callie I remember. You were always able to find the good in everything."

Levi's comment shocked me. Had I really been like that?

"Let me bless this food so we can eat," Levi said. "It smells so good, and I'm starving."

I nodded and bowed my head. While Levi prayed over our food I tried to listen, but my head was so full of thoughts and voices, I couldn't concentrate. I was startled when he said my name.

"I'm done, Callie. Is there something else we should pray about?"

I raised my head and found him studying me. "No," I said quickly. "I'm sorry. Guess I was somewhere else."

"That's okay." His blue eyes searched mine. "As long as you come back. I'm glad you're here with me."

"Me too." I scooped up a spoonful of stew and put it in my mouth. Delicious. "Lizzie is such a great cook," I said gratefully. "I hope you won't be disappointed with my cooking after we're married."

Levi chuckled and put his spoon down. "I'm not hard to please. Besides, I'm sure you'll do very well. You cooked for your father all those years."

"Yes, but toward the end all he could eat was oatmeal . . . and pudding."

Levi held up his spoon. "Then we'll live on oatmeal and pudding. Sounds good to me."

"Levi," I said his name slowly, drawing it out. "You . . . you said we needed to open up to each other. I'm still concerned about your counseling sessions today. I can't get them off my mind."

He dropped his spoon into his bowl, causing some gravy to run over the side. "Please, Callie."

"But you seemed so upset. I'm worried for you."

He started to say something when suddenly a strong gust of wind shook the building, and one of the large windows at the front of the room shattered. I heard Levi shout my name and felt arms grab me, throwing me to the floor. Next came the sound of breaking glass all around me, but all I could feel was Levi's body sheltering me. The room, which had been warm because of the fire, became instantly cold.

"Levi," I said, after waiting for the sound of breaking glass to cease, "it's over. You can let me up." There was no response, and I began to panic. I felt crushed beneath his weight. "Levi!" I called loudly. "Levi!" Still no response. Slowly I began to wiggle out from underneath him. As I tried to free myself, I cut my hands and arms on several small pieces of glass that covered the floor. Finally I pulled my body free. Levi lay motionless on the floor, his head resting against the table leg. I lightly touched the side of his head and found a large lump. It was then that I noticed his dark-blue shirt was almost black with blood. Several large shards of glass stuck out of his back.

CHAPTER 10

At first I was frozen with fear, but then I began to pray with all my might, calling on God to help us. I ran upstairs, grabbed some towels and a large quilt, and then I hurried back down, taking the towels to the washroom. As I ran, glass crunched under my shoes. After the towels were damp, I rushed back to where Levi still lay on the floor. Praying for wisdom, I began to remove each shard of glass from his back, putting pressure on the wound from the largest shard so the bleeding would stop. When the last piece of glass was gone, I turned Levi onto his side and then pushed the broken shards on the floor away from him with a napkin I took from our table. Once the area was clear, I pulled the quilt next to him and began removing his shirt. It took a while because I had to push him back over on his stomach to get the blood-drenched shirt off. When I finally had him settled, I began cleaning his wounds with the wet towels. Thankfully, most of the wounds weren't very deep. Once the bleeding slowed down, I went to the medicine cabinet and got some mercurochrome. When I returned, Levi was trying to push himself up from the floor.

"Please, don't move," I said. "I need to put medicine on your cuts."

He lowered himself back down onto the quilt. "What happened?" He saw the broken glass on the floor. "Oh, the window." Once again he started to raise himself up.

"Levi!" I said sternly, "stay down. You'll start bleeding if you move too much."

"Are . . . are you all right?" he asked, his voice weak.

"I'm fine, thanks to you. And you'll be fine too. Your cuts are shallow, but you've lost a lot of blood, and you hit your head. You may feel faint for a while."

"Why is it so cold?" he asked, his voice quaking.

"Because of the broken window. And I had to remove your shirt."

"My shirt? Oh, my goodness, Callie. It's not proper. I need—"

"Levi Housler! You could have died, and you're worried about a silly shirt! You're being ridiculous."

He started to say something but then seemed to think better of it. "Okay, but when you're done, do you think you could find me something to wear?"

"Fine. But right now, I need you to be brave. This is going to sting. A lot."

"I doubt I could hurt any worse than I do now."

"I wouldn't count on that," I said gently. "Hold on."

I dabbed at his cuts with a liberal amount of mercurochrome. He didn't say a word, but the muscles in his back clenched with pain. When I felt the wounds were clean enough, I got up from the floor. "How's your head?"

"Frankly, I hurt in so many places it's hard to figure out where the pain is coming from." He touched his scalp gingerly. "I think I hit my head on the edge of the table when I grabbed you."

"Well, before you put on another shirt, I need to bandage your back. Don't move."

He didn't argue this time. The wind was blowing snow into the dining room. Now the floor was covered with snow as well as glass. I was afraid we'd lose the fire in the fireplace, but the added air seemed to only fuel it. Unfortunately, it was no match for the bitter cold. It was almost unbearable. I got the first-aid kit in the kitchen, grateful to discover that it was stocked with gauze and tape. It took me only a few minutes to bind up Levi's back. I hurried to the basement to check the clothes Levi had worn earlier in the evening. I'd thrown them into the dryer right after he'd changed. Fortunately they were dry, so I brought them upstairs.

When I reached the dining room, I discovered Levi sitting in a chair.

"I wanted to use the quilt to cover myself, but it's full of glass now," he said when I came into the room. He shivered and shook from the cold.

"Here. Put these on." I held them out, but he didn't take them.

"Callie, you're bleeding!" he cried.

I'd forgotten about the cuts on my arms and hands and was dismayed to see blood dripping from my arms. "Take these clothes before I get blood on them," I said.

Levi grabbed them and started to lay them down on the table next to us.

"No, Levi! There's glass on the table. Just go in the bathroom and change. I'll clean myself up. I'm fine. Really."

Although I could tell he was reluctant to leave me, he got up and walked slowly to the bathroom. While he was gone, I went into the kitchen, pulled up my sleeves, and washed the blood off my arms and hands. I was glad Levi hadn't noticed the blood running down my legs. My knees were shredded, but I was happy to see that all the cuts were superficial. I cleaned myself up the best I could. Using cold water slowed the bleeding. When I got back to the dining room, I found Levi waiting for me.

"Sit down. Now I'm going to tend to you."

I shook my head. "I'm fine. They're just tiny scratches."

"Sit, Callie. I mean it." With a sigh I plopped down in a chair that had been cleaned off. Levi applied mercurochrome to the larger scratches, and bandaged one long one that had started to bleed again. I didn't tell him about my knees. There was no way I could lift my skirt in front of him.

"I appreciate the help," I said, "but maybe we should do something about the window."

Levi stood up but swayed a bit. I reached out to steady him. "You're weak. You need to rest."

He shook his head. "It's freezing. I don't suppose there's any plywood around here?"

"Noah brought some supplies from the house and stored them in the basement. I'm not sure what's down there."

"You stay here and start sweeping up the glass. I'm going downstairs to see what I can find."

"Are you sure you should be going down the stairs? You're as white as a sheet. Besides the blood loss, you hit your head pretty hard. I'm afraid you might have a concussion. "

"I'm okay, Callie. I'll hold on to the railing, and if I feel like I'm going to pass out, I'll sit down. I promise."

I let him go, even though I was worried about him. As soon as he disappeared from sight, I cleaned the scratches on my knees and legs and applied bandages. When I finished I got the broom and tried to sweep up the broken glass. It was a losing battle. The wind kept blowing the smaller pieces around the room. Eventually, I got most of it into a pile in the corner and managed to dump several loads into a large trash can. There was no way to clean up everything with the intermittent blustery gusts that raged through the dining room.

As I waited for Levi to come back, I realized my head felt uncomfortable. When I reached up to touch my hair, I found tiny slivers of glass under my fingertips. I went to the bathroom and checked in the mirror. Sure enough, my hair was a mess. The only thing I could do was pull my bun apart, hang my head down, and start brushing out the fragments. My hair really needed to be washed, but right now, taking care of Levi and covering the window were more important.

I heard a noise in the dining room and came out. Levi was pulling two large pieces of board across the room. When he saw me, he almost dropped them. I'm sure I looked like a wild woman with my long, curly red hair flying everywhere in the wind. But he didn't say anything. He just went back to dragging the wood toward the front window. I could see he was struggling. Every step he took forward, the wind pushed him back two. The large pieces of wood caught the strong gusts just right, making it almost impossible for him to make any progress. I ran over and grabbed the other side of the boards, trying to help him get them next to the empty space where the window had once been. We fought to get the first piece of wood in place. Levi took some long nails and started hammering the plywood into the wall. We stood behind it, somewhat protected from the storm. After a quick breather, we struggled once again to get the other board in place. It took some time to steady it enough for Levi to get the first nail in. By the time it was secure, I was exhausted. If it wasn't for the remaining glass scattered around, I would have just slumped down to the floor. One look at Levi told me he was in much worse shape than I was.

"Lean on me," I ordered.

He didn't argue. His weight was almost more than I could bear, but I managed to get him to the one chair we'd already dusted off. The room was beginning to warm up again.

"You sit here while I finish cleaning up this mess."

Levi pointed at the bowls of stew we'd been eating when the glass was blown out. "I don't think we'll be able to finish that." He shook his head. "I'm sorry, Callie, but I feel faint. Is there anything hot I can eat? I'm sorry to cause so much trouble."

"Don't be silly. You need food to help you build your strength. There's more stew on the stove, and it doesn't have glass in it." I pointed to the stairs. "Why don't you lie down for a while?"

"I can't go up there."

"Levi, if you pass out, I'm too small to carry you. For my sake, please go upstairs and rest. I'll bring you some food in a little while."

He stood up, and I went to his side. It took us some time, but I finally got him to my apartment. I started to take him to my room, but he resisted.

"The couch is fine."

I got him settled on the couch with a pillow and a quilt. The fire in the corner stove had kept the upstairs nice and warm. Levi was asleep almost as soon as he laid his head down. After pulling the quilt up, I kissed him lightly on the forehead and started toward the stairs. A small mewing sound from behind me made me stop and go back. I got down on my knees and found Prince and Dora huddled under the couch.

"Oh, you poor things," I whispered. "You must be terrified." I couldn't believe I'd forgotten about them in the ruckus. I got up and ran downstairs. It only took me a couple of minutes to put some tuna in a bowl and carry it back up the stairs. It took even less time for the two frightened cats to crawl out from their hiding place and start eating their special treat.

I checked on Levi again. He was sleeping so soundly I decided not to wake him, even though he'd asked for food. At this point, sleep might be better for him. I tiptoed out of the apartment, careful to shut the door behind me. I didn't want the cats around the broken glass.

It took me a long time to clean up glass, blood, and melted snow. After that, I went to the basement and got in the shower. I washed my hair several times, trying to make sure all the glass was out of it. The scratches on my arms and legs stung when the hot water hit them, but it was worth it. By the time I came upstairs, I felt much better. The dining room was back to normal except for the plywood on the front window. I took a quick peek outside through another window, not wanting to get too close in case it broke as well. The storm didn't seem to be letting up. I'd decided to turn on the radio in the kitchen to see how long it would last, when suddenly the lights went out.

I shook my head in the dark. Maybe losing electricity was a major disaster in the outside world, but in a Mennonite town, it really wasn't a big deal. I felt my way into the kitchen, found the flashlight, and then went to the basement and gathered up several oil lamps, putting them into a large box. When I got upstairs, I lit a couple of them and set them on tables. After that, I went upstairs and lit two more. With fires burning in the fireplace downstairs and in the stove upstairs, the rooms were cozy and warm. Tomorrow, when the wind settled down some, Levi could go outside and start the generator. That would keep Lizzie's food from spoiling.

At first I couldn't find the cats, but finally I discovered Prince curled up next to Levi, who was dead to the world. Dora was in my room, sleeping on my bed. My small bed looked so inviting, but I couldn't sleep upstairs with Levi in the other room. For his sake, if not my own, I'd have to find another place to rest. I gently pushed Dora off the bed and yanked on my mattress. It wasn't heavy, but it was a little awkward. I scooted it out of the room, past Levi, and over to the stairs. It took a while, but I finally tugged it down the stairs and into the dining room. Then I hauled it over near the fire. One more trip upstairs to retrieve my pillow and my quilt, and I finally had a place to lie down. At first it felt strange, trying to sleep in my clothes, but I was so tired it didn't take long for me to nod off. Although most people in Kingdom might have found our situation untenable, I was comforted by the knowledge that our hearts were pure.

As I drifted off to sleep, I thanked God for keeping us safe.

CHAPTER / 11

Startled awake by a strange noise, I sat up, confused as to why I was downstairs and fully dressed. Then I remembered the events of the night before. I flung off the quilt and got to my feet. My body ached all over. It felt as if every joint was on fire. I tried to brush the wrinkles out of my skirt, but it didn't help much. I was surprised to see Levi standing by the door, peeling off his coat and gloves.

"What are you doing?"

He jumped at the sound of my voice. "I thought you were still asleep. You almost gave me a heart attack."

"Well, you might warn a person before you sneak out."

"I most definitely was *not* being sneaky. When I got up this morning, I discovered our electricity was out, so I started up the generator. Now Lizzie's food will be safe, and we can cook."

I laughed. "*We* can cook? So you'll be fixing breakfast?"

He came over and kissed my cheek. "I'll have you know that I'm a pretty good cook. Why don't you have a seat and let me show you?"

I lifted my hand and felt my hair. It was sticking out all

over. "Oh my. If you don't mind, I'd like to make myself presentable before we eat."

He smiled. "I think you look wonderful, but if you need to freshen up, go ahead. I'm going to put a few more logs on the fire."

I hobbled up the stairs, willing my sore legs to move. When I got to my apartment, I went into the bedroom to get a change of clothes. Although I tried to ignore the mirror on the dresser, I felt drawn to it. The image that greeted me was shocking. My hair was a mass of flattened red curls sticking out every which way. I grabbed my brush and shaped it into a bun. Reaching into my wardrobe, I grabbed a fresh dress and a prayer covering and changed out of my wrinkled clothes. Finally, the girl staring back at me from the mirror more closely resembled the Callie I knew.

Before going downstairs I glanced out the window. Dark clouds covered the sky and snow still fell, although it was much lighter than it had been last night. When I reached the dining room, I found Levi waiting for me.

"How are you feeling?" I asked.

He smiled. "With my fingers."

I chuckled. "I take it that means you're stronger this morning?"

He took my hand and led me to a table. "You relax and let me get you some coffee." He swept his hand around the room. "It's clear you worked hard last night, cleaning this up. Taking care of me." He took my other hand and grasped my small fingers in his large ones. "I should have been the one to sleep downstairs though. I'm sorry I didn't wake up in time to move to the dining room."

"You needed your sleep. Besides, my mattress is light, and

160

it wasn't any trouble." I grinned at him. "But if we spend another night here, I think I'll trade with you."

"Agreed." He paused for a moment. "Callie, I can't thank you enough for everything. You've tended to my outside wounds as well as my inner ones."

"I wasn't aware I'd done anything that dramatic," I said, unable to keep the emotion out of my voice. "You're being too modest, you know. You probably saved my life last night. Throwing yourself on top of me like that." I shook my head. "If anything serious had happened to you . . ."

He pulled my fingers to his lips and kissed them. "But it didn't. I'm fine. You're fine." He gently released my hands. "Now you rest. You must have been very tired. You slept pretty late."

"What time is it?"

"According to the battery-operated clock in the kitchen, it's a little after two o'clock."

I couldn't believe my ears. "I'm shocked. I wonder what time I went to bed."

"I have no idea, but you deserve to be waited on." He gave me a wide grin. "Your wish is my command. How about coffee to start? Even though it's past time for lunch, I think breakfast is still in order. Whatever you want. As long as it's bacon and eggs, since that's the only thing I'm confident enough to make for you."

I laughed. "Well, then I guess I'll take bacon and eggs. But are you sure . . ."

Levi held his hand up, his blue eyes full of humor. "There is nothing I'd like better than to make you breakfast. My mother made sure Noah and I knew how to cook a few dishes. She said she didn't want to worry about us starving to death if we were ever out on our own. Certainly helped Noah when he was at college those two years."

"My thanks to your mother, then." Thinking of Dottie Hostettler made me remember her frantic call from the night before. "Oh, your mother. I don't suppose the phone's working yet."

Levi shook his head. "Tried it first thing after I got up. It's still dead."

"Your mother has strong faith," I said gently. "She knows God will take care of you." I sighed. "I wish I were more like her. Sometimes I feel so powerless."

Levi crossed his arms across his chest and raised an eyebrow. "Are you serious? I don't think a powerless woman could have done what you did last night. You took care of me, and you cleaned up a mess so big it would have taken three men to match you. You're not weak, Callie. You're just not confident." He frowned. "I blame your father for that."

I felt the blood rise to my face. "My father? How can you say that? I swear, you and Lizzie seem to have something against him."

Levi studied me for a moment. "I'm going to start breakfast. Why don't we talk about this later?"

I started to protest, but he put his finger up to his lips. "Later. Right now I need to throw some bacon into a pan and scramble some eggs. It's been a while. A small prayer for your protection may be in order."

He left the room but returned a few minutes later with a carafe of coffee and a cup. He set them down in front of me. "I've never made coffee before. I hope it's the right strength. It looks a little dark."

I poured some coffee into my cup and took a sip. Even

though I tried not to react, I shuddered at the bitter liquid. Trying to smile, I said, "It . . . it's fine."

Levi's hearty laugh made me giggle. He shook his finger at me. "Lying is a sin, Callie Hoffman. If we're going to spend the rest of our lives together, you need to start telling me the truth."

I took a deep breath. "Okay, Levi Housler. This may be the worst coffee I've ever had in my entire life."

He grinned. "Boy, when you tell the truth, you jump in with both feet." Levi picked up my cup and took a quick sip. "Oh my. This really is bad." He picked up the carafe and the cup. "Easy to fix. A little diluting is in order." With that he went back to the kitchen.

His comment about Papa had upset me, but his antics made me feel lighthearted and happy, so it was easy to overlook. While he was gone, I got up and walked over to the front windows. I couldn't see much out of the remaining window since it was covered with frost. Although the room was warm near the fireplace, the closer I got to the door and windows, the colder it got. I slowly pulled the door open. Even though the bitter air made me gasp, I was overwhelmed by the beauty in front of me. Kingdom was covered with thick, white, glistening snow, and the trees looked as if they were encased in white lace. I couldn't guess how much snow had actually fallen, but it appeared to be more than a foot. Main Street wasn't even visible. The steps up to the porch had disappeared too. Drifts blown up next to buildings were very high, as tall as me. I wondered how much more we would get before it was over.

How would Levi and I ever get out of here? We were blessed to have plenty of food, and I wasn't really worried about others in our community. Kingdom was a very self-sufficient town, and we all prepared carefully for the winters, knowing they could be harsh in this part of the country. But in my lifetime I could only remember one other storm that had dropped this much snow or blown with the ferocity of this winter monster. It had happened right before my mother left. The snow was so deep we were trapped inside for a week. I thought playing in the snow was fun, but Mama, who was already depressed, saw it as one more hardship in a long line of difficult circumstances.

I pulled the door shut just as Levi came back with the coffee. I could smell the bacon cooking, and my stomach rumbled from hunger.

"I think you'll like this better," he said as he set my cup down.

"It couldn't be any worse," I quipped.

"Very funny. It's beautiful outside, isn't it?"

"Yes, but it's still snowing. We may be here awhile."

Levi frowned. "I keep wondering if I should have tried to make it home last night. It was rough outside, but—"

"Stop," I said firmly. "We did the right thing. Besides, we would have had to get your buggy upright, and I don't think I would have been much help." I smiled at him. "We just need to have faith that everything will turn out all right."

"I trust God to defend us. It's just that I don't like putting you in this position. People are people. There's bound to be talk."

I shrugged. "Well, we'll just have to ignore it, won't we? The people who matter will believe us."

"I know. But a pastor has to think about appearances. I don't want to cause anyone to stumble in their faith."

I shook my head. "This is silly. We've been over this and over this. It's time to drop it. I thank God we made it to shelter." I slid back into my seat at the table and picked up the cup of coffee Levi had filled for me. Although I was a little hesitant, I took a sip. It was perfect. My smile must have given Levi some assurance, because the muscles in his face relaxed.

"I know you're right," Levi said. "Guess I need to let it go."

I could hear the hesitation behind his words. "Look," I said with a smile, "let's have a nice breakfast. We'll be here for a while, and I don't want to spend our time worrying about what other people might say. Besides, it's entirely possible that except for our families, no one will ever know."

Levi's expression brightened. "Maybe you're right. You know, we won't get this much time together again until after we're married. We might as well enjoy it. Breakfast coming right up!"

He hurried out of the room, and I could hear him banging around in the kitchen. It felt odd to have a man cook for me. Very few Mennonite men cooked, but all the women were expected to. After my mother left, I had to pick up where she left off. I wasn't very good at it in the beginning. It took a while to bake biscuits that were as light and fluffy as hers. And I burned more than one roast before figuring out the right way to do it. Eventually, I learned to hold my own. I wasn't as good as Lizzie, but working with her had allowed me to pick up some of her recipes and skills.

I could hear Levi humming while he prepared breakfast. Tears filled my eyes as I thought about how blessed I was to have found a man like him. There wasn't anyone else in the whole world I'd rather spend my life with. There were several women in Kingdom who seemed unhappy with the match they'd made. Divorce was not allowed in our community, so they were destined to spend their lives in an unfulfilling union.

The night before I hadn't read my Bible as I usually did every evening before bed, so I ran upstairs, got it from my nightstand, and brought it back down. How wonderful it would be to hear Levi read some Scriptures this morning. Prince and Dora followed me, deciding it was safe to venture downstairs. I needed to feed them but decided to wait until Levi was finished in the kitchen so we wouldn't get in his way.

"Here we are!" Levi proclaimed proudly as he came out of the kitchen. "Breakfast for my lady."

I giggled as he carried two plates to the table. Prepared for the worst, I was surprised to find bacon fried to just the right crispness and a pile of fluffy scrambled eggs. A piece of Lizzie's homemade bread sat on one edge of the plate. It was beautifully buttered and toasted.

"One more thing," Levi said after putting our plates on the table. He jogged back to the kitchen and came back with a bowl of Lizzie's homemade apple butter.

"Oh, Levi. It all looks so good."

He raised one eyebrow and looked at me with suspicion. "You didn't think I could do it, did you?"

I laughed and shook my head. "Noah prepares meals whenever Lizzie is sick, but you're the only man who's ever cooked just for me."

He smiled sweetly. "It won't be the last time. I like doing things for you."

I shook my head. "I've never known anyone like you, Levi Housler."

"You brought your Bible?" he said, pointing at it. "Were you really that afraid of my cooking?"

I laughed. "I thought maybe you could read to me after we eat."

He broke out in a wide smile. "I would love that."

"Um, Levi. There is one little problem with the breakfast."

He frowned and stared down at our plates. "A problem? Everything looks fine to me. We have hot coffee. Not too strong. Eggs, bacon, toast." He looked at me with a confused expression. "I know Lizzie always serves hash browns, but I've never made them. I don't know how to—"

"That's not it," I said chuckling. "Are we supposed to eat with our hands?"

"Oh my. I guess I wouldn't make a good waiter. I'll be right back." He jumped up and made another trip to the kitchen, this time returning with utensils. "How you do this job all day long is beyond me. I'm already tired, and I'm only taking care of you and me."

"It's not easy on my legs, but I really do enjoy it. I love talking to everyone, feeling like I'm part of a large family."

He raised one eyebrow. "You know the church will probably want you to quit after we're married, right?"

"I know. Whatever they ask me to do, I will." I smiled at him. "Being your wife is more important to me than anything else. And besides, I'm sure there will be lots to do in the church that will keep me busy."

"Yes, I suppose that's true," he said slowly. "Well, I'll ask the blessing, and then you can judge my talent in the kitchen."

We bowed our heads and Levi prayed, blessing our food and also thanking God for keeping us safe in the storm. He prayed for everyone else in Kingdom and that God would give him wisdom about dealing with our circumstances. I loved to listen to him pray. Levi's prayers sounded so personal. Not like Papa's, which had been formal and distant. When I was young, I'd prayed just like him. Not long after Mama left Kingdom, Ruth Fisher befriended me. She prayed like Levi, and after hearing her, I began to get more intimate with God. At first it was a little scary. Something she said once popped into my head. *"God loves you like a perfect Father,"* she'd told me. *"Not like our earthly fathers, who may not know how to love little girls in the right way."*

I heard Levi say "Amen" and repeated it. But Ruth's words stuck in my head. It was true that my father was distracted when Mama left, but he was a good father, wasn't he? I sighed and shook my head. Lately, it felt as if I was continually defending Papa. Why?

"What are you sighing about?" Levi asked.

"Nothing. Eat your breakfast." I stuck a piece of bacon in my mouth. "Oh my. It's so good. For some reason I've been ravenous ever since last night."

"Me too, although I ate some fruit and bread after I got up. I was hungry and weak. I felt a lot better after I got a little food in my stomach." He leaned back in his chair, and I saw him wince.

"Oh, Levi. Your back. I need to check the bandages. Do your injuries hurt? And what about your head?"

"My head feels fine today. The bump is almost gone. But for some reason my back stings more today than it did last night."

"Your wounds are healing. There's some aspirin in the medicine cabinet. I'll get it for you."

"Please finish your breakfast first. I went to all this trouble. The least you can do is to eat it while it's hot."

He smiled when he said it, but I could tell he was uncomfortable. I ate quickly, although it was so good, it would have been nice to savor it a little longer. When I got the last bite of eggs down, I went to the bathroom and located the aspirin. I hurried back and handed it to him before I realized he had nothing to take it with.

"You can't take aspirin with hot coffee," I said. "I'll get you a glass of water."

I patted him on the shoulder and headed toward the kitchen. When I opened the door, I was shocked by what I found. It was a mess. Levi had left all the dirty pans sitting around and grease was splattered on the floor. I almost slipped and fell. Lizzie had complained more than once about Noah not cleaning up after himself. Obviously, it ran in the family. Not wanting to offend Levi, I quickly rinsed some dishes and put them in the dishwasher. I'd have to come back later and clean up the rest of it. I guess Lizzie was right when she told me that men only see what they want to.

I pushed the door open and called out, "Here's some water," but Levi wasn't sitting at the table. Looking around the room, I saw that the front door was open. I put the water on the table and went to the door. As I got closer, I could hear an engine running. Levi stood outside on the front porch. Parked in front of the restaurant was a large tractor with chains on its tires. It took me a moment to make out the figure sitting in the cab. It was Marvin Hostettler.

"It's Marvin," Levi said when he saw me. He didn't sound too happy, and frankly, I wasn't either. Although I knew I should be thrilled that rescue had come, I'd been looking forward to spending a little more time alone with Levi. I quickly blinked away tears. The last thing I wanted was for Marvin to think we weren't grateful for his help.

Marvin pushed open the door of the cab and climbed out. He immediately sank into the snow, and Levi went out to help him to the front porch. Marvin's face was red with cold and exertion. His large frame may have helped to keep him warm, but by the time he got inside the restaurant, he was huffing and puffing. We led him to a chair, where he sat down to catch his breath. Finally, he sputtered, "I been lookin' all over for you, Levi. Your mama's been frantic all night."

"I'm fine, Marvin. You didn't have to go to all this trouble to find me."

Marvin took a deep breath and let it out slowly. "You know your mama better than that, boy. She dotes on you and Noah. When you didn't come home, she started prayin'. When that woman prays, I know somethin's gonna happen, and it usually involves me. So I got in the tractor this morning and came lookin' for you. I went by the church first, but when I found out you weren't there, I figured this was the only other place you could be." His eyes searched the room and then settled on me. "Where's Noah and Lizzie? I thought they'd be here too."

"They went home last night before the storm moved in," Levi said. "I'm sure they're fine."

Marvin's eyes widened. "You mean to say you two been here all night by yourselves?"

I could feel my face grow hot, probably making me about as red as Marvin.

"Yes," Levi said slowly. "We were here all night, thanking God for giving us a place of refuge."

Marvin didn't say anything, but his expression grew somber. He looked over at the table where Levi and I had been sitting. "Sure would love some hot coffee. I'm freezin' inside."

"Sure," Levi said. He got up to get the coffee when Marvin stopped him.

"Levi, you're bleedin'. What happened to you?"

One of Levi's cuts had reopened and blood was staining his shirt. "Sit down," I ordered. "I'll get a fresh bandage."

Levi finished pouring Marvin's coffee from the carafe on the table, then obediently sat down while I fetched the first-aid kit. In the meantime, Levi filled Marvin in on the broken window and its aftermath.

"My goodness," Marvin said when Levi finished. "You two was surely sheltered by God last night. I expect it had something to do with your mama prayin' like she was."

"You're probably right," I said as I came back into the room. "We're grateful to be safe and sound today." I asked Levi to lean forward. When he did, I raised the back of his shirt and worked at removing the bloody bandage. I quickly took off the old gauze and taped a new piece in its place.

"Look, I know that some folks would frown on Callie and me being here together last night," Levi said. "But I'm going to ask you not to spread it around. There was nothing inappropriate in our behavior. I would rather not give fuel to anyone who might like to turn this into something it's not."

"Well, Son, I'd be glad to do as you suggest," Marvin said, "but I'm afraid all of us are gonna have to account for our whereabouts last night."

"What are you talking about?" I asked as I pulled Levi's shirt down.

Marvin shook his head. "No way for you to have heard, bein' cut off and all."

"Heard what?" Levi said. I could hear the tension in his voice.

"A friend of Dottie's called from Washington last night before the phones went out. Someone reported findin' a body on the turnoff for Kingdom. Looks like the same killer."

"Oh, my goodness," I cried. "Not another one."

"Yep, and this time we know her."

I felt as if the blood was rushing from my head, right into my toes. I slumped down into a chair, feeling as if I might faint. "Who . . . who was it?"

"Mary Carson. Roger's wife. You knew her as Mary Yoder."

CHAPTER/12

It took me a few seconds to comprehend what Marvin had told us. "Oh no," I said finally. "Poor Mary. I can't believe it." I wiped the tears that began to spill down my cheeks. "Are they sure? I mean, are they positive it's her?"

"Well, the sheriff said it's definitely Mary," Marvin said gently. "I wish I could tell you somethin' different, but I can't."

"Do you know any other details?"

Marvin wrinkled his forehead in thought. "Just what Dottie told me. A body was reported found somewhere near the turnoff toward town. It was pushed over to the side, buried in brush. No idea how many people went by without seein' it. Seems someone stopped to check their tire chains and found her."

"So she was hidden, just like the first woman?" Levi asked.

"Was the other woman found under brush as well?" I asked. "Noah mentioned she was near some trees."

"No," Levi said. "She was lying in that small section of red cedar trees that line the road about halfway between the main road and town. We didn't tell anyone because the sheriff said they didn't want all the details reported." He sighed. "Mercy Eberly thought her cat might be hiding there. He's done it before. That's how she found the dead woman."

"I guess I pictured her as being more visible than that," I said.

Marvin shook his head. "Too many people passed her by. If she was easy to see, it woulda been reported a lot earlier. Seems like the killer wants the women found, but not too fast."

I shivered. Thinking about where a body might be hidden from view put a more vivid picture in my head than I was willing to allow.

"Lizzie is . . . was friends with Mary," I said. "She'll be devastated." I looked at Marvin. "Does she know?"

He shook his head. "Noah and Lizzie just put a phone in at their house, but it's been pretty unreliable. Sometimes it works and sometimes it don't. We tried callin' them last night, but we couldn't get through. Then ours went out too." He cocked his head. "Yours workin'?"

"No. We lost it last night," I said.

Marvin sighed. "This news is gonna hurt Lizzie a lot. I don't look forward to tellin' her about it." He rubbed his gloved hands together. "Now, what are we gonna do with you two?"

"Do with us?" Levi asked. "What do you mean?"

Marvin looked uncomfortable. "This storm isn't over. It's gonna hit again real hard tonight. I can't leave you two here. Don't look . . . proper."

Levi nodded. "I feel the same way, but I'm not sure what to do about it."

"I think you should come back with me, son," Marvin said. "Leave the young lady here. She's got plenty of supplies." He gazed around the room. "Did you lose your electricity?"

I nodded. "But the generator's going."

"Prediction is that this second system will move out in a few days. After it's done with what it's doin', our farmers will

start comin' into town with their tractors and snowplows.
You'll be fine."

"You can't guarantee that," Levi said, frowning. "I can't
leave her here alone with a killer on the loose."

"It's all right, Levi," I said. "I've got heat and food. And
like Marvin says, it won't be long before the tractors start
showing up. I won't be alone for long." I didn't mean a word
of what I'd just said, but I couldn't see any other choice. If
Levi could leave, he had to do it. Truthfully, the idea of staying here by myself after finding out about Mary frightened
me. Would I be safe?

"No," he said firmly. "I have no intention of leaving you
here without protection. Not with some crazed killer running around."

"I doubt any killer can get through all this snow," Marvin
said with a smile. "Don't think he'd risk drivin' a big tractor
down the middle of the main street of Kingdom just to get
at Callie." He put his hand on Levi's shoulder. "Look, son,
if I thought the young lady was in any danger, there ain't no
way I'd take off. But the truth is, she's safe. She'll be fine.
We'll get to her before anyone else."

Marvin's point about the snow made me feel better—and
even more determined to protect Levi's reputation. "Maybe
this is the time to break out that famous faith of yours, Levi,"
I said. "Can't you believe God will protect me?"

I knew my comment was somewhat challenging, but Levi's
faith was the one thing I knew he'd respond to. The only
thing that might make him leave with Marvin. If he really
believed God would watch over me, how could he be afraid
to leave me at the restaurant?

"I do have faith, Callie," he said, "but that doesn't mean

I should be reckless in regards to your safety. If I can't stay with you, we'll all have to leave together."

"All three of us can't ride outta here in my old tractor," Marvin said, rubbing his beard. "I can barely fit in." He patted his large stomach. "There's no way we can get all of us in that cab." He shook his head. "It ain't safe, son. I'm takin' a chance just with you."

"Callie can sit on my lap," Levi said firmly. I recognized the look on his face. When Levi made up his mind, that was it. It would take an angel sent straight from heaven for him to change his opinion.

Marvin studied him for a moment before saying, "I want to say yes, Levi, but I can't. I'm sorry."

"Then I'm staying here. There's no other choice." He nodded at his stepfather. "You better get going before that bad weather moves in. I'm sure Mama's worried about you."

I was wondering just how much worse the weather could possibly get when I heard the sound of another engine outside. I got to the window just in time to see Noah's truck pulling up in front.

"It's Noah," I exclaimed.

"Reinforcements," Marvin said, relief evident in his voice. "That big truck of his can get through anything."

We hurried outside to greet Noah. I stayed near the doorway, but I could see heavy chains wrapped around his tires. I knew some of the farmers, like Marvin, used chains in the winter, but I had no idea Noah had them too.

"Lizzie sent me to check on Callie," Noah said, climbing out of his truck. "She's worried about her." The snowdrift in front of the restaurant was so deep he immediately sank up to his knees. "What are you two doing here?"

"I just got here a little while ago," Marvin called out. "Your mother was worried about your brother, since he didn't come home last night."

Noah stopped in his tracks and gaped at Levi. "You didn't go home? Where were you?"

"I was here," he said defensively. "With Callie. I drove her back from the church, thinking I'd go home after that. But the storm was too bad, and we had no choice but to hunker down here."

Noah frowned, but he didn't say anything about our situation. "Well, I'm thankful you're both safe." He pushed through the snow, grabbed hold of the railing, and pulled himself up. "If you don't mind, I'd like to come in and get a cup of coffee. It was a long ride over here." He stopped and pointed at the boards protecting the front window. "Looks like you had some damage."

"Wind blew out the window," Levi said. "Made a big mess, let me tell you."

I held the door open. "I'll get you some coffee, Noah. Come inside."

All three men trudged back into the dining room. I pulled an extra rug up for them to wipe their feet on.

"Sit down," I ordered. "I'll bring out more coffee." With that, I turned around and went to the kitchen. Once I got there, I quickly put another pot of coffee on the stove just in case we were here for a while. Not wanting to put too much strain on the generator, I ignored the large metal coffee makers. I poured the rest of the hot coffee from the other pot into a new carafe, grabbed a couple of cups and headed for the dining room. As I entered, Marvin smiled widely at me.

"We got the situation figgered out," he said. "I'm takin' Levi with me. You'll go to Noah and Lizzie's. That way, everyone's safe, and you and Levi aren't left in a . . . compromising situation."

"I think it's for the best," Levi said. "At least I'll know you're safe."

"And it might just save your reputations," Marvin said.

Levi bristled. "I would hope our friends know us well enough to trust us."

"They do, Brother," Noah said. "But it's our job to think of the weaker members of our church family. Any appearance of evil—"

"Saving our lives wasn't evil," Levi snapped.

Noah's eyes widened. "I didn't mean . . ."

Levi waved his hand toward his brother. "I know. I'm sorry. This is the right decision. I just get a little weary of worrying about what people will say."

Marvin grunted and took a quick sip of coffee. "I guess I gotta point out that it's a pastor's job to consider what's best for his flock."

Levi took a deep breath. "You're right. This has been quite an ordeal. And then to find out about Mary Carson . . ."

Noah stared at his brother. "Mary? What about her?"

"Your mother got a call last night from Julene Klassen," Marvin said. "You know, the lady with the dog rescue group in Washington?"

Noah nodded, looking confused. I could tell Marvin was having a difficult time telling him the news about Mary. Noah and Roger Carson were close friends, and Mary had grown up in Kingdom.

"I'm sorry, Son," Marvin said gently. "But they found Mary

dead, not long before the storm moved in last night. It looks like the same killer."

Noah's face crumbled. "I . . . I can't believe it," he said, his voice breaking. He looked at his brother with tears in his eyes. "First it was someone we didn't know, but this time it's too close to home."

Marvin got up and put his hand on Noah's shoulder. "I'm sorry, boy. I really am. Bringin' you bad news isn't something I enjoy."

"I know." Noah cleared his throat and fought to regain his composure.

"At some point, the sheriff will be askin' everyone where they were when Mary was killed," Marvin said. He looked back and forth between Levi and me. "You're both gonna have to tell the truth about where you've been."

"Maybe we can tell him privately," Levi said. "Since we didn't have anything to do with Mary's death, perhaps he'll allow us to give him our—" He stopped and frowned.

"Alibi," Noah finished for him. "It's called an alibi."

"Thank you, Brother. Our *alibi* behind closed doors."

I didn't say anything, but for some reason, I felt sick to my stomach. The idea that I even needed an alibi was extremely disturbing.

"Why don't you pack a suitcase, Callie?" Noah said. "We should get going."

"I agree," Marvin said. He quickly told Noah about the second system moving in.

Noah shook his head. "I didn't know that. The batteries in our radio are dead."

"Aren't there extra batteries here?" Marvin asked.

"A whole drawerful," Noah said sheepishly. "Lizzie told

me more than once to take some home. When we couldn't listen to the radio last night, she wasn't too happy with me. I'll grab some now." He got up and went to the kitchen.

I stood to my feet. "I'll go pack. And I've got to make sure the cats have plenty of food."

"I'll help you with the cats," Levi said.

I nodded and he followed me to the kitchen. When I opened the door, we found Noah putting batteries in a plastic bag.

Levi leaned against the sink and waited for his brother to leave. "I'm sorry about all this, Callie," he said once Noah was gone. "I really don't think I could have left you here alone. I feel a lot better knowing you'll be safe with Noah and Lizzie."

"I do too, but now I'm concerned about Lizzie and Charity. They're by themselves. The news about Mary makes me fear for their safety."

"I hadn't considered that." He sighed. "I think you're right. You and Noah need to get back as soon as possible." He grabbed my hands in his. "I'm going to miss you. I loved having this time with you. I can hardly wait until we're married. You know, last night was the most relaxed I've been for quite a while—and that's even with broken glass sticking out of my back."

Love for him washed through me. "I don't know what I'd do without you, Levi."

He let go of my hands and wrapped his arms around me. "From now on, we're not going to let anything or anyone come between us."

I buried my face in his chest. "I hope you're right. I really do love you."

"I love you too, Callie. More than I can say." He leaned down and kissed me. "We won't be apart much longer."

I didn't respond, just nodded.

"You get packed," he said, his voice husky with emotion. "I'll feed the cats, and then I've got to check on Stormy. Make sure he has everything he needs until I can get him home."

"Okay. Be sure to leave all the animals plenty of food. We don't know how long we'll be gone."

"I will."

I hurried upstairs. It took me a while to pack because I couldn't decide what to take. When I was done, I put on my cloak and picked up my valise. Then I stood and looked around. Leaving the apartment made me sad, but the idea of spending a day or two with Lizzie would be good for me. I needed her calming influence and her sound judgment.

As I came down the stairs, Levi was just coming out of the kitchen. He shook his head as I joined him. "Those cats didn't wait a minute before they started devouring what I put down for them. It's a wonder they don't weigh more than I do."

"What about Stormy?"

"He's fine. Matthew has lots of hay in the barn. I'll have to pay him back when this is all over. I hope he'll understand."

"Matthew may have a hard time loving people, but he is very kind to his own horse. I'm sure he'll agree with our decision to put Stormy there." I sat my valise down near the bottom of the stairs. "I've got to clean up the kitchen before we leave. You'll have to entertain your brother and your stepfather."

Levi gave me a sheepish grin. "I left the kitchen in kind of a mess, didn't I?"

"It's not too bad. Won't take me long to clean it. Besides, it was worth the great breakfast."

"I'll bring in the dishes. It's the least I can do."

I clucked my tongue. "Yes, it is."

Levi laughed and headed to the dining room while I went to the kitchen. By the time everything was cleaned up, it was almost five-thirty and already getting dark outside. Between the clouds moving in and the sun going down, it looked like midnight. I joined Noah, Levi, and Marvin at the front door.

"I've put out the fire, and I'll turn off the generator as we leave," Noah said. "It's so cold, the food should keep."

"What about the cats?" Levi asked. "Will it be too cold for them?"

I shook my head. "The basement stays pretty warm. I left the door open just wide enough for them to go down there if they want to. They'll be fine."

"Okay. Let's get going before it gets any worse out."

Levi took my valise, carried it out the front door, and put it in Noah's truck. Then he helped me inside. "Don't worry about anything," he said earnestly. "Everything will be all right. I'll come to see you as soon as this new storm passes."

"All right. Be careful going home. I'm not sure how safe that tractor is."

"I'll be fine. I love you."

"I love you too," I said.

He kissed me one last time and then closed the truck door. I watched as he climbed up into the cab of Marvin's tractor. It looked like an incredibly tight fit, making it clear it would have been impossible for the three of us to ride together. Marvin started the engine, and it roared to life. After turning off the generator, Noah watched to make sure the large machine got turned around and headed in the right direction.

"They'll be okay," he said as he got into the truck. "Don't worry."

"I wish your phone was working," I said. "I'd like to hear that they made it home safely."

Noah put the truck into gear. "I'll take a look at it when we get home. Sometimes it works, sometimes it doesn't. Could be the storm that's affecting it now though." He smiled. "It's a new world, isn't it? A phone in the house. And we're planning to add electricity in the spring."

I looked at him in surprise. "Really? Why?"

"With the electric company expanding this way, I want to make sure my family has what they need. This past summer was so hot that Charity got sick. She wasn't brought up without air conditioning the way we were. I don't want to put her through that again. That doesn't mean we'll be ordering a TV anytime soon. I saw some television when I was away at college. There are some great programs on TV, but most of it I can do without. Besides, I don't think we need it. But no matter what we choose for our family, people in our community must make their own decisions." He looked over at me. "Living a simple life should be by choice, not by edict."

"What about news and weather?" I asked. "I wonder sometimes if we're cutting ourselves off from some important information. None of us knew about the killings in this area until the sheriff came here."

Noah shrugged. "I have a weather radio that gives me important updates." He grunted. "When I keep batteries in it, that is. And as far as news reports . . ." He looked out the window for a moment. "With some of the awful things happening in the world, I'd rather count on the sheriff to notify us when there's something that might directly affect Kingdom. I don't want all that terrible stuff in my head."

As we passed by the school, I suddenly thought about

Leah. "Noah, what about Leah? She lives behind the school. Shouldn't we check on her?"

Noah shook his head. "She went to stay with Lizzie's parents before the first storm moved in. They always keep a close eye on her. They treat her like their second daughter."

That explained why I hadn't noticed her lights on last night. "Oh, good." I settled back into the seat of the truck. The heater warmed up the interior nicely, and I felt very comfortable. I tried to put worries about serial killers out of my head for a while. It didn't take long before I felt my eyes beginning to close. I'd just decided to give in and grab a short nap when I felt a hard jolt and heard Noah cry out.

"Hold on, Callie!"

I looked out the window and realized that the truck was spinning on the snow. Everything seemed to be moving in slow motion. It was only at the last second that I realized where we were. With a sickening thud, the truck slammed into the trees on the side of the road. The red cedar trees.

CHAPTER / 13

At first I was too afraid to move. Then I looked over at Noah. His head was slumped forward, and I realized that the truck's engine was racing in an ear-piercing whine that seemed to be getting louder and louder. Although I'd never driven a car or truck, I'd ridden with Lizzie in this one to pick up supplies. At least I knew enough to turn off the engine. I reached over and turned the key. The truck jerked and then became quiet.

"Noah?" I said. "Noah, can you hear me?"

There was no response. I took off my seat belt and scooted over closer to him. He was ashen. Fear gripped me as I felt for a pulse in his neck. Thankfully, I could feel a strong beat. He was just unconscious. I checked him over carefully, trying to see if he was hurt, but I couldn't find any injuries. Lizzie had told me once that wearing seat belts was important, but that in an accident, they could cause bruising. I put my hand to my own chest, and it felt very tender. I hoped that was all that was wrong with Noah. The force of the impact had knocked the wind out of him.

I tried my door to see if it would open. It did, but the sound of metal rubbing against metal told me that it would be hard to get it closed. I stepped out carefully and scooped up a handful of snow, trying not to think about where we were. It was almost as if death had cursed this spot and tried to take Noah and me as well. Feeling foolish for thinking something so ludicrous, I climbed back into the cab. As I suspected, the door wouldn't close completely. I leaned over and said Noah's name a few times. Still no response. Duplicating something I'd seen my father do when a new calf was born in our barn but didn't breathe on its own, I opened Noah's coat, unbuttoned the first few buttons of his shirt, and quickly put the ball of snow directly on his chest. Just like the calf's, his reaction was immediate, and he yelped.

"What? Where?" Noah looked around, obviously disoriented. Then he started pulling at his shirt. "What in the world?"

"I'm sorry, Noah," I said. "I had to make sure you were just unconscious."

"Well, I'm awake now. And wet. And cold."

"Sorry."

"That's okay, but remind me never to pass out around you again."

He tried to move so he could survey the damage to his truck, but he winced with the effort.

"I'm not sure, but I think the seat belt bruised you," I said. "Are you okay?"

"A little sore, but fine. I can't say the same for your truck."

The interior of the cab was growing colder by the minute. "Did you turn off the engine?" he asked.

"Yes. It was making a loud noise. Like it was screaming."

Noah raised an eyebrow. "That's not good. I don't think we're going to be able to drive out of this." He tried the door handle, but his side wouldn't open. "Can you scoot into the back seat? I need to get outside and look at my truck."

"Okay." I turned to look at the space between the two front seats. It wasn't very big, but I knew I could manage it. Being small does have its advantages. I carefully wiggled my way into the back seat. It wasn't very ladylike, but I made it. I waited for Noah to move over, but he stayed right where he was.

"Are you okay?" I asked finally.

He shook his head slowly. "No. I can't get the seat belt undone."

I pushed my way between the seats and tried to undo the belt. It was jammed. "I . . . I can't get it either, Noah. What should we do?"

"I don't know. I'm in a lot of pain. I hope I didn't break a rib."

"Just in case, I don't think you should move." I squirmed my way back up into the front seat and looked out the window. "I don't think anyone's going to be coming this way. Not with the roads the way they are."

His expression was tense, and when he tried to move, he grimaced. "I've got to get out of here."

Trying to think of what to do, I remembered that Noah and Lizzie had another truck. It was an old one, only used when this one wasn't available. "What about Lizzie?" I asked. "Will she come looking for us?"

He shook his head. "The snow is starting to pick up. She'll probably think I decided to stay at the restaurant." He turned his head to look at me. "Callie, I'm sorry. But if I can't run the engine, we're going to get cold. Very cold. I'm stuck here and in a lot of pain. We're only about a mile from the house. Do you think you can walk it? If you can get to Lizzie, she can bring the other truck and pick me up."

The wind had increased, and with it the snow. Nevertheless, I'd walked from my father's house to town many times, and that was almost five miles. Surely one short mile wouldn't be too much for me.

"I can do it, Noah. It's not that far."

"Listen," he said, gasping, "get the flashlight out of the glove compartment. Take it with you. It will make it easier to see your way, and if you get lost, it could help someone find you."

A sliver of fear cut through me. I'd had to battle terrible blizzards twice. Last night with Levi and once not long after Papa got sick. The chickens had to be rounded up and put into their coop. The snow was blowing so hard, I couldn't see a foot in front of me. Both times had frightened me. Now I was about to confront another intense storm, and this time shelter would be a lot farther away.

"Thanks," I said, trying to keep my voice level. "But I don't like leaving you here in the dark."

"It's all right," Noah said, his voice beginning to shake. I couldn't tell if it was from the cold or from his injuries. "If I need light, I'll turn on the truck lights. But I can't imagine why I'd need to."

I grabbed a blanket from the back seat of the truck. "I'm going to put this around you. It will help keep you warm. Try to stay still until I get back."

Noah offered me a sickly smile. "You really don't have to worry about that. I'm not planning to go anywhere. Tell Lizzie to bring something to cut this belt off."

I tucked the blanket around him. "I will. We'll be back for you. Everything will be all right." I sounded a lot more confident than I felt.

"Be careful, Callie," he said in a weak voice. "If you think you can't make it, turn around and come back. We'll wait here together until someone finds us."

I nodded as if I agreed with him, but if he was badly injured, he might not last long enough for the truck to be discovered. Everyone in Kingdom was probably hunkered down, prepared to ride out this new storm.

With a silent prayer, I slowly opened the door and slid out into the snow. After pushing the door closed the best I could, I fought my way to the road. The snow was its highest on either side, having been blown against the trees on one side and a long fence that ran along the other side. Even though I stayed away from the drifts, the snow was deep enough to make walking difficult. I wrapped my cloak around me tightly, the hood over my head. The wind seemed to grow stronger with each step I took.

"Oh, Lord," I prayed, as loudly as I could, trying to be heard over the wild screeching of the storm, "please help me! I don't know if I'm strong enough to make it to Lizzie's." As soon as the words left my mouth, I heard a voice whisper inside me. *I can do all things through Christ which strengtheneth me.* I began repeating the precious words over and over. With each step, I could feel a new resolve. The wind and the snow increased, but so did my determination.

I felt as if I'd been walking for only a few minutes when a bright light cut through the blizzard. Lizzie and Noah's house was silhouetted in its glow. The electric company had been stringing poles on the main road, and some of the poles had lights. I had no idea there was one near Lizzie's house, but I thanked God for it. It kept me on track. I made it to the main road and turned right, toward the large white house where the Houslers lived. I'd just reached the driveway when

I took a step and fell, rolling into the ditch. I lay there for a moment, almost buried in snow. Then I heard it again. *I can do all things through Christ which strengtheneth me.* I struggled to my feet and clawed my way back up.

When I finally found my way out of the ditch, I tried to stand up, but my feet and legs felt so numb from the cold that all I could do was crawl toward the front door. Thankfully, the light from the electric pole made finding the porch easier. I crawled up the steps to the top and was happy to find it almost clear of snow. On my hands and knees, I made my way to the front door and began pounding on it. My fingers were frozen, and try as I might, I couldn't make a fist. Every time I slammed my hand against the solid wood door, it fell limply back to my side. Lizzie would never hear me. I tried again, but I still couldn't raise a sound. Suddenly, someone jumped up on the porch behind me. My first thought was that the serial killer had found me, but when my attacker began licking my face, I realized it was Muffin, Lizzie and Noah's small dog.

"Help me, boy," I whispered. "Get Lizzie. Please. Get Lizzie."

Muffin stopped licking me and backed up, staring at me quizzically. Then he began to bark. Long, loud yips that turned into howling. He kept it up, stopping only to take a breath, and then started yowling again. A few moments later, the front door swung open. I fell inside, right at Lizzie's feet. Muffin ran past me, wagging his tail.

"Callie! What in heaven's name?" I looked up into her frightened face. Her eyes were wide with alarm. "What in the world are you doing here? Are you okay?"

I tried to answer but could only whisper.

"Let's get you up," she said. "You've got to get out of those wet clothes."

"No," I murmured. "Need . . . to get . . . Noah."

Lizzie grabbed me, pulled me up, her arm wrapping around my chest as she half dragged me into the living room where a fire burned brightly in the fireplace. I cried out in pain. My body was tenderer than I'd realized. She lowered me gently onto the couch. Muffin followed, planting himself right next to me.

"Where is Noah?" she asked. "Were you with him?"

It took all the strength I had left to explain what happened. When I finished, Lizzie called loudly to Charity.

"Charity! Come here. Right now."

Almost immediately, Charity came around the corner, her special princess doll clutched tightly in her arms. She stopped in her tracks when she saw me.

"Mama, is that Callie?"

"Yes, honey. I need to take the truck down the road a bit and pick up Daddy. Will you get some of my clothes out of the closet and help Callie get dressed? She's got to get out of these wet things before she catches a bad cold. Can you do that for me, Cherry Bear?"

At first Charity just stood there, staring at me like she'd never seen me before. Then she nodded. "Yes, Mama. I can do it. You go get Daddy."

I took hold of Lizzie's arm. "I'm going with you."

Lizzie shook her head. "You're not going anywhere. You stay here by the fire."

"But . . . I promised Noah I'd be back."

"Callie, you've done enough tonight. It's my turn."

I started to argue, but I could see Lizzie had made up her mind. My body felt so sore and weak, I honestly wasn't sure I could make it anyway.

Muffin whimpered and Lizzie seemed to notice him for the

first time. "Charity, dry Muffin off. He's soaking wet. Why did you let him outside without telling me?"

Charity shook her head slowly, looking confused. "I didn't let him out, Mama."

Lizzie got up, hugged her little girl, and then leaned over and put her hand on my cheek. "I'll be back soon, okay?"

"Yes," I said. "Just go. Noah needs you. You'll need to take something to cut off his seat belt."

She nodded and ran from the room. A few seconds later, I heard the front door slam.

"I'm gonna go upstairs and get some dry clothes for you," Charity said. "You need to take off that wet stuff." She put her doll down in a nearby chair and ran into the other room. Then she came back with a large plastic bag and put it next to me. "Put all your clothes in here." She put her hands on her hips. "And I mean all of 'em."

With that, she ran out of the room, Muffin close on her heels. Even though I was weak, in pain, and freezing, I couldn't help but be touched at the way she'd taken charge.

I slowly peeled off my soggy clothes and put them in the bag. When I got down to my undergarments, I hesitated. What in the world was I going to wear under Lizzie's clothes? After some hesitation, I wrapped myself up in the quilt on the couch, and then slipped off everything left and added them to the bag. The couch underneath me was wet, so I got up and moved to a dry chair that was closer to the fire. Although I was beginning to feel warmer, I couldn't stop shaking. I'd been sitting there for a few minutes when I heard Charity clumping down the stairs. When she came into the room, her arms were full of clothes.

"I picked out what I thought Mama would want you to

wear." She handed the garments to me. "You can go in the bathroom and change if you want to."

"Thank you, Charity." My teeth were chattering, so it took a while to get the three words out. I stood up, holding the quilt around me. Unfortunately, the only bathroom was upstairs. It took me quite a while to make it up the steps. I found it hard to breathe and assumed it was because of all the cold air I'd sucked into my lungs. Although it felt as if it took forever to get to the bathroom, I finally made it. I went inside and closed the door. Looking around, it was a lot like the bathroom at the restaurant, but much nicer. All the fixtures were new, and there was a large mirror over the sink. I opened the bundle of clothes and found a pair of jeans and a sweatshirt. There was underwear too. The underpants were in a package, brand new and unopened. I wasn't picky when it came to wearing someone else's clothes. Since I didn't have much money after Papa got sick, a lot of my dresses were donations from women in the church. But I had no desire to wear hand-me-down underwear.

I felt strange pulling on Lizzie's jeans. I'd never worn a pair of jeans in my life. Papa had always insisted on plain dresses. After he died, I'd made a few dresses with colors and patterns because other women in town were wearing them. Some of the ladies wore pants when they worked around their farms, but this was a first for me.

I had to take off my prayer covering. It was not only wet, but it was torn and dirty. Beyond repair. Two prayer coverings gone within a few hours. At this rate, I'd have to make some new ones. I dropped it in the trash can and worked to get the pins and ribbon out of my hair. There was a brush on the counter, next to the sink, and I brushed my hair out the best I could. When I looked in the mirror, I didn't recognize the girl who stared back at me. Lizzie's jeans and sweatshirt had turned me into a different person. With my hair down, I looked like someone who could fit in with most of the young women I'd seen in Washington during my trips with Lizzie.

For what seemed like a long time, all I could do was gaze at the stranger in the mirror. Could clothes really change me so much? At first I felt panic and wanted my dress and my prayer covering back. But gradually another sensation began to build in me. Something I couldn't put my finger on, but it felt good. I turned from the mirror, pulled on the socks Charity had given me, and started back down the stairs. Charity was waiting on the couch, and Muffin was lying on the floor beneath her.

"Oh, Callie," she said when I came in. "You're so beautiful. Just like Mama."

I didn't think badly of Lizzie for the way she dressed, so why did I feel guilty? Somewhere inside, I could hear my father's disapproving voice. My stomach turned over, and I had to steady myself as I sat down next to Charity.

"You should dress like that more often," she said simply. "I like the way you look."

"Thank you, Charity," I said. "But I'm not sure this is . . . me."

She frowned up at me. "Then who are you?"

I stared at her, trying to find an answer. I didn't notice the tears streaming down my face.

Charity put her hand up to my cheek. "Don't cry, Callie. I know who you are."

Her words made me sob harder. I tried to stop, but it was as if something had broken open inside me. Charity jumped up from the couch and ran into the other room. She brought back a paper towel, and I wiped my face. Once my emotions were under control, I tried to apologize.

"Don't be sorry, Callie," Charity said with a smile. "Mama says that God gave us tears so we could get our sadness out. There's nothing wrong with crying." She lowered her voice to a whisper. "I cry too."

I was touched by her attempt to comfort me. "Thank you, Charity. I didn't know that. I feel much better now."

"Good. I'm glad."

I suddenly remembered that the couch was wet when I went upstairs, and I ran my hand on the material. It was dry now.

"I turned the cushion over," Charity said with a smile. "Mama did it once when I spilled lemonade on it."

"Thanks for doing that. It's more comfortable." I reached down to stroke the small white dog that lay at my feet. When he looked up at me, he appeared to be smiling.

Charity tugged at my sleeve. "Is my daddy okay? Why did Mama have to go and get him?"

Not wanting to frighten her, I explained that the truck had quit running and that Noah needed a ride home. She seemed to accept this, but then it occurred to me that my account wouldn't explain her father's injuries. I told her that he got a few bumps when the truck stopped fast, but that I was sure he would be okay. That seemed to satisfy her.

Although I didn't say anything to Charity, I was beginning to worry why it was taking so long. What if Lizzie couldn't get Noah out of the truck by herself? I started to wonder if I should have gone with her, to help with Noah, when bright lights suddenly flashed across the room. Charity and I both got up and went to the windows. Muffin followed along behind us.

"It's Mama!" Charity exclaimed gleefully. "She's back!"

Lizzie pulled the truck up close to the door. I went to the front closet, not able to move quite as fast as I wanted because my chest was so sore. I found a pair of boots and an overcoat and put them on. Warning Charity to stay inside, I opened the front door and trudged through the snow to the passenger side of the old truck. When Lizzie opened her door, the interior light came on, and I was thrilled to see Noah leaning against the window. He gave me a faint smile, which made me feel even more relieved.

"Can you help me get him inside?" Lizzie yelled as she came around the front of the truck. I nodded. She cut in front of me and opened Noah's door. He moved slowly and almost fell into her arms. I got on one side, and she got on the other. Fighting the wind and snow, we painstakingly made our way toward the house. I had to clench my teeth to ignore the sharp spasms that coursed through me. Noah was actually walking, although he definitely needed our assistance. I took it as a good sign, since he hadn't been able to move much right after the accident.

"Just a little farther," Lizzie said loudly to her husband. "We're almost there."

Getting Noah up the stairs was difficult, but we finally made it. Charity stood on the other side of the door, her face puckered with concern.

"Is Daddy all right?" she asked, her bottom lip trembling.

"I'm okay, sweetheart," Noah said, trying to reassure her. "Remember when you fell off the front porch after we first moved here?"

She nodded. "Yes, it hurt."

He smiled, but I could feel him flinch with pain. "Well,

it's just like that. Daddy got hurt, but you got better, and I will too."

"Okay," she said slowly. "If you say so."

"I do."

We steered Noah to the couch where I'd collapsed almost an hour earlier.

"Where's the quilt?" Lizzie asked. "I want to put it under him."

"I-I'm sorry," I said. "I used it earlier after I took off my wet clothes. It's still upstairs."

"That's okay." She looked at Charity. "Honey, go upstairs and get a couple of quilts out of the linen closet. And hurry."

Charity nodded and ran toward the stairs.

"Don't run on the stairs, Charity," Lizzie said. She looked at me and winked. "One injured family member a night is my limit."

I was amazed at how calm she was. In her situation, I would be frantic with worry. We held Noah upright until Charity came back with the quilts. Lizzie told her to spread one out on the couch. Then we carefully lowered Noah down. He grimaced even though we tried to be as gentle as possible. Once he was settled, Lizzie covered him with the second quilt.

"We need to get him to a hospital," I whispered to Lizzie so that Charity wouldn't hear.

"No, I don't need that," Noah said quickly. "If I get any other symptoms—something that might indicate some kind of internal injury, I'll go. But for now, I'm just going to sit here and rest." He smiled at my worried expression. "Believe it or not, I've had this kind of pain before. At the most, I cracked a rib. Happened once on the farm. There's nothing doctors can do about it. It has to heal on its own. I'll be fine."

Suddenly, Lizzie grabbed me in a hug. "Noah told me about Mary," she whispered into my ear. "I don't want to talk about it in front of Charity. We'll discuss it later, when she's in bed."

I nodded. The sorrow in her eyes was awful to see, yet her expression was set and resolute. Protecting her family was her priority now. She turned away from me and struggled to help Noah out of his wet coat.

"Stay with him, Callie," she told me. "I'm going to get him some dry clothes." She left the room, and Charity followed her.

"What if it's more than just a cracked rib?" I asked Noah.

"I won't get into details," he replied, "but when this happened before, the doctor at the hospital told me what signs to watch for in case there was something wrong inside. If I see any of those symptoms, I'll be the first one to tell Lizzie to take me to the hospital. Okay?"

"Okay."

"Are you sore at all?" he asked.

I touched my chest without thinking. "Yes. I checked myself out when I changed clothes. There's no bruising. I'm just red. But I'm definitely tender." To be honest, I was in quite a bit of pain, but I didn't want to draw attention to myself. Since I'd made it from the truck to Lizzie's, surely I couldn't be hurt as badly as Noah.

"Just wait. In a couple of days, you'll be black and blue. Some guy ran a light in Washington a few years ago and slammed into my truck. At first my chest turned red. A couple of days later it was almost black. Looked a lot scarier than it really was though. It didn't hurt much after it turned colors. Unless I touched it."

I was relieved to hear that my symptoms were normal and

that the pain would subside. Realizing I was still wearing Lizzie's coat and boots, I took them off and returned them to the coat closet.

As I walked back toward the couch, Noah looked me over carefully and frowned. "You sure look different dressed like that."

"I feel different dressed like this."

"Oh, Callie," he said, "I just remembered your suitcase. We left it in the truck. I wasn't thinking—"

"It's okay," I said. "We'll get it later. I'm just relieved you're home."

"Thanks. Still, I wish I'd thought of it."

"Really, Noah. It's fine. Right now I'm just so grateful we're all safe. My valise isn't the least bit important to me."

Lizzie and Charity came down the stairs. Lizzie carried an armful of clothes. "Callie," she said, "could you take Charity into the kitchen and heat up some coffee for Noah? There's a pot on the stove." She obviously wanted us both out of the room so Noah could change.

"Of course, I'd be glad to."

"Um, Callie," Noah added. "Could you also make Noah a huge sandwich with a side of potato salad? He's starving."

As if responding to Noah's words, my stomach rumbled loudly. At first I was embarrassed, but Noah burst out laughing. "And could you make yourself a nice big sandwich too?"

The comical expression on his face put me at ease, and I giggled. That made Charity laugh, seeming to ease her anxiety.

"You look good in my clothes," Lizzie said to me, "but it's hard to get used to."

I started to tell her that she didn't need to get used to

seeing me like this, since it was a onetime thing, but something stopped me. I just smiled and nodded. "Do you want something to eat too?" I asked her.

"No, Charity and I ate earlier. We're fine."

"Could I have a cookie, Mama?"

"If you go with Lizzie and help her make sandwiches, you can have a cookie. But you eat it in the kitchen, okay?"

"Okay."

Charity skipped off toward the kitchen, and I followed her. I hadn't seen the kitchen since it had been renovated. I was surprised to discover how modern and cheery it looked. I'd been to the house a few times while Noah was working on it and had watched the inside gradually transform from decrepit to beautiful. The old fireplace in the living room had a new stone front, and all of the wood floors had been refinished. The walls had been repaired and painted, and the stairs had been ripped out and completely rebuilt. The changes were incredible, but no room had been altered as much as the kitchen. The old woodburning stove had been replaced with a sleek stainless steel stove. And the old white refrigerator had been tossed out. A shiny new refrigerator stood in its place. Both appliances ran on propane, and I wondered if Lizzie planned to keep them after they added electricity. Although many of the modifications needed to switch to electricity were easy, for the most part, propane appliances had to be completely replaced.

I gave Charity a cookie from the cookie jar, and set about making two sandwiches. When I was finished, I carried the plates into the living room, along with a glass of water for me.

"Thank you, Callie," Lizzie said when I handed her Noah's plate. She frowned at my glass of water. "I'm so sorry. I meant to make a pitcher of tea earlier, but I got distracted when

Noah didn't come home. I'm afraid the only other cold thing we have is milk, and I know you never drink it."

"Callie doesn't drink milk?" Noah said.

Lizzie shook her head and grinned at him. "Surely you know that. Callie's been working at the restaurant more than a year now."

He chuckled. "I guess I haven't been paying attention to her drinking habits."

"No reason you should," I said.

After a short blessing, Noah and I started in on our sandwiches. I noticed that Noah was eating with gusto and his color had improved.

"You look like you're feeling better."

He nodded. "I do. Fortunately, I still have some pain medication left over from wrenching my back a couple of months ago. I took a couple and it helped a lot."

"Oh yes. I remember that. You tried to move the stove at the restaurant so Bud Gruber could get behind it and work on the outlet."

Lizzie laughed. "Yes, Bud told him to wait until he could help, but my mighty man of valor decided he could do it alone."

I shook my head. "You should have waited. Bud is really strong."

Noah raised his eyebrows and grinned. "*Now* you tell me. Believe me, I won't do it again."

"So how long until the work at the restaurant is finished?" I asked.

"There's not much more to do," Lizzie said. "And it worries me."

I put my sandwich down and looked at her quizzically. "Why would it worry you? Shouldn't you be happy about it?"

She nodded. "I am."

"She's worried about Bud," Noah said. "Ever since his wife died, he's been really lonely. I think we've kind of become his family."

"He's such a nice man," I said.

"Yes, he is," Lizzie said. "I can't help but compare him to John Lapp. They both lost their wives around the same time. John has become even nastier, yet Bud has kept his kind temperament."

"Does Bud go to church?" I asked.

Lizzie shook her head. "And don't think I haven't wanted to ask him to ours."

"Then why don't you?"

"She's afraid he'll be snubbed," Noah said.

"Surely not. We wouldn't do that."

"When's the last time anyone who wasn't Mennonite darkened our doors?" Lizzie asked.

I couldn't think of anyone except for Ruby, but I was sure Lizzie was talking about an adult, not a child. "Is . . . is that right?" I asked. "I mean, wouldn't Jesus expect us to welcome everyone?"

"Yes, he would," Noah said emphatically. "And so would I."

"We're just not sure about some of the other elders or members," Lizzie said. "And I can't put Bud through that."

I didn't say anything, but the idea that our church would turn away people who needed the Lord made me ache inside. Surely that didn't please God.

Noah held out his empty plate and Lizzie took it.

"Boy, you were hungry," she said with a smile.

"Famished. Now I'm warm, comfy, and sleepy."

Lizzie handed the plate to Charity. "Cherry Bear, will you

please take Daddy's plate into the kitchen? And you can have one more cookie."

Charity got up and took the plate from her mother. "But I gotta eat it in the kitchen again?" she asked.

"Yes, in the kitchen."

"Okay, Mama."

As soon as she left, Noah smiled at me. "Callie, I can't thank you enough for what you did. You may have saved my life. After you left the truck, I was worried that I'd sent you out into the storm to do the impossible. With the wind blowing so hard, I'm shocked you found your way."

"I am too, Callie," Lizzie said, her eyes glistening with tears. "You could have gotten lost or fallen into a snowdrift. You really shouldn't have tried it, but I'm glad you did. There's no way we can ever repay you."

"It wasn't that bad," I said, blushing. "To be honest, if it hadn't been for that bright light on the electric pole outside, I probably would have gotten lost. I just followed it to your house."

Lizzie frowned, and Noah looked confused. "The electric pole?"

"Well, I thought it was on the electric pole. Maybe it's a different pole." I got up slowly, since my chest was throbbing, and walked over to the big window in the living room. I drew the curtain back and gazed out into the front yard. It was pitch black. Not a light to be seen.

"Where is it? Did the light go out?"

Noah's eyes widened as he said, "Callie, there's no pole . . . or light out there. Never was."

CHAPTER 14

Not long after we finished eating, Noah dozed off on the couch with Muffin curled up next to him. Lizzie decided to leave him where he was and let him sleep.

After putting Charity to bed, Lizzie and I went into the kitchen. Lizzie and Noah had rejoiced over the mysterious light that led me to their home, saying it was God guiding me through the storm. They also couldn't understand how Muffin got outside, since no one admitted to letting him out. The small dog hated going out and only did so when he had to do his duty. Then he'd run right back inside. For him to venture out alone, especially in a storm, didn't make any sense. Lizzie chalked it up to a miracle. I wanted to believe that too, but my mind searched for some other more reasonable explanation. Maybe the light had just been installed and they didn't know about it. Maybe Charity had let Muffin out and didn't want to admit it. It wasn't that I didn't believe in miracles. I did. It's just that I'd never experienced one before. Things like that happened to other people. Not to me. Why was it so hard for me to believe that God loved me enough to do something miraculous?

"I'm going to put you in the spare room," Lizzie said. "It's the only bedroom downstairs. You're the very first person to stay in it since it's been remodeled. Let me show it to you, and then I'll heat up some cider, and we can talk for a while."

"There's cider?" I asked. "I didn't notice it earlier."

"It's in the pantry. I'll move it to the fridge so you can have some later if you want."

I followed her through the kitchen and into the extra bedroom. It was lovely. An old iron bed sat in the middle of the room. There was an antique dresser and a beautiful carved rocking chair in the corner. A vented propane heater was mounted on the wall.

"I'll turn on the heater, but you'll want to keep it low. This room gets hot fast."

"It really doesn't feel that cold in here." Papa and I had used a fireplace and a couple of potbellied stoves to warm our house. For the most part, they did a fine job.

"Noah put vents all around the house. They help to keep the heat from the living room circulating through the rest of the rooms. We stay pretty warm. Some rooms are colder than others though. This room is okay now because I've been baking and the heat has drifted in here. Later tonight, it could get extremely cold. You'll appreciate the heater then. Oh, and there are several blankets and quilts in the closet. You're welcome to use any of them."

I couldn't help but notice the quilt covering the bed. It was a log cabin quilt made out of different shades of blue. It was striking.

"That's the quilt Hope made for you, isn't it?" I asked.

Lizzie smiled. "Yes, it is. Isn't it gorgeous? She's so talented."

"Have you ever made a quilt?"

She nodded. "When I was a child. But not since I've become an adult. I just don't have the time. How about you?"

"Yes, a few. To be honest, I haven't had much time for quilting either. When Papa got sick, I couldn't seem to find a spare moment. Besides taking care of him, helping Leah at the school, and working for you, the only time I had left was for sleeping."

Lizzie nodded. "I understand." She pointed at the dresser. "I'll bring some clothes down from upstairs and put them in here. Nightgowns and other things." She smiled at me. "I'm having a tough time getting used to you in my clothes. You look like someone else."

"I really don't feel like myself. I asked Papa once if I could stop wearing my prayer covering all the time. You know, like you do. He said no. Said if I didn't wear it, I would be dishonoring God."

"Do you think I'm dishonoring God, Callie?" Lizzie asked quietly.

"Of course not. I know you love God."

"I wear a prayer covering on Sundays because it's expected. But God isn't honored by what we wear. He's honored by our love for Him. Our obedience to Him because of that love."

"But all the women wear coverings except you," I said. "Why? If it isn't necessary, why do we do it?"

"Let's get that cider, and I'll try to answer your question. But you must remember something. The only person you should follow is God. Not me. All I can do is tell you what I believe. You have to decide what *you* believe for yourself."

As I followed her into the kitchen, I couldn't help thinking that I'd really rather have someone just tell me what to think and do. Papa always seemed to have the answers, so I didn't have to make many decisions. Life was easier that way, but in my heart, I knew it wasn't right.

"Sit down," Lizzie said. "I'll start heating the cider."

I slipped into the wooden nook Noah had built into the corner of the kitchen. An oil lamp on the table added to the cozy feeling in the room, although most of the light came from another propane lamp mounted on the wall.

"Are you ready to talk about Mary?" I asked.

Lizzie shook her head. "Not yet. If you don't mind, let's discuss her later. Honestly, right now I'd rather concentrate on Noah . . . and you. Do you mind?"

"Not at all." I was being completely honest. My mind was so full of thoughts, I felt that if I tried to put one more thing in it, it might explode.

The storm outside wailed in the dark. Sometimes the sound reminded me of a child crying. Sitting in Lizzie's house, I felt safe and secure. As if nothing bad could possibly get in. Somewhere out there a killer sat, probably hearing the same storm. Was he planning his next evil deed? The thought gave me chills, and not the kind caused by the cold.

I decided to bring up a question I'd been waiting to ask. "Lizzie, did you and Noah stop by the church the night of the storm?" I tried to sound casual. The last thing I wanted was to alert Lizzie to the fact that I was trying to worm information out of her.

"Yes, but Levi was having a counseling session." She sighed. "We told him about the storm, and that he needed to get home, but obviously he didn't listen."

"Yes, Aaron Metcalf was still there when I arrived," I said.

Lizzie was busy pouring cider into a pan, which she set

on the stove. The flame under the burner made a whooshing sound when she turned it on.

"Aaron Metcalf?" She shook her head. "He wasn't there when we stopped by. Levi was with Margaret Harper."

Margaret's presence wasn't a surprise. I already knew she saw Levi frequently. Not so much for counseling, but to get help from the church. I was pretty certain the frail woman wasn't a serial killer.

"I wonder who else he saw that night. Maybe they took so long that Aaron's appointment got pushed back."

Lizzie snorted. "That's entirely possible. John Lapp was leaving as we pulled up. You know how self-centered he is."

"John Lapp?" I couldn't keep the surprise out of my voice. "Why in the world would he go to Levi for counseling if he thinks he doesn't qualify to be our pastor? That doesn't make sense."

"I have no idea. I was as shocked as you are. Maybe it had something to do with Frances's death."

"Maybe." John Lapp? What was it the sheriff said? To be on the lookout for someone who had experienced a change in their life? "Lizzie, weren't John and Frances married about twenty years?"

Lizzie turned to look at me. "Not quite twenty years, I think. Not too many people know this, but my mother told me John was married when he was younger. His wife died tragically."

I felt my heart race. "I'd never heard that. Do you know how she died?"

"Mother told me, but I'm not sure I remember. Seems like it was some kind of accident or something." She frowned at me. "Why?"

I took a deep breath. "Lizzie, remember what the sheriff

209

said? To look for someone whose life has changed in some way? Someone who starts acting oddly?"

After staring at me a moment, Lizzie burst out laughing. "You think old John Lapp is a serial killer? Oh, Callie. Really."

I bristled at her attitude. "Look, the killer murdered women twenty years ago. Right about the time John gets married to Frances, the killings stopped. Then Frances dies, and the murders start again. Isn't this exactly what Sheriff Timmons was talking about?"

Lizzie turned around and took the cider off the burner. She was quiet for a moment. "But he isn't acting any differently."

"Yes, he is. He didn't oppose Levi's election at the time of his appointment. Now, suddenly, he tries to start a campaign against him."

"Well, maybe. . . but I don't think John Lapp could kill anyone. That man's blood is pure Mennonite. You know how we feel about violence."

"Then what about Aaron?" I said. "You know there's some kind of secret from his past that the elders won't reveal. Don't you find that suspicious? And Aaron isn't old. He could certainly kill a woman."

"For crying out loud, Callie. First of all, Aaron isn't old enough to have killed anyone twenty years ago."

"I know that," I snapped. "But he could be copying the murders. We don't know what his secret is, Lizzie. Maybe he killed someone else."

Lizzie raised her eyebrows. "Aaron moved here from Iowa. He couldn't have heard something about a serial killer in Kansas that wasn't even considered a serial killer until recently." She took a deep breath. "Besides, his secret has nothing to do with murder."

My mouth dropped open in surprise. "You know what it is? How could you?"

She grinned. "Let's just say that running a restaurant affords me lots of chances to overhear things."

"I don't know if you should repeat . . ."

She looked around the corner, making sure Noah was still asleep. After checking, she leaned in close to me. "I can't have you thinking poor Aaron is a crazed murderer. The truth is, he's divorced."

"Divorced? Is that all?"

Lizzie straightened up. "In our church, that's pretty major. His wife left him for another man. When he came here, he wanted to start fresh. That's why he went to the elders and told them. Even Noah and Levi don't know. I overheard Elder Wittsman talking about it to Elder Scheer. They didn't realize I was standing behind them at the time."

I frowned as I considered this information. "Doesn't mean he isn't a murderer," I said softly.

"Oh, for crying out loud. Why are you—" Lizzie poured the cider into two mugs, picked them up, and carried them to the table. She sat down and eyed me suspiciously. "Wait a minute. First you try to find out who Levi met with last night, and now you think Aaron or John might be a murderer. Why? Did Levi tell you something that made you suspicious of them?"

"Oh, Lizzie." I tried to say more, but I choked up.

"Callie, what's wrong?" She reached across the table and took my hand. "You can tell me, honey. What's going on?"

I fought to gain control of myself, but it took a few seconds. Finally, I said, "If . . . if I tell you, will you keep it between us? Levi would be so upset if he knew I said something."

"Whatever you say will stay between us. You know that."

211

I nodded. There was no one in my life I trusted more than Lizzie. I cleared my throat, still unsure about revealing something Levi had told me in confidence. What if he found out? Would he ever trust me again? My concern for the safety of other women who might be in danger made me decide to confide in Lizzie.

"Lizzie," I said slowly, "I believe Levi knows who the serial killer is."

Lizzie's eyes grew wide and her mouth dropped open. "Callie! Are you serious?"

I wiped the tears off my face with the back of my hand. "He told me that himself."

She turned her head sideways and looked at me suspiciously. "Exactly what did he tell you?"

I tried hard to think back on our conversation. "He was upset after his counseling session yesterday. I asked him if it had anything to do with the murders."

"And what did he say?"

"He didn't deny it."

Lizzie let go of my hand and sank back into her chair. "He didn't deny it? Oh, Callie. That doesn't mean he knows who the killer is. Maybe he just didn't want to say anything else about his sessions. You know what's said in counseling is—"

"Confidential," I said with a big sigh. "I've heard that enough lately, thank you."

"What in the world makes you think he's keeping something secret that would help the investigation?"

"It's just . . ." I could feel irritation replace worry. "Look, Lizzie. You weren't there. I could tell he was concerned about the murders. He heard something that's connected to them in some way. You'll just have to trust me."

Lizzie looked unconvinced. "Did you ask him directly if that was true?"

"I . . . I think so." Had I? I couldn't remember exactly what I'd said.

"And how did Levi respond?"

Levi's voice drifted into my mind, and I suddenly felt foolish. "He said that if he knew something that would stop the murders, he'd go to the sheriff."

Lizzie shook her head. "Callie, I love you to pieces, but you've blown this way out of proportion. Turned it into something it isn't." She picked up her cup and stared at me. I looked away, not wanting to meet her eyes. "You're going to have to learn to trust Levi, or your marriage has no hope. You know that, right?"

"But I know it has something to do with these killings."

Lizzie sighed. "And how do you know that?"

"Like I said, he didn't deny it."

Lizzie took a sip of her cider and then put the cup down on the table. "Callie, has it occurred to you that it could be something besides a confession of murder?"

"Like what, Lizzie? What else could someone possibly say that's connected to these killings? Something that upset Levi so much? I can't think of a thing."

"What if one of these people voiced their own suspicions as to who the killer might be? Someone who couldn't have possibly done it? Or what if someone saw the body earlier and didn't report it? Or what if someone knew something about Levi's book? Or what if—"

I held my hand up to stop her. "That's enough. You're right." Relief flowed through me for the first time since Levi mentioned his disturbing counseling session. There *were*

213

other reasons for his reaction. "I guess I did jump to conclusions. But Levi didn't do or say anything to make me think otherwise."

Lizzie chuckled softly. "Maybe he didn't think he had to. I imagine he asked you to trust him."

"Okay, okay. Obviously I'm wrong." I pushed my cup toward her. "Can I have more cider, even though I'm a terrible human being? It's delicious."

Lizzie laughed as she took my cup and stood up. "You're not a terrible human being, sweetie. You're a woman who cares about right and wrong. Maybe a little too much. Sometimes you have to let others decide what's right for them. Levi would never allow anyone to be put in danger if he could stop it. You should know that."

I watched Lizzie as she filled my cup. "Yes, I should. Then why did I automatically jump to the wrong conclusion?"

She shrugged and walked back to the table. The wind screamed again, rattling the windows. "Just because you were wrong about Levi doesn't mean you should close your eyes to everything that's happening. We all need to be on alert. Maybe the killer's not Aaron or John, but that doesn't mean we shouldn't consider other possibilities."

"I've been thinking about what the sheriff said and trying to come up with someone else who might be acting oddly or has something to hide. I guess my mind is just running wild, but I still say John qualifies."

"Maybe you should suspect yourself," Lizzie said wryly. "Because you're the one who's been acting weird."

"Very funny."

Lizzie sipped her cider and studied me.

"You forgot the cookies," I said, trying to ignore her.

She got up without saying anything and took some cookies out of the cookie jar. After putting them on a plate, she brought them over and set them down on the table. When I reached for one, the pain almost made me gasp. Determined not to let Lizzie know how much I was hurting, I kept quiet. She would worry and try to take care of me. I felt certain I'd start feeling better before long.

"Please be careful, Callie. You don't want to accuse someone falsely of something like murder." She took a sip of her cider before saying, "And you definitely don't want to betray Levi's trust. If you have concerns, take them to him. No one else."

"Thanks, Lizzie. I know you're right. I'm so glad I had the chance to talk to you."

Another huge blast of wind shook the house. Lizzie got up again and looked out the window. "This storm is getting worse." She shook her head. "I still can't believe Mary is dead. Poor Roger. I never liked him much, but I sure feel sorry for him."

"You warned me to do the right thing and not cast aspersions toward other people, but you're still holding a grudge against Roger for the way he treated us in school all those years ago."

Roger had been a bully when we were in grade school, calling the kids from Kingdom names and making our lives miserable. When Mary left Kingdom and ended up marrying Roger, everyone was shocked. But Roger was a different person now and had not only been a wonderful husband to Mary, he'd also shown nothing but friendship to the residents of Kingdom.

"Funny that you brought up our childhoods, Callie," Lizzie

said softly. "Because that's exactly what I want to talk to you about—if we're past the serial-killer discussion."

I immediately felt a wall go up. Was Lizzie going to say something unkind about my father again?

"Look, Callie," she said as she sat down again, "I can't put off discussing something with you. Something you don't seem to want to talk about." She stared into her cup and cleared her throat. "You're getting ready to get married. I'm afraid . . ."

The look on her face made my heart sink.

"I'm afraid if you don't deal with some things now, before the wedding, they'll pop up later and will affect your marriage." She hesitated for a moment. Then she took a deep breath. "Do you know why you got so angry with Elmer Wittenbauer?"

"Because of the way he treats Ruby." My voice rose out of frustration.

"It's more than that, Callie. You identify with Ruby. Why do you suppose that is?"

"I don't know what you mean. If this is about Papa . . ."

She shook her head vigorously. "Callie, it's not just your father. It's about you." She paused again as if gathering her thoughts. "I've known you since we were children. Maybe I was gone for five years of your life, but I still know a lot about you."

"Just what is it you think you know?"

She took a sip of her cider, put the cup down, and sighed. "Well, I know that your life was shattered when your mother left. And your father made you feel unwanted and unloved. I believe that was the point when you started hiding your true feelings. You became the dutiful daughter. The faithful friend. The young woman who unconsciously created a kind of shield around herself so she wouldn't feel pain. The problem is, you've done such a good job, you don't feel much of anything anymore. Not when it comes to yourself. That protection is costing you a lot, Callie."

She gazed at me solemnly. "Sweetie, you can't spend your life stuffing your emotions into a closet. One day that closet will burst open, and the result won't be good. I saw this more than once when I worked with abused women at the shelter. Not facing the truth can cause all kinds of problems. It can actually ruin your ability to trust anyone. Ever."

I wanted to stop her. To tell her to be quiet, but it was as if my mouth had frozen shut and wouldn't open. Why couldn't I talk? Why couldn't I defend myself?

"You're a sweet little Mennonite woman because that's who you think you're supposed to be. But it isn't real. It isn't you." She reached out and squeezed my hand. "Don't get me wrong, Callie. If that's who you *want* to be, that's great. The problem is that you've never made a decision about who you are or what you believe. You've just followed the path your mother and father laid out. And that's not right."

"I don't know what you're talking about," I said finally. "I'm exactly who I want to be." I realized with a start that I'd said those words while dressed in jeans and a sweatshirt. My right hand instinctively reached up to touch my head.

"No, you're not wearing a prayer covering, Callie. And you know what? You're still the same person. Head covered or uncovered."

"But the Bible says—"

"The Bible says we're free. Free from the laws of man." She smiled. "If you want to wear a prayer covering, that's great. It's not much different from women in the world who wear cross necklaces. They do it as a reminder of the love they have for God. To honor Him. But don't turn an old tradition into a new law. Just because women in the early church covered their heads doesn't mean it's important now. And besides, even if you want to make that Scripture into more than it is, it does say *in church*. It doesn't say all the time."

"Is that why you wear your prayer covering only in church?"

Lizzie shrugged. "No, not really. I don't believe God cares if I wear it there either, but I do it out of deference to those who would be offended if I didn't. I don't have to, but I want to. Out of love for my brothers and sisters in Christ." She frowned at me. "And that's the point, Callie. I make a choice. I don't just follow what my father wants."

"You think that's what I'm doing?"

She squeezed my hand. "Yes. I think that's exactly what you're doing. Look, honey, I don't care if you decide to wear your prayer covering in the shower and in bed. That's not the point. The point is, I think it's time Callie Hoffman found out the answer to a very simple question: Who are you?"

Charity's words from earlier came back like a ghost whispering in my ear. *Then who are you?*

I looked at Lizzie with tears in my eyes. "I have no idea," I said finally.

CHAPTER 15

Lizzie and I stayed up late and talked. It was well after midnight when I fell into bed. Unfortunately, my sleep was anything but restful. I dreamt my father was saying things to me. Hurtful words that stung. *"It's your fault your mother left. My life would be better if you weren't here."* When I woke up, I realized the words were real. He'd actually said them—and more. That I'd never amount to anything. That I'd never get a good husband. And my mother left because she didn't love me. Letting those terrible words into my heart hurt almost more than I could bear. I lay in bed and cried until it felt that there were no more tears inside. Remembering his hateful statements answered another question. Why I had changed when I was about twelve years old. Levi was right. That was when Papa started hurling mean-spirited insults my way.

Although it was still dark outside, I could hear noises in the kitchen. I had no idea what time it was. There wasn't a clock in my room. The only light was from the wall-mounted heater.

I pulled my legs over the side of the bed and stretched. Pain shot through my chest. I sat there for a few minutes, trying to take deep breaths until it ceased. Strangely, my breaths seemed shallow and small. Eventually the pain subsided, and I felt better.

I continued to sit for a while, trying to gather my thoughts. How could I face Lizzie today? Should I tell her what I'd remembered? How could I say bad things about my father? I'd been taught to honor him. Would God be mad at me if I told Lizzie the truth? Would he turn His back on me the way my earthly father had? Even as I pondered my questions, I knew the answer. It was rooted inside my heart. God's love was perfect. Not like Papa's. As I remembered the light that had guided me to Lizzie's house, I became certain God's light would also guide me through this dark time in my life.

I didn't have all the answers yet, but there was one thing I knew for sure. Lizzie was right about stuffing my feelings into a closet. And Papa was right too. I had been living in a dream world. Maybe I'd wanted a happy family so badly I'd painted a picture of my life the way I wanted it to be. And I'd seen Papa, not realistically, but through rose-colored glasses. No matter what, I'd always love him. And that was the challenge. To love him but see him for the person he really was. A bitter man who hadn't given his daughter the love she needed.

Papa hadn't always been cruel. I could still remember good times before Mother left, and toward the end of his life, he'd mellowed quite a bit. He'd thanked me for taking care of him and had even told me he loved me. But his hold on me remained. Whether it was of his making or mine, I would probably never know. But at least I could see him clearly now. And that gave me the power to forgive him.

The core of anger inside me felt drained, but in its place was sorrow. I had no confidence that all my rage was gone, but at least now I understood it.

I reached over to the clothes that were on the chair, slowly pulling on the jeans and sweatshirt I'd worn last night. I didn't want to move too quickly and aggravate the pain from my bruised chest. After making my bed, I turned off the heater and opened the door. Lizzie stood in the kitchen, putting strips of bacon into a large cast-iron skillet. A pot of coffee percolated on the stove.

"Good morning," I said.

She looked over at me and smiled. "Good morning. Coffee will be ready in a few minutes."

"Great. I need to use the bathroom, but I'm afraid of waking up Noah and Charity."

Lizzie shook her head. "Noah's out like a light on the couch. Those pain pills will keep him asleep for a while. And you couldn't blast Charity out of bed with a cannon. I've never known anyone who can sleep like that girl."

"Okay, thanks."

I started to walk out of the room when Lizzie stopped me. "I put some fresh clothes in the bathroom in case you'd like to take a shower. It's up to you. Breakfast won't be ready for at least thirty minutes."

"Okay, thanks. A shower sounds good."

Lizzie nodded and went back to her tasks.

I walked on tiptoes through the living room. Sure enough, Noah was snoring away. I hoped he wouldn't be so sore today. At least he looked comfortable. I walked slowly up the stairs, hoping their creaking wouldn't wake him. When I reached the bathroom, I turned on the light. Sure enough, clothes were waiting for me. Two sets. My dress and underthings, along with another pair of jeans and a sweater. Lizzie had washed out my clothes, but instead of putting just them in the bathroom, she'd given me a choice.

I showered slowly because of the pain. Then I looked at my chest. Noah's prediction about the skin turning black and blue was true. I found it odd that the seat belt installed in Noah's truck to keep me safe had caused so much damage. It was certainly a mixed blessing.

There was a hamper in the bathroom, so I put my dirty clothes in it. After cleaning up the bathroom the best I could, I fixed my hair and went back downstairs. Lizzie was putting scrambled eggs on a plate as I walked in.

"Just in time," she said. She smiled and put the plate on the table. "Have a seat, and I'll get you some coffee."

"Thank you."

She turned back to the stove and took the pot off the burner. After pouring coffee into two cups, she carried them over to the table. "I have an extra prayer covering if you want it," she said.

I smoothed my dress. "I don't think so, thanks." I smiled at her. "One step at a time, Lizzie. It may take some time for me to discover the real Callie who lives under her clothes. For now, though, I'm determined I'll find her in my own way. I know I need to stop trying to be the person other people want . . . or expect me to be."

Lizzie filled another plate with food and then slid it into the oven to keep warm. Probably for Noah. "That's the way it should be." She came over and sat down. "Callie, a lot of people never find the person God created them to be. They're too busy trying to live up to other people's expectations, or they try to create themselves in the image of a person they admire or envy. Just because we respect someone or think their life might be more exciting than ours doesn't mean God created us to be just like them. Sometimes we have to ignore the people in our lives so we can hear the voice of God."

"That sounds rather selfish. Aren't we supposed to prefer others before ourselves?"

"Sure. But making a decision to put someone else first out of love isn't the same thing as putting them first out of fear. Because you're afraid they won't love you if you don't act the way they might want you to."

I stared at her in surprise. "Is that what I've been doing?"

"I don't know. Is it?"

That simple question hung in the air like the smell of rain after a storm. Had I lived my life trying to please my father so he'd love me? And what about Lizzie? Had I done the same with her?

Lizzie bowed her head and prayed over our food. I listened to her, but my mind was somewhere else. It was as if I were seeing my life for the first time.

When she raised her head, I quickly told her about my dream. About remembering the things my father had said.

"Oh, Callie," she said with tears in her eyes. "I'm so sorry. I know it must hurt, but facing the truth is better than hiding it."

"The truth will set me free?" I asked softly.

She nodded and wiped the tears from her eyes with her napkin. "I believe that. We can't be our true selves if we have secrets hiding in our hearts."

I didn't say anything, but what she said made sense.

"It's stopped snowing for a while," Lizzie said, changing

the subject. "But clouds are moving back in. We may be here another day or so."

I sighed. "I think that's good. Maybe by the time I face Levi again, I'll know what to do."

"What to do about what?"

I gazed past her, trying to organize my thoughts. "What to do about him." I picked up a piece of bacon and took a bite. I chewed and swallowed it, followed by a sip of Lizzie's perfect coffee. What was it about breakfast? There was no other meal like it. Somehow it had the ability to set the tone for the rest of the day. I felt comforted and warm inside.

Lizzie didn't say a word, just waited for me to continue. Which was good because it took me that long to figure out what I wanted to say.

"How can I marry Levi when I'm just now beginning to figure out who I am and what I want out of life? It's entirely possible the woman Levi wants to marry doesn't exist."

"Oh, Callie. I think she exists. I believe she's a compassionate woman who cares about her friends. Who will go out of her way to help anyone who needs it. Who loves children and animals. And more than anything else wants to please God." Lizzie smiled at me. "Getting out from underneath manipulation and control won't wipe those things away. It will only make them stronger. And you'll do them because you want to. Not because you think you have to. Do you understand?"

I nodded while I moved the scrambled eggs around on my plate with my fork. "Y-yes, I think so."

"Look, I believe you really love Levi. No one forced you to get engaged to him. That was your decision. Your father wasn't even around when that happened."

"But what if I decide to . . . I don't know, dress like you. Stop wearing my prayer covering. Levi's our pastor. He could never allow that."

Lizzie raised an eyebrow. "*Allow that?*" She shook her head. "I think that's the point, Callie. It isn't up to Levi to allow anything. You're responsible for your own decisions. That doesn't mean you won't acquiesce to some things because other people's feelings are worth more than what you want to do—or what you don't want to do. You have to pick your battles though. Being true to yourself is the first one."

"But Levi—"

"But Levi," she said with emphasis, "deserves honesty, Callie. If you two are meant to be together, it will work out. If he can't accept you for who you are, a successful marriage would be impossible. Trust me. I know what I'm talking about."

"I do trust you," I said. "And thank you, Lizzie. I don't know what I'd do without your friendship."

"I don't know what we would have done without you last night. If it hadn't been for you, today might have been very different. The worst day of my life."

I had to smile. "Well, if I hadn't gone for help, this might have been a pretty bad day for me too. Noah and I both could have frozen to death out there."

Lizzie blanched. "You're right. I've been so focused on Noah, I forgot that your life was at stake as well. You saved two lives yesterday. The lives of two people I love very much."

"I don't think I'm the one who should get the credit," I said. "God not only gave me strength, but He lit the way."

"Yes. Yes He did."

I smiled and got busy eating my breakfast. To be honest, I

was still amazed by what had happened the night before. I'd always believed God was a God of healing and miracles, even though Papa told me the day of miracles was past. Obviously, Papa had forgotten to explain that to God, who seemed to think He could do one anytime He felt like it.

The kitchen was chilly but warming up fast. I felt relaxed sitting in Lizzie's cozy kitchen. Would it be like this when Levi and I were married? Would I be fixing breakfast in our own kitchen while Levi sat and talked to me? The picture in my mind made me happy and sad, all at the same time. There was no way I could predict what was going to happen next. If I changed too much, would he break off our engagement?

Lizzie had just put more bacon in the pan, and I was getting up to get another cup of coffee, when the sound of a loud motor got our attention. Lizzie and I got up and went to the living room. Who in the world had braved the huge snowdrifts to get here? The answer was quickly evident. Levi was pulling his stepfather's tractor up to the front of the house, a huge snowplow attached to the front.

"It's Levi!" I said. At first I was thrilled to see him, but then reality hit. Was I ready to confront him? What could I say to him? Suddenly, an idea struck me. "I'll be right back, Lizzie," I said. I walked slowly toward the stairs.

"Callie, are you sure about this?" Lizzie asked, her face a mask of concern. "Maybe it isn't a good idea."

I marveled at her perception. She knew exactly what was on my heart. "I have to know, Lizzie. I have to. This is the only thing I can think of right now."

She didn't say anything else, just nodded at me.

I walked up the stairs to the bathroom and changed out

of my dress. Pulling it over my head was difficult. During breakfast, my discomfort had grown. Again, I felt the sensation of being able to take only short, quick breaths. I forced myself to quit thinking about my injury and got busy putting on Lizzie's jeans and sweater. Then I unwrapped my bun, pulled out the pins, and ran my hands through my long hair. The young woman who looked back at me in the mirror had fear in her eyes. Was this girl me? Or was she the girl in the plain dress and prayer covering?

At this point I had no idea. But I had to find out if Levi would be able to accept me, no matter who I turned out to be. With a sigh, I put my hand on the doorknob and stood there for a moment.

"Help me, God," I whispered. "Help me to know you better. And to find the person you want me to be. And please, please, if it's at all possible, help Levi to love me no matter who I am." I turned around and took one more quick look in the mirror. For just a moment, I thought about putting my dress back on. Was this fair to Levi? Was I thinking of him—or of me? Gathering up my courage, I forced myself to open the door and start for the stairs. I could hear his voice from the first floor. Walking slowly, I came down the stairs. As I neared the living room, all talking ceased abruptly.

I saw Levi standing near the front door, staring at me with his mouth open. Fear almost made me turn and run, but instead I pasted a smile on my face.

"Levi! What are you doing here?" I asked. "The snow is so deep—"

"I came to check on you," he said slowly. "And to make sure Lizzie and Noah are all right. I found the truck on the road."

"I was just telling Levi about how you saved Noah," Lizzie

227

said. She kept her eyes on me, not looking at Levi. Was there a warning on her face? Did she think I'd made a mistake?

"You . . . you must have ruined your clothes," Levi said. I couldn't read his expression. His eyes were narrowed. Was he angry?

"I was pretty wet," I said, "but my dress is dry now." I walked the rest of the way into the room to find Noah sitting up, his gaze darting between me and Levi.

"Then why . . . ?" Levi frowned at me and shook his head. "Forget it. I'm just grateful you're okay. That all of you are okay." He held out his arms, and I went to him. His hug was firm and reassuring, and I felt the tension leave my body.

"That tractor isn't made for snow this deep," Noah said in a scolding tone. "I wish you'd stayed home where you were safe."

Levi let go of me and smiled at his brother. "It wasn't that hard. With the plow in front of me, I was as safe as I could possibly be. It just took a long time to get here." He sniffed the air. "I'm not sure if that's bacon I smell, but if it is, I could sure make use of a hot breakfast."

Lizzie got a strange look on her face. "Oh, my goodness. The bacon!" She ran to the kitchen.

"How does burned bacon sound, Brother?" Noah said with a grin.

"Believe it or not, it sounds fantastic."

"How long did it take you to get here?" I asked.

"I started this morning around four. What time is it now?"

"It's a little past eight," Noah said, scowling. "You were out there for four hours? You could have frozen to death."

"Nonsense. The cab's nice and warm." He smiled sheepishly. "I did get stuck a couple of times though."

Lizzie walked back into the room. "The bacon's okay. I caught it just in time. If you're hungry, Levi, get in here. I'll give you Noah's plate. It's all ready." She pointed at her husband. "You stay there. I'm making a fresh plate for you, and I'll bring it to you. No sense in you getting up from that couch."

Noah got a funny look on his face, and I was surprised to see him blush. "Actually, there's a very good reason for me to get off this couch." He motioned upstairs with his head. "I'm really feeling better, Lizzie. If you don't mind, I think I'll go upstairs for a few minutes."

She put her hands on her hips and stared at Noah as if she wasn't certain he should make the trip alone.

"Lizzie," Noah warned. "You're going to have to trust me here. I might be a little sore for the next few days, but I'm fine."

"Okay, but take it easy." She pointed at Levi. "You watch him. Make sure he gets up and down the stairs okay."

Levi smiled. "I'll stand guard until he returns. I promise."

Lizzie cast one more serious look Levi's way before turning on her heel and heading for the kitchen.

"Don't let anything happen to him," I said softly. "Lizzie would never forgive you."

Levi grinned and nodded. Noah got up from the couch and walked slowly toward the stairs. I was relieved to see him moving under his own power. I followed Lizzie to the kitchen. She was getting eggs out of the refrigerator.

"I'm glad Levi made it here safely," she said when she saw me. "I can't believe he spent four hours trying to make it through the snow."

I slid carefully into the nook, my chest sore and aching. "I can't tell if Levi's upset about the clothes."

She turned around to frown at me. "Callie, don't worry about it. Levi loves you." She pointed at me with her spatula. "You know you have to talk to him, right? Just wearing different clothes doesn't tell him what's in your heart."

I nodded. "I know."

"I'm going to eat breakfast with Noah in the living room. That will give you two a chance to visit. I wouldn't take too long though. Charity will be up any minute."

"What am I supposed to say to him?"

Lizzie put the spatula on the counter and sat down next to me. "You tell him the truth, Callie. Whatever it is. And you tell him about your father. What you've remembered."

I couldn't respond. Tears dripped down my face and splashed on the table. Suddenly I was afraid. Would Levi understand? Would he still want me? A desire rose up inside of me to run upstairs, change my clothes, and turn back into the girl Levi had fallen in love with.

Lizzie leaned over and hugged me before she got up and went back to the stove. She finished the eggs and made toast while I tried to figure out what to say to Levi. By the time she'd made up two more plates, Levi came into the kitchen.

"Noah's back on the couch," he said, shaking his head. "I think he's milking this as much as he can. He loves being waited on."

Lizzie chuckled. "I know that. But after last night, I'm grateful to God he's okay. Babying him a little is fine with me. Everyone needs special attention once in a while."

"It wouldn't be a bad idea to have him checked out," Levi said. "Marvin broke a rib once. We had no idea he was badly injured until he passed out from the pain. Sometimes people feel fine until that broken part of the rib moves."

"When the phone's back up, I'll call the doctor in Washington and make an appointment," Lizzie said.

"Noah said you've been having trouble with it," I said. "It keeps going out."

She nodded. "That's true, but since last night, it's been deader than a doornail. I think all the phone lines are down in this area. Hard to know when they'll be up again."

"Speaking of injuries, how are you feeling?" Lizzie asked me.

"Very sore," I said. "My entire chest is turning dark."

"You're hurting?" Levi asked.

"Just from the seat belt. It bruised me pretty bad, and it hurts worse today. But I'll be fine."

Levi frowned at me. "We need to keep an eye on you too. If you start hurting more or if you have any other symptoms, you've got to let us know, okay?"

"I will. But really, I'm okay."

Lizzie wiped her hands on her apron. "If you want a pain pill, let me know, Callie. They really helped Noah."

I smiled at her. "I might take you up on that a little later, but I don't want to be sleepy right now."

"Okay." She pointed at Levi. "You sit down. I've got your food ready. Noah and I will eat in the living room."

Levi started to protest, but Lizzie held up a hand to silence him. "No arguments. You need to trust me."

Levi seemed puzzled and looked over at me. I couldn't read him, couldn't tell what he was thinking, but my stomach clenched with fear. I had to walk a path that would lead me to the truth, and Levi would have to deal with whatever waited at the end of that road. Would it be the end for us as well?

Lizzie picked up her plate and Noah's and left the room. The silence that followed her departure was so deep, I was afraid to broach it. To disturb it. I knew my life would never be the same when the words I had to say finally came out.

"What's going on, Callie?" Levi's eyes searched mine. "And why are you dressed like that? Lizzie has more appropriate clothing you could borrow. You . . . you look like someone else."

My heart sank at his words. "Levi, something . . . something has happened, and I need to explain." With that, I began to tell him everything. The truth about my father and how I'd hidden from it all those years. That I'd been living in my father's shadow for so long I'd never allowed myself to have opinions or feelings that didn't line up with the church or with my father's strict teachings. When I finished, he just sat and stared at me.

"I'm sorry you were treated like that, Callie," he said finally. "Really sorry. I had no idea—"

"Of course you didn't. We weren't close when we were kids, and my father didn't share his feelings with anyone else. Lizzie knew because she overheard some of the things he said to me."

"One thing I don't understand. You actually forgot about his treatment of you? How is that possible?"

"I can't pretend to comprehend it all yet, Levi. Lizzie knows more about it than I do because she worked with abused women in Kansas City. I guess it was a kind of emotional protection. A way to keep myself from the pain inside. It started when my mother left, and from there, it got worse. Lizzie said it was like stuffing all the hurt into a closet. But it didn't really stay inside. Sometimes I'd get so mad. The other day when Ruby came into the restaurant, it all came to the surface. My closet burst open." I shook my head. "The anger was so intense. Almost uncontrollable."

"Ruby reminded you of your own situation."

"Yes. I believe that's exactly what happened."

Levi clasped his hands together, his breakfast forgotten. "What can I do to help you?"

I sighed and shook my head. "I don't know. Give me some time. I'm confused."

His blue eyes were locked on mine. "But we're still getting married. This doesn't change how I feel about you."

I reached over and grabbed his hand. "Oh, Levi." I felt a tear slide down my cheek. "I'm twenty-two years old, and I've just discovered that I have no idea who Callie Hoffman really is." I looked down at Lizzie's sweater. "I don't even know how Callie Hoffman dresses. If she believes in our Mennonite way of life or not." I brought my face up and met his gaze. "Please understand that I love Kingdom. And I love you. But I've never been given the chance to choose. Even my relationship with God is based on what my father told me it should be. Shouldn't every person have the chance to decide what they believe? I mean, if they don't, how can their beliefs mean anything?"

Levi was silent, and his taciturn behavior frightened me. Why couldn't he sweep me into his arms and offer me reassurance? Let me know that no matter what, he'd stay by my side?

"Say something, Levi," I said finally, unable to keep the impatience out of my voice.

"Callie, the truth is . . . you're right. Completely right. You do have the right to choose. No one should follow Christ just because their parents did." He sighed deeply, as if releasing something painful from his body. "Nor should you marry someone because you think you should. Marriage should be out of love, no matter what our ancestors thought."

"Levi, I'm not saying I don't love you. Please don't assume that. My feelings for you are the same. And I do love God. With all my heart. I'm just afraid that my choices will hurt you. You're a Mennonite pastor. Your wife should be . . . I don't know . . . the perfect Mennonite woman. I'm not sure I can be that."

Levi stood up and walked over to the stove where he poured himself another cup of coffee. I could see that the muscles under his shirt were taut.

"I don't want you to be upset. . . ."

He brought his coffee cup over to the table and sat down again. "I understand what you're saying, but I'm not sure how you want me to respond." He stared into his cup for a moment. "I love you, Callie. You. No matter what you wear or don't wear. I wanted to marry you before you told me these things, and I still want to marry you. We can work through all of this . . . together." He gazed into my eyes. "But if you need some time, I will give it to you. I don't want us to be apart, but I have no desire to push you into something you're not ready for."

"Thank you. Just give me a little time to process everything. That's all I'm asking." I hesitated for a moment. I was grateful for his understanding and didn't want to make him angry. "Levi, there is one other thing I'd like you to do for me though. If it might help in any way, please go to the sheriff with what you know about these killings."

He sighed deeply. "Callie, I told you very clearly that what I know has nothing to do with who killed those women. Why won't you believe me?"

"I do believe you. This is the last time I intend to bring it up. I just think the sheriff should determine whether or not your information is important. Not you."

"What I know has less to do with the murders than it does with . . . you."

"What are you talking about?" My voice trembled with emotion. What in the world did he mean? "How could it have anything to do with me?"

Levi leaned against the kitchen cabinet and stared out the window. "Look, this isn't the right time to talk about this. I'll tell you all about it later, Callie. I promise. But not right now. You're going to have to trust me."

"All right."

He came over to where I sat and put his hand on my cheek. "I need some time to think, and so do you. I'm leaving. Let's talk again in a few days. But please know that I'm willing to work through anything. I love you, but you need to decide if you feel the same way."

With one last, long look, he left the kitchen. I tried to get up and go after him, but pain stabbed me in the chest as I struggled to scoot out of the nook. By the time I got to my feet, I heard the front door slam. I hurried into the living room as quickly as I could.

"Where's Levi going?" Lizzie asked.

I stared at the front door, my body throbbing. I wanted to run after him and ask him to come back. Dresses and prayer coverings didn't mean as much as Levi did. I'd do whatever I had to do to make things right. I suddenly felt Lizzie's arm around me.

"He thinks we need time to ourselves, Lizzie," I said, my voice breaking. "I don't want to lose him."

"Let him go, Callie," she said softly. "He's right. You both need time to sort out your feelings. If you're meant to be together, it will only strengthen you. You need to be honest with each other, and I'm not sure you're ready to do that yet." She hugged me. "It's all right, honey. Come over here and sit down. Everything will be okay."

"I hope you're right," I whispered. "I really hope you're right."

CHAPTER 16

It took several minutes for me to calm down after Levi left. Lizzie and Noah tried to reassure me that Levi and I would find our way and work things out. In the end, I understood why Levi left, but it didn't make me feel any better. I was having a hard time breathing as I struggled to control my emotions.

"Levi said the storm is finally moving out," Noah said once I'd settled down some. "He's going to clear off the road all the way to Kingdom. We could take you back to town tonight, but I suggest we wait until tomorrow. Others will be working on the roads as well, and it should be much safer when they're through."

"I think that's wise," Lizzie agreed. "That gives you another day to get yourself together, Callie."

"I feel better," I said, "but I have a lot of thinking to do." I put my hand up to my chest. The steady ache I'd felt all day was sharper now. Getting upset wasn't helping me emotionally or physically.

"I truly believe everything will work out," Lizzie said gently. She sat on the end of the couch by Noah's feet. I was in the overstuffed chair next to the fire. The flames were warm, but my heart felt like a block of ice.

"I don't want to force anything. Levi deserves to marry

the kind of woman who will make him happy. Help him to be the best pastor he can be."

Lizzie started to say something else, but I shook my head. I didn't want to debate the situation anymore. My head was full of confusing thoughts that needed to be sorted out before I could find the path I should take.

"Mama?"

We looked up to see Charity standing on the stairs in her pajamas. She'd slept late. Not surprising after all the late-night commotion.

"Good morning," Lizzie said with a smile. "Why don't you get dressed and then come back downstairs? I'll make you some breakfast."

She nodded slowly. "Is Daddy all right?"

"I'm just fine, honey," Noah said.

"Okay." Charity didn't seem convinced. She loved Noah. Finally having a father meant everything to her. "Nobody move. I'll be right back." She turned on the stairs and padded back up to the top.

"Nobody move?" Noah said, chuckling. "No problem. I'm so comfortable, I could stay here all day."

Lizzie pulled the quilt up and covered him. "I know you feel better, but you might as well get a little more rest. You've been through a lot. Levi and some men from town will tow the truck back here after they clear the roads. There's nothing you need to do right now."

That seemed to mollify him, and within a few minutes, he was snoring away. Lizzie got up and motioned for me to follow her into the kitchen.

"More coffee?" she asked once I was settled into the breakfast nook.

"I'm too nervous already. I think I've had at least six cups."

"How about some decaffeinated tea? With a little honey?"

I smiled at her. "That sounds perfect."

She busied herself, putting water on to boil and getting cups out of the cabinet.

Though it was still morning, I suddenly felt exhausted—and old. "Levi said the oddest thing, Lizzie."

She sat down across from me while we waited for the water to boil. "What's that?"

I sighed and ran my finger along a ring on the hand-stitched tablecloth. "He said whatever he knew about the person who killed that woman on the road to Kingdom had more to do with me than the murder itself."

Lizzie's forehead wrinkled and she tilted her head to the side. "What does that mean? What could you possibly have to do with the murder?"

I shrugged. "Maybe I'm really a serial killer and don't realize it."

Lizzie snorted loudly. "Oh, for crying out loud, Callie. That's ridiculous."

"I guess so. It's very disconcerting to realize you're a stranger to yourself."

She smiled at me. "You're not a stranger. And you're certainly not a serial killer. I think you know yourself more than you realize. You just need to face some things you haven't before. I'll help you. We'll do this together."

"Thanks."

"What else did you two talk about?" she asked.

I went over everything I could remember. As I repeated the things Levi and I said, once again fear began to build up inside me, and with the fear, my pain increased. I tried to change my position to see if I could get some relief. It didn't work. After telling Lizzie, she made me go in the bedroom and show her my chest.

"Oh, my goodness," she said, lowering my sweater. "It's a wonder you're still on your feet. Here I've been focused on taking care of Noah and practically ignoring you. I'm so sorry, Callie. Why don't you take one of Noah's pain pills and lie down for a while?"

"I don't like pills," I said. "They make me feel out of control."

Lizzie chuckled. "And we can't have that."

I tried to take a deep breath but couldn't. I grimaced with pain. "Maybe I should take you up on your offer after all. I'm really starting to hurt."

"You don't look so good," Lizzie said. Her voice sounded like it was coming from a barrel.

"What did you . . ." I suddenly found myself gasping for breath. "I . . . I can't . . ."

She reached for me, but before she could catch me, I collapsed to the floor. I could hear Lizzie's voice, but I couldn't understand what she was saying. Everything was blurry, and I could have sworn someone was crying. It sounded like Charity. I wanted to tell her I was okay, reassure her that there wasn't anything seriously wrong, but I couldn't get any words out.

I was gasping for air, trying to cry out, but it was useless. Images started floating around like specters without bodies. I could hear people speaking, but I couldn't understand them. I kept passing out and coming to. At one point I could have sworn I was moving. Eventually something loud, like a siren, surrounded me. Hands touched me, picked me up, and then finally, everything became silent, and I drifted away.

CHAPTER 17

"Callie? Callie, can you hear me?"

I could hear Lizzie's voice, but it sounded so far away, I could barely make out her words. It took a while to get my eyes to stay open. Once they were, I found myself looking up into her worried face.

"Where . . . ?"

"You're in the hospital in Washington," Lizzie said, stroking my hair. "You're going to be fine."

I tried to sit up but couldn't. "What . . . what happened?"

She took my hand. "Your lung collapsed, sweetie. You've also got a broken rib."

"But how did I get here? The snow . . ."

Lizzie smiled down at me. "Levi came back. He couldn't shake the feeling that something was wrong. When he saw you had collapsed, he started clearing the road so Noah could follow behind him with you in the truck. He was prepared to go all the way to Washington, but Sheriff Timmons was out in an SUV checking the condition of the roads. Noah met him a couple of miles out of town. The sheriff called the hospital and they sent an ambulance. It was a miracle any of them got through the snow."

"Levi came back?" I asked. My voice was so weak I wasn't certain Lizzie could hear me.

"Yes, and he's been here almost constantly since you've been in the hospital."

"How long . . ."

"Three days. The pain medication the doctor gave you to keep you comfortable made you sleep a lot. You woke up several times, but you probably don't remember because you were so groggy. He's decreasing the medicine so you'll be able to stay awake, but I'm afraid you're going to hurt."

"I don't remember anything since the house." I tried to move my head and look around me. Just as Lizzie had predicted, even that small movement was painful. "You said Levi is here?"

She shook her head. "He left once the doctor said you were going to wake up and start becoming more aware. I have no idea why, but I'm sure he's coming back. He's been so worried about you. I've never seen him so upset. We couldn't get him to leave your side."

"Is Noah okay?"

Lizzie chuckled softly. "He's fine. Back to normal." Her smile disappeared. "Why didn't you tell us you were in such pain?"

"I thought it was because my chest was bruised. It never entered my mind that there was anything else going on."

Lizzie rubbed my hand. "That sounds just like you."

I tried to sit up, but the pain made me stop. "Can this bed be raised up?"

She let go of my hand and got up from her chair. After fiddling around with some controls on the side, the bed began to move. Sitting up, even a little, felt much better than lying flat.

"The doctor says you can go home Monday morning."

"I don't know what today is."

"It's Saturday."

"I have to stay two more days?"

Lizzie nodded. "They want to be absolutely certain you're okay." She grinned. "Look at it this way—you get to lie around in bed and be waited on."

I sighed. "I just want to go home."

"You can't go back to the apartment, sweetie. You're coming to our house. Just until you can get around by yourself."

Actually, I didn't mind going back to Lizzie's one bit. Being alone right now wasn't very appealing.

"Lizzie, have there been any more . . . ?"

"Murders?" Lizzie asked. "No, thank God. Not since Mary."

"Have you talked to Roger?"

She nodded slowly. "He's a wreck. Blames himself for leaving Mary alone. I guess he feels that if anyone should have been safe, it should have been his wife."

"That's not rational."

"I know," Lizzie said, "but he's grieving. I guess it's hard to think clearly when you're experiencing that kind of loss."

"I'm sure it is. It was hard to lose Papa, but I knew he was dying. His death wasn't violent and sudden like Mary's. Roger must be devastated."

"We'll all help him through this. It's important that he doesn't feel alone."

I smiled at her. "You almost sound compassionate. I thought you didn't like him."

She waved her hand at me. "Suddenly, it seems childish to hold something against him that happened so many years ago. I guess I was being ridiculous."

"Yes, you were."

"Hey," she teased, her eyes crinkled with humor. "You don't need to agree with me so quickly."

I laughed, but as soon as I did, pain gripped me. "Oh my. Quit making me laugh. It hurts too much."

Instead of responding with laughter, Lizzie's expression grew solemn. Now that some of the grogginess was lifting, I realized she was distracted.

"What's wrong?" I asked.

She looked back toward the door before getting even closer to the bed. "Listen," she said quietly. "I probably shouldn't tell you this, but something happened that concerns me."

I raised my eyebrows in a silent question.

She cranked her head around once more. Seemingly satisfied, she leaned in close. "Remember what you told me about Levi counseling someone who had information about the killings?"

"Of course. Aaron Metcalf, John Lapp, and Margaret Harper. He was upset about something one of them said."

"I saw Leah in town yesterday, and she told me something interesting." Lizzie's voice was barely above a whisper. "She wanted to know if we had a copy of the book of martyrs, you know, like the one Levi lost? She wants one for the school. One of the children borrowed the school's copy and their dog chewed it up."

Lizzie seemed upset, and I was beginning to feel alarmed. "So?"

"So when I told her we didn't have one, she mentioned that she saw John Lapp with a copy. At church. On the very day Levi lost his."

"Oh, Lizzie. That book is all over town. John probably has his own book."

"I'm not stupid, Callie. I know that. But here's what's interesting. When Leah asked John about his copy, he denied having one. In fact, he got very belligerent about the whole thing."

I just stared at her. Why would John say he didn't have a copy of a book that was well-loved by the Mennonite community? There wasn't anything wrong with it.

"There's more," Lizzie said quietly. "John traveled on the road to Kingdom early Monday morning. He could have dumped that body, Callie."

"You told me I was imagining a link between John and the murders. You said whatever Levi heard in counseling couldn't be a confession to the killings."

She gave an exasperated sigh. "I know what I said, and I still believe it. Forget about the counseling sessions. This is something totally different. Don't you think it's a little odd that John would deny having the book?"

I turned the question over in my mind. It did seem strange. "But what about Mary? She lives . . . I mean, she lived in Washington. I can't see John driving his buggy to Washington and luring her away so he could kill her."

"I made a few calls yesterday to Washington. John was in town Tuesday afternoon. Right around the time Mary disappeared."

"Oh, Lizzie. Really? John Lapp? How old is he anyway?"

"He's in his late fifties or early sixties, Callie. And still strong enough to kill someone. That's how old BTK was."

"When I brought up John's name, you acted like I was crazy."

"Well, I don't think you're crazy now." She fastened narrowed eyes on me. "I called the sheriff about it."

"You what?" Although I found Lizzie's information disturbing, hearing that she'd actually turned John's name over to the sheriff shocked me. What if she was wrong? What if I was wrong? Lizzie's excited demeanor alarmed me. She was usually the calm, rational voice in our friendship.

"Look, Callie," she hissed, "you're the one who originally brought John up. You gave me several reasons why John could be the killer. Now I'll give you one more." She paused dramatically. "John's first wife died under suspicious circumstances."

I frowned at her. "I thought her death was an accident."

Lizzie nodded enthusiastically, her dark hair bouncing. "She fell down the stairs and broke her neck. Doesn't that sound suspicious to you?"

I considered it. Although none of the facts by themselves seemed particularly ominous, together they did seem unusual.

"What did the sheriff say?"

"He thanked me for bringing all of this to his attention. He's going to do some digging around into the circumstances surrounding John's first wife. Just in case he killed her too."

"Oh, Lizzie. I . . . I just don't know."

She pointed her index finger at me. "For goodness' sakes, Callie. You're the one who put the thoughts in my head." She leaned back in her chair, a look of triumph on her face. "I did think you were imagining things until Leah told me about the book. Then everything came together. It all fits."

I nodded. Lizzie had put together a rather convincing argument. Could John Lapp actually be a crazed killer? But the whole idea was so foreign to someone who had lived a life committed to nonviolence. How could it be true?

"Sounds like the authorities are finally convinced the killings are the work of the same serial killer."

Lizzie sighed. "They're so closemouthed, like they don't want to admit to anything. But the sheriff told me they're confident it's him."

"Do people in Kingdom know that? We need to be careful."

"Levi and the elders are warning everyone they can. We're all looking out for each other, but no one knows about John."

Suddenly, I felt incredibly tired, like I'd just run out of steam. "I guess you did the right thing in contacting the sheriff," I said, "but please don't tell Levi. He'd be furious if he knew."

"This has nothing to do with his counseling sessions. I don't know why he'd be angry."

"Who wouldn't be angry about what?"

Lizzie jumped, and I turned too quickly, cranking my head toward the door where Levi stood with his hat in his hand and a deep frown on his face. I cried out in pain from the sudden move, and Lizzie turned back to comfort me. She shook her head just slightly, a silent message not to tell Levi what she'd done. I clamped my mouth shut and looked the other way.

"Nothing you need to know, Levi," Lizzie said. Although she answered him calmly, I was certain he wasn't fooled. "Just girl talk."

"If it has something to do with me, I'd like to know." Although my head was turned away, I could hear his shoes on the linoleum floor as he approached my bed. "Callie, is there anything you need to tell me?"

I turned my head, slowly this time, and found him standing next to Lizzie. His eyes were locked on mine. I was shocked to see dark circles under his eyes. I remembered Lizzie saying he'd been spending most of his time at the hospital. His concern for me touched me deeply.

"Like Lizzie said, it's nothing." I tried to sit up straighter in the bed, and was rewarded with a sharp jab to the side. When I cried out, Levi's expression changed from one of suspicion to one of compassion. Although I was ashamed of myself, it's what I'd counted on.

"You're still in pain." He glanced over at Lizzie. "Can't they do anything for her?"

Lizzie gave me a quick look, rolling her eyes. We both knew we'd just escaped an incredibly awkward moment.

"No," she said, addressing him. "They've reduced her pain medication so she can remain conscious. Now she has to heal."

"I'll be fine," I said with a smile. "Have a little faith."

A flicker of a smile crossed his features but then slipped away. "I'm confident you're going to recover, but I hate to see you hurting."

"Which reminds me," I said, my voice slurring. "Why am I so sore? I understand about my rib, but why is it worse now?"

Lizzie patted my cheek. "Oh, sweetie. They had to inflate your lung with a chest tube. That's what's making you so uncomfortable. But it will get better. Unfortunately, your rib will take a little longer."

"How much longer?"

I saw Lizzie and Levi exchange a quick look, and my heart sank. "How long, Lizzie? Tell me the truth."

"There's nothing the doctors can do," Levi said. "They'll give you some medicine to take with you."

"You have to take it easy, Callie," Lizzie said, frowning. "If you don't, you could develop pneumonia."

I felt my frustration level rising. "I want to know how long I have to *take it easy*."

Lizzie cleared her throat. "Anywhere from six to eight weeks, Callie."

My fatigue vanished. "Did you say six to eight weeks?"

Lizzie nodded, and Levi looked uncomfortable.

"There's no way I can lie around for two months." I knew I sounded somewhat hysterical.

"You don't have a choice," Lizzie said matter-of-factly. "It's simply the way it has to be."

I tried to blink away the tears that sprung to my eyes. "But what about the restaurant? My job?"

Lizzie smiled. "You don't need to worry about that. Noah and I will take care of things."

"And my apartment?"

"You're going to stay with us for now. We'll see about the apartment a little later."

I started to protest, but Lizzie held a finger to her lips. "Hush. You're going to have to be brave and work with us. I know you want to go home, but you're going to need help for a while."

I sighed in frustration. "I'm sorry. I appreciate everything you're doing for me. It's just . . ."

Everything seemed to be falling apart all at once. My engagement, my health, my job, my emotions . . . even Kingdom itself was in turmoil. Where was God in all this? Suddenly, the light I'd seen the night of the accident popped into my mind again. A sweet peace settled over me, and I smiled.

"I'm sorry." I reached out my hand, and Lizzie clasped it. "I'm grateful to have friends who love me. Who want to take care of me. I really am blessed."

"My, that was a quick turnaround," Levi said. He looked relieved and dubious all at the same time.

I sighed. "Being upset isn't going to help anything. I might as well deal with the situation."

Lizzie grinned. "Good for you. You're facing some challenges, but we're all here to help."

"That's right," Levi said. "No matter what happens, I'll always be here for you, Callie. Always."

Overcome by another rush of emotion, all I could do was nod. Those were the words I wanted to hear. They gave me hope. In my heart, I knew my love for Levi was real. With God's help, we had a chance of finding our way through whatever changes came. And I wanted that chance. More than anything.

Lizzie leaned over and kissed me on the forehead. "Everything will be all right, Callie. I know it."

"I'm beginning to believe it," I said, looking past her and catching Levi's eye. "I really am."

At that moment, a nurse opened the door and came into the room. She smiled when she saw me. "So you're finally conscious. Your friends have certainly waited patiently for you to wake up." She walked around to the other side of the bed and lifted up the covers. Then she pulled my gown up. Thankfully, I was hidden from view. "You're looking pretty good," she said. "How are you feeling?"

"Sore. Very sore."

She nodded. "And you will for a while. I'm going to give you a little medicine to help the pain. It will make you sleepy but not like the last time."

I grunted softly, but even that hurt. "I hope not. Sleeping for three days is rather disturbing."

The nurse took a syringe out of her pocket and started to inject it into my IV line, but before she did, Levi stopped her.

"I'm sorry, but could you wait just a little bit? Someone's coming to visit Callie, and she needs to be awake for it."

The nurse, whose name tag read *Ellery Adams* frowned. "We need to keep ahead of her pain, sir. How long . . . ?"

At that moment, Noah walked into the room. I was thrilled to see him and smiled at Levi. "Is this who you wanted me to—?"

Someone else stepped from behind Noah. I was taken aback to see Margaret Harper, the odd woman from the restaurant, standing there.

"I don't understand," Lizzie said.

"I don't either," Noah said. "I'm just following instructions." He pointed at his wife. "You and I need to leave. Levi will take Margaret home after her visit with Callie." He shook his head at his brother. "You're going to have to explain all the secrecy later, Brother. This isn't like you."

Lizzie crossed her arms and stared at Levi. "I hope you know what you're doing."

"I do," Levi said. "Now if you don't mind . . ."

Lizzie shrugged. "I'll see you tomorrow, Callie. If you want to talk to me before then, you can try to call me. The phone still isn't working all the time. I wrote our number down and put it next to the phone in case you don't have it already."

"Thank you. I don't." I nodded at her and said good-bye. After Noah and Lizzie left, Levi asked the nurse to leave too.

"I'll be back in fifteen minutes," she said. "I'll have to administer her medication. She needs to rest. Understood?"

Levi nodded. "I understand."

When the door closed, Levi grabbed a nearby chair and pulled it near the bed. Margaret sat down in it. She looked frightened, and for some reason, I was too.

"I'll be in the hall," Levi said to her. "You can do this."

"No, Pastor. Please stay."

Although he looked reluctant, Levi closed the door to my room and stood next to it.

Margaret wouldn't look at me and didn't say anything. She just stared down at her hands, which were folded in her lap.

"Margaret, I don't understand," I said slowly. "Please explain what's going on. You and Levi are scaring me."

When she looked up, her eyes were full of tears. "First of all, my name isn't Margaret Harper," she said, her voice trembling. "It's Esther. Esther Hoffman."

At first her words didn't make any sense. I opened my mouth several times, but nothing would come out. Finally I managed to croak, "Mother? Mother, is it really you?"

CHAPTER 18

The woman I'd known as Margaret stood slowly and came up next to my bed. "I felt sure you'd recognized me," she said, her lips trembling and her eyes brimming over with tears, "even with the scar. I even tried to drop hints. Like about my sensitivity to milk—just like yours. But no matter what I said, you didn't seem to make the connection." She shook her head slowly. "I wanted to tell you, Callie, but I've been so afraid. Afraid you would tell me to leave before I had the chance to explain."

Levi stepped up next to her. "Esther came to me the other day and told me the truth," he said. "I couldn't tell you, Callie. She had to do it herself." He sighed. "It's been so hard, keeping it from you."

"But then I found out you'd been hurt," my mother said, "and I realized I couldn't wait any longer."

I felt stunned—as if someone had just slapped me in the face. Yet there was a part of me that wasn't surprised. As if I'd suspected the truth all along. "Who else knows about this?" I asked Levi.

"I haven't told anyone," he said. "After the doctor reduced your pain medication so you'd be more awake, I decided

Margaret should see you right away. Maybe it would have been better to wait a few days until you were stronger, but I was afraid Margaret—I mean Esther—would lose her resolve. I couldn't take the chance. You had to know the truth. I didn't want to keep it from you any longer."

"I felt I had to come now," Mother said. "What if something happened and I never got the chance?"

Levi gave me a quick smile. "You *are* getting better. Please don't see this as a death-bed confession."

"Ruth Fisher recognized me," Mother said. "I was surprised. I've changed so much. That's what we were talking about the other day in the restaurant. She threatened to tell you if I didn't. Ruth said it was wrong to hide it from you." She shook her head. "I don't think anyone else knows who I am."

"Esther came to me after her talk with Ruth," Levi said gently. "She didn't know what to do."

I kept my eyes focused on the bathroom doorknob. Although I wanted to respond, my emotions were exploding in so many directions, I couldn't seem to sort them out. I honestly had no idea how I felt about my mother—or toward Levi. He'd kept this from me for days. Whether it was right or wrong, a sense of betrayal overwhelmed me.

"You should have told me," I said to him. "This was a secret you shouldn't have kept. It involved me, and I had a right to know."

He stepped up next to the bed and took my hand. Although my first reaction was to pull it away, I didn't.

"Callie, I didn't know what to do. I wanted to tell you, I really did. But I was trying to do the right thing. For you, and for your mother. Finally, the only solution I could find was to get Esther to confess the truth herself." He squeezed my hand. "You know I love you. Please believe me when I tell you this was one of the hardest things I've ever gone through."

I took a deep breath. "I believe you. I know this isn't your fault." I turned my head to stare up into my mother's face. "I blame you, Mother. You should have come to me when you first got to town. Instead, you hid the truth. Then you forced Levi to carry your secret. One more example of how you always put yourself first. I had the right to know. And the right to tell you I don't need you anymore. I don't want you in my life."

The color drained from her face. "I . . . I understand how you feel, Callie. I really do. But please . . . please give me a chance to explain. It may not make any difference, but after you hear me out, if you still want me to go, I'll go. And I promise to never bother you again."

"It's too late, Mother. Fourteen years too late."

She swayed a little, and Levi let go of my hand. He reached out to steady her. Then he helped lower her back into her chair.

"Callie," he said, "if you don't want to talk to your mother, that's okay. I understand. It's your choice. But I'm asking you to listen to her. Just this once. Then, as she said, if you want her to leave, she'll go. I'll even help her get out of town."

I started to refuse, but the look on Levi's face stopped me. My love for him overshadowed my anger.

"All right. As long as you both stick to the agreement. After you're done, Mother, you'll leave and never come back?"

"I promise," she said, her voice cracking with emotion. She stared down at her hands and clasped them together before she spoke again. "A friend in Kansas City who knows all about me found your father's obituary online. It was posted in the Washington paper. I decided I had to see you. I wrote to the Kingdom church elders with a story about being related to a man I knew used to live here who had died. I assumed they couldn't confirm the truth and would let me come. I was right."

"Another lie," I mumbled.

"Yes. Another lie," she repeated. "I was afraid if I told the truth, they wouldn't allow me to live here."

"Why wouldn't the elders let you move back, Mother? That doesn't make sense."

"It does, because of what happened," Mother said quietly. She wouldn't look at me, kept her head bowed. It made it harder for me to hear her.

"Life with your father was . . . difficult," she said. "But I want you to know that I'm not blaming him for my actions. I'm responsible for the bad choices I made. At the time, I was confused. If I could go back and do things differently, I would. But that's impossible, isn't it?"

"Yes, it is," I acknowledged. I sighed. "The nurse will be here soon, Mother. You need to say whatever it is you feel you have to say."

Her head bobbed up and down. "Yes, you're right. I'm sorry. I want you to know that when your father and I first came here, we were looking for a safe place to raise you. A place where you'd be content and secure. The world seemed scary and dangerous. We were happy then. Excited about you. Excited about our lives together. But after we got here, things began to change. The pastor of the church was a harsh man. A man who believed in rules. A man who taught that God was always angry with us. I watched your father change before my eyes. Nothing I did was right or was good enough. I tried to be a good wife, I really did."

She finally looked up. There were tears running down her face. "I loved him," she whispered. "I didn't want to give up on our dream of having a wonderful life together. But after a few years, I could tell it wasn't going to happen. James became someone else. Someone I didn't know." She took a deep shuddering breath, her thin shoulders trembling. "At first it was just verbal abuse. But then he began to hit me." She shook her head and gazed at me. "He never tried to hit you, Callie. I was thankful for that. His anger seemed directed toward me."

"He never struck me, Mother. And I don't remember him hitting you. Not once."

"No, you wouldn't. I made sure of that. When he got angry, I sent you outside to play."

A memory flashed through my mind. Something I hadn't thought of for years. My father's face red with rage. Mother telling me to go play at Lizzie's house. I'd forgotten all about it.

"Your father kept a tight rein on me," she continued. "I was rarely allowed out of the house, except to go to church. But there was a man . . ." She sobbed and covered her face with her hands.

Levi reached over and put his hand on her shoulder. There were tears in his eyes.

Mother looked up at him and seemed to gather strength. "There was a man," she said again. "A veterinarian from Washington who cared for our horses and cows. He was a kind man, and he overheard your father and me . . . arguing. He knew your father was abusive, and he tried to help. I . . . I began to have feelings for him. Your father figured it out and fired him. James also threatened to kill this man if he ever came around me again." Her tear-filled eyes locked on mine. "Nothing happened between us, Callie. I swear to you. Nothing. But your father went to Pastor Linden and told him we'd had an affair. Pastor Linden ordered me to leave town. That's why I left. It wasn't my choice."

"You could have fought to stay," I said. "Or you could have taken me with you." The anger I'd felt earlier was turning into something else. A kind of deep grief.

"They never gave me the chance. Your father and Pastor Linden drove me out of town and dumped me off on the road with nothing. Just the clothes on my back and not a dime to my name."

"In all these years, no one ever told me about this, Mother. Why am I just hearing this story for the first time?"

She shook her head slowly. "I don't know. If anyone else knew about it, maybe they didn't tell you because they didn't want to hurt you. They didn't want you to know that your mother had been branded an adulteress. But my guess is that your father and the pastor kept it to themselves. I wasn't called before the elders, nor was I allowed to speak to anyone before I left. Not even you."

"I-I'm sorry you went through that. But it doesn't explain why you never tried to come back and see me."

"I planned to, even though I was told the church would never allow me to get near you. My plan was to sneak back and get you. Take you with me."

"Then why didn't you?" I glanced at the clock. The nurse would be back any moment. But I realized to my surprise that I wanted my mother to finish her story.

"This . . . this is difficult," she said, her voice catching. "I ended up in a women's shelter for a while in Kansas City. At first, all I could think about was coming back here and finding you. But I didn't have any self-esteem, Callie. In the end, I became convinced I wasn't worthy of you. That leaving you in Kingdom would be better for you. I couldn't support you. I had no job skills. No money. But being without you devastated me.

"Another woman at the shelter gave me drugs. At first, they made me feel better. Happy for the first time in years. Eventually I became hooked. I was thrown out of the shelter and lived on the streets, doing anything I could to get the drugs I craved."

The horror in my mother's eyes brought tears to my own.

"I even—"

"Stop, Mother. You don't need to go any further."

She nodded and pointed to the scar on her face. "This was caused by a drug dealer I couldn't pay. My life was a nightmare. I wanted to die, and in fact, I tried more than once to take my life. Then one day a church opened a ministry downtown. I went there for food and ended up finding God. The real God." A look of wonder crossed her face, and for the first time since coming into my room, she smiled. "The loving God. Not the angry deity your father believed in. And I changed, Callie. I really did. I'm a new person. A better person." She blinked hard, trying to control the tears that ran down her face. "Once I was clean, I decided to come back to Kingdom, but I was so afraid. Then my friend showed me that obituary. I took it as a sign." She gulped and wiped her face with a tissue Levi handed her from a box on the nightstand next to me.

"My plan was to take you back to Missouri with me, but

when I got here I discovered you were planning to be married. My number-one goal was to stop the wedding. I didn't want you to experience the kind of unhappiness I had. I didn't know Levi then. He seemed different from your father, but I didn't know if I could trust him. Then I went to see him. Got to know him. And finally, I told him the truth. I found him to be a wonderful man who truly loves you. He counseled me to tell you who I was, and he promised to stand by me when I did." Mother let go of a sigh so heavy it seemed to come from somewhere deep inside her. "I'm not blaming anyone but myself for my life, Callie." Her eyes searched mine. "I'm so sorry for all the pain I've caused you. I wish I'd been a better mother. All I can do is hope that someday you'll find it in your heart to forgive me." She grasped the railing on my bed so hard her knuckles turned white. "You don't need to say anything today. I've told you everything I can . . . for now." She stood to her feet. Levi grabbed her arm to support her. Her body was limp, as if all the strength had gone out of her.

"I'm sorry for you, Mother. Really. But right now I can't promise anything. You have to give me time. I need to think." Suddenly a wave of weariness swept over me, which seemed silly, since I'd been doing nothing but sleeping lately.

"You're tired," Levi said. "Get some rest. I'll come back after church."

I nodded. "All right."

He started to say something else, but just then the door to my room opened and Ellery came back in. "Sorry, folks, but that's it for now. I'm going to have to ask you to leave."

"We're going," Levi said to my nurse. Then he leaned over and kissed me on the cheek. "I'll see you tomorrow, Callie. I love you."

"I know."

After they left, Ellery checked me over and added the contents of her syringe to my IV line. As I drifted off to sleep again, a disturbing thought jumped into my mind. Was my mother's revelation the thing that had upset Levi so much the other day? If so, what could it possibly have to do with the murders?

CHAPTER 19

I spent a restless night full of odd dreams. In the most dis-concerting, I searched through Kingdom, trying to find something, but I had no idea what it was. I knew it was very important, and that I had to discover it, yet Kingdom was empty. No one was there. Every building, every home, had been deserted. I had the strangest feeling there were people all around me, hiding in the shadows, watching me. I could see them out of the corner of my eye, but every time I turned to look, they disappeared. Muted voices came at me from shadowy corners, but I couldn't make out the words. After a while I became frantic—and frightened.

Toward the end of the dream, I began to call for my mother, but I couldn't find her either. Finally I thought I saw her walking down the road, and I began to run after her. Before I could reach her, she disappeared, and I started shouting her name. At last I spotted her again, but when I approached the spot where I'd seen her, I realized I was standing amid the red cedar trees that lined part of the road to Kingdom. I cried out her name, but she wasn't there. Just before I woke up, I found myself lying on the ground, the trees standing over me, and something wrapped around me. Plastic. I opened my mouth to scream, but before I could get any sound out, I woke up, sweating and breathing heavily.

"Are you okay, honey?" A new nurse stood next to my bed, watching me.

"Y-yes," I stuttered. "B-bad dream."

She nodded. "I've seen it before with the medication you're on. Some people have nightmares. We'll switch you to something different. Pills that will help the pain but shouldn't cause dreams."

"Thank you. What time is it?"

The nurse looked at her watch. "Almost ten. You missed breakfast, but I didn't want to wake you. I'll get you something now. The doctor wants you to eat light though. Do you like oatmeal?"

"Sounds great. And some toast and coffee?"

She smiled. "I think we can do that. Dry toast though."

"Still sounds good."

"How's the pain today?" she asked.

I tried to move a little. "Still there, but I think it's getting better."

She smoothed my sheets. "You have a long way to go, but in the next few days your pain should begin to ease a bit."

She looked at my Bible lying on the nightstand. Lizzie must have brought it. "It's Sunday morning. How about a nice Christian program on TV?"

I started to explain that I didn't watch TV, but instead of refusing her offer, I just nodded. I remembered Noah saying that there were some good television shows, and my curiosity got the better of me. Papa had said that everything on TV was evil and it would break down families and ruin the spiritual character of the nation. I wanted to see if he was right. No one from Kingdom would be here until later in the afternoon, after church services, so no one would know about it.

The nurse picked up a small black instrument and pointed it at a television mounted on the wall. Suddenly, a picture appeared. Some man was pointing toward an automobile, saying he could help anyone buy a car, no matter how bad their credit was. I had no idea what he meant, although some of the business owners in Kingdom allowed residents to pay later. Especially the farmers who had to wait on selling their crops in the spring and summer. Could that mean people in the world could get a car and pay for it later when they had the money? That didn't sound like a bad deal to me.

"I think you'll like the next show," the nurse said. "I watch it a lot. Really helps me to feel closer to God."

"That sounds great. Thank you."

She smiled. "You're welcome. I'll see about that breakfast now."

She left the room, and I turned my attention back to the television. The man finished talking about cars, and then a big picture came on the screen that seemed to be announcing the name of the station I was watching. This wasn't actually the first time I'd seen TV. When he was healthy, Papa had driven us into town for groceries and supplies many times. I'd seen a few televisions inside some of the stores we visited. Papa had instructed me not to watch them, but I'd sneaked a quick look more than once. Most of the time, I didn't understand what was happening anyway.

I'd also seen some television when Lizzie and I went to town. Many of Lizzie's supplies for the restaurant were ordered through Maybelle Miller, who ran Maybelle's Restaurant in Washington. Usually, she didn't have TV in her dining room, but if the weather was bad, or there was a sports game on that was important to her customers, she brought in a large set.

Some of the things I saw confused me, and Lizzie had to explain the difference between actual shows and what she called "commercials." According to her, commercials were like quick shows that gave people information about products they might want to buy. That might be so, but some of the images I saw horrified me. Women in skimpy outfits dancing around, men drinking alcohol, and one where they were speaking about a personal product for women that shouldn't be talked about in public. There were men in the restaurant, watching this announcement. I remember being so embarrassed that I left and went to the truck. Lizzie came out a few minutes later to see if I was all right. I explained how horrified I was by the commercial.

"I still remember how I felt the first time I saw a commercial like that," she'd said, smiling. "I guess now I see both sides of the issue. On one hand, they're very personal and probably shouldn't be broadcast in public to children who don't understand what those products are. Yet in Kingdom, things like this are never discussed. Normal and natural functions of the human body are hidden. It can cause young people to feel that everything that has to do with the body is wrong. They can end up in trouble like I did."

"But, Lizzie," I'd wailed. "Men shouldn't see these things."

Lizzie had hugged me. "Oh, honey. That's nothing. I've seen some things on TV that would curl your hair if it wasn't already curly."

Thinking back to her words made me wonder if I should have allowed the nurse to turn on the television at all. Then the program started, and I was shocked to discover that the speaker was a woman! Women weren't allowed to teach men in Kingdom. I grabbed for the little device the nurse had used to turn on the set, but when I looked at it, all I could see were buttons, numbers, and words that meant nothing to me. Not having any other choice, I stared up at the woman who was talking. I noticed that she had a very kind face.

"Feelings buried alive never die," she said, looking at me through the television screen. "They only cause problems that can derail God's plan for your life."

It was as if she were in the room with me—as if she knew me. "God doesn't want you to bury pain from the past. Even though it hurts, He will allow it to surface because He wants to set you free. And you *can* be free. It will take inner strength and a commitment to face the truth you've been running from. Until you confront the situations that hurt you, they won't go away."

I couldn't stop the tears that ran down my face. For the next thirty minutes I listened, enraptured by this woman God was using to minister to me. I felt like an onion being peeled, one layer at a time. One layer was my inability to trust Levi's love because I'd never been able to trust anyone. My mother had deserted me, and my father had injured me through hurtful words and actions. But none of that had anything to do with Levi. The woman on TV had been abused by her father too, but in an even worse way than I had. As a result she began to treat her husband as if he was the one who'd hurt her, and it almost destroyed their marriage. When she faced what had happened and let God heal her heart, she began to change. She started to love her husband, and she quit trying to make him pay for her father's sins.

Then she began to talk about forgiveness, and I realized that for me to be truly free, I had no choice but to forgive. My father, my mother, anyone who had hurt me. Little by little, years of self-protection began to crumble. By the time the nurse returned, I felt like a dishrag that had been wrung out.

After the show concluded, another came on, but it was for some kind of strange utensil that cut up vegetables into flowers and odd shapes. I tuned it out and thought about the woman teacher. How could God have used her to minister to me in such a strong way if women were only supposed to teach each other how to be better wives? I was still mulling this over when the nurse came back into the room.

"I see the show is over," she said. "How did you like it?"

I shook my head. "I've never seen anything like it before. It was as if that woman knew me personally."

She smiled. "That's the anointing of God, dear. God knows you, and that lady knows Him. People can do great things for God if they'll let Him guide their lives. Too many folks end up following God the same way their parents did. Or the way their church teaches. But God has a unique path for each of us. " She pulled a small table over to me and put the tray she held in her hands down on it. "God asks us to follow Him—not anyone else. We all have to find our own distinctive calling, don't we?"

I looked into eyes full of kindness and something else. Something deep and special. It was like seeing God. I was overcome with emotion again and held the tissues up to my eyes.

"You go on and cry, honey," she said. "I understand. Been there. Done that." I felt her pat my arm. "You eat your breakfast. I'll be back in a bit."

I took the tissues away from my eyes. "What's your name?" I asked. I couldn't see her name tag through my tears.

"I'm Lynne. Lynne Young." She smiled. "If you need anything else, you just call for me, okay?"

"I will. And thank you so much, Lynne."

She smiled once more and closed the door behind her. I ate the breakfast she'd brought, but when I finished, I couldn't remember what I'd eaten. Lynne's words and the words of the woman on TV kept running through my head. Had I ever made a conscious decision on my own? Or more important, had I ever once asked God what He wanted from my life?

After thinking for a while, I bowed my head and prayed softly. "God, please take my life and make me the person you've called me to be. I honestly have no idea who that is. But if you really do have a plan for me, then please bring it to pass. I'll try very hard not to get in your way." I thought for a moment and added, "You'll probably have to help me with that though. I want to forgive my mother—I really do—but I still feel angry. Thank you."

After my prayer, I felt better. Lynne came back, gave me a sponge bath, and helped me to the bathroom. I was happy to be on my feet, but the trip back and forth was uncomfortable. She was patient and took things slowly. While we were up, someone else came in and changed my bed. When we returned, it felt wonderful to be clean and to climb into fresh sheets.

Once I was settled, it was already time for lunch. Lynne brought me a bowl of chicken soup, some crackers, and some red gelatin. Although Lizzie certainly made much better soup, it was still good. I settled back into my bed feeling refreshed and more awake than I had since I first woke up in the hospital.

I opened my Bible, deciding to read the Lord's Prayer, which was a favorite part of Scripture for me. But instead of stopping at the end, I read further and came across a verse I'd seen before. However, today it seemed to speak to me in a way it never had in the past. *But seek ye first the kingdom of God, and His righteousness; and all these things shall be added unto you.* This verse had been read to us in church many times, but for some reason, it felt like the first half of the Scripture was being shouted at me. What had I been seeking? Was I seeking God's kingdom first? Or had I been seeking after the church I'd grown up in? Or the father who'd told me how to live my life? Charity's words echoed in my mind: *"Then who are you?"*

"Aren't you going to say hello?"

Lizzie's voice startled me. I hadn't seen her come into the room. Lizzie, Noah, and Levi stood just inside the door.

"I'm sorry," I said with a smile. "I was thinking."

"I guess you were," Lizzie said, walking over to the bed. "Must have been deep thoughts."

At that moment Lynne came back. Yesterday, Lizzie had on regular clothes, but today she wore her church dress and her prayer covering. Levi and Noah also had on the suits they normally wore to church. Lynne looked surprised, but she greeted them warmly. After giving me a couple of pills, she excused herself and left the room.

"She seems very nice," Levi said. "Are you getting good care?"

"Excellent. I could get used to this."

Lizzie laughed. "Noah and I will do our best when you get home, but we can't promise it will be the same. You might have to do a little more for yourself than you do here."

"Actually, much more of this, and I'll end up spoiled rotten."

I put my Bible back on the nightstand. More than anything, I wanted to ask Lizzie what was going on with John Lapp. It was as if she'd read my mind, because she asked Levi and Noah to go to the hospital café and get all of us a cup of coffee. After they left, she sat down in the chair next to my bed.

"Levi told us all about your mom," she said excitedly. "So how did it go yesterday? Were you shocked? I know I was. I remember your mother, but Margaret—I mean Esther— looks so much different than she used to. I honestly didn't recognize her."

"I know this sounds strange, but I think part of me knew who she was. It's one of the reasons I've been so upset lately." I sighed. "She tried to explain why she left, and I realize now that she was going through a lot. I've asked God to help me forgive her, but it will take some time."

"I can't even imagine how you feel. What a shock this must be."

I nodded. "Look, let's talk about my mother later, okay? I want to ask you about John Lapp. You know, before Noah and Levi get back. Have you heard anything?"

"Not a word. I can't keep calling the sheriff. Noah will get suspicious. I guess if Timmons is checking John out, his past and stuff like that, maybe Sunday isn't a good day for it. I expect we'll hear something tomorrow." She paused for a moment. "Do you think I did the right thing, Callie?"

"I don't know. At first I thought it was a mistake, but after thinking about it, the sheriff did ask us to tell him if we noticed anything unusual. That's all you did."

Lizzie sighed. "John fits everything the sheriff said to watch

271

out for. And the book clinched it for me. Whatever happens, I'm not sorry I gave his name to the sheriff."

"I hope you feel that way later."

"I do too. But no matter what, this is on me, not you. My conclusions came from John's suspicious behavior. What you told me about his counseling session with Levi has nothing to do with it."

I shook my head. "I don't know. John Lapp has always had suspicious behavior."

Lizzie giggled and covered her mouth. "Oh, Callie. I'm trying to be serious, and you're making me laugh."

I smiled at her. "I don't mean to."

"I know." She stared past me, out the hospital window. "The last thing I want to do is to accuse an innocent man of something so horrible. But if there's nothing to it, the sheriff will let it drop and look somewhere else."

"I hope so."

We heard Noah's and Levi's voices in the hall.

"We'll talk more about this when you get home," Lizzie whispered. She quickly scooted her chair back several inches.

"By the way," I said, "how in the world are you going to take care of me and run the restaurant?"

"That's easy," Noah said as he came into the room. He and Levi were carrying foam cups of coffee. "We've set up some volunteers to come by and watch you."

My mouth dropped open. "Are you serious? Who?"

Lizzie began reeling off a list of names, including Leah, Belle Martin, Hope, Ruth, Myra Fisher, and several other women. Lizzie's mother was included. When she finished, she laughed. "Levi said something in church today about needing help, and we actually had more volunteers than we could use."

Although that made me feel good, the idea of being *watched* by others didn't appeal to me. "Will I ever get another moment alone?" I grumbled.

"Not many," Levi said, "because as soon as you're better, we're getting married. I don't intend to let you spend much time alone anymore. You get into too much trouble."

"But . . ."

He waved his hand. "I know. What about your prayer covering? What about your clothes? I don't care about that, Callie. I love you, and I don't intend to spend my life without you. This accident woke me up to the fact that I can't live without you. And I won't. No matter what that means. If I remain the pastor of Kingdom Mennonite Church, so be it. If not, I'll be a farmer."

Noah laughed. "You're a lousy farmer."

Levi smiled at him. "Then I'll be the happiest lousy farmer in the world because I'll be with the woman I love."

At that moment, I wanted to jump for joy. Levi wanted to be with me no matter what happened, but would he really be happy if he wasn't a pastor? I wasn't so sure.

"Levi offered to stay with you too," Lizzie said with a smile.

"He can't do that. We'd be right back in the same situation that happened the night of the storm." I frowned at Levi. "Which reminds me. What's happened with that?"

Lizzie and Noah exchanged a look between them that made my stomach turn over.

"You don't need to worry about it," Levi said. "I'm handling it."

"The truth is, my father is doing everything he can to cause Levi trouble," Lizzie said. "But so far, most people aren't listening to him."

"What do you mean *most people*?" I asked.

Noah shot Lizzie an unhappy look. "We can talk about this more when you're feeling better," he said. "But everything's fine. Matthew's tried to get a few people to side with him, but he's not having much success. It's obvious to almost everyone that you were both stuck in a situation where you had no other options."

"Don't worry about it," Levi said. "Really. Everything will be fine."

"Okay," I said slowly. "I hope you three aren't trying to pacify me."

"Noah's telling you the truth," Lizzie said. "Your reputation is intact."

She seemed sincere, so I let it go. "How's your back?" I asked Levi.

He smiled. "It's just fine. Your nursing skills are exemplary." He shook his finger at me. "I didn't realize you'd cut your knees up so much. We found out how bad it was from the doctor. They had to give you stitches."

"I totally forgot about my knees. Haven't even thought to check them."

"They're healing nicely," Lizzie said. "It's a miracle you and Levi weren't killed by flying glass that night."

"There have been several miracles lately," I said. "God has been wonderful, hasn't He?"

"So you're accepting miracles now, are you? My, you are changing."

"Yes, I am," I said, remembering some of the words the woman teacher had said. "I've decided that it's time I face the past head on. I won't let the past affect my future anymore."

Lizzie stood up and came over to the bed. There were

tears in her eyes. "I'm very proud of you, sweetie. Very proud indeed."

"Thank you, Lizzie. For everything. I don't know what I would do without you."

"Sisters forever, honey."

I nodded, unable to say anything over the lump in my throat.

"Oh, Levi," Noah said in a high-pitched voice. "If you weren't in my life, I would just die."

"Oh, Brother," Levi said, grinning. "You are my hero. Brothers forever."

"Oh, you two!" Lizzie whirled around and pointed at them. "You're both incorrigible!"

I giggled and winced at the same time. "Stop it. Don't you realize there's a patient trying to recover here? Laughing hurts!"

"I'm sorry, Callie," Levi said. "That wasn't very nice of us."

"Let's change the subject," Lizzie said. "For Callie's sake." She sat down. "Do you want to talk about your mom now?" Lizzie handed me the coffee she'd gotten from Noah.

I sighed. "There's not much to talk about. She was here for only a few minutes. We're going to get together after I get out of the hospital. We have a lot of things to sort out."

"Yeah, like why she abandoned you," Lizzie said wryly. "I'd like to hear that explanation. There's nothing in this world that would make me walk away from Charity."

Levi cleared his throat. "I don't think you should judge her too harshly. Sometimes people think they're doing the right thing at the time. Your mother's situation was . . . dire. Just give her a chance, Callie."

"I'll try," I said. "Although I'm not sure anything can

justify what she did. In the end, all I can do is forgive her and move on."

I asked about the town and how we'd fared through the storm. The streets were in pretty good shape, thanks to our farmers and their snowplows. Noah's truck had been towed back to the house, and he'd been working on it.

"I've got it going, but it will need more work on the engine and extensive body work. Once the snow is gone, I'll take it to Washington. My insurance will pay for repairs."

"I'm opening the restaurant tomorrow," Lizzie said. "Do you know what time you're leaving the hospital?"

"She should be ready to go in the morning." Lynne had come back into the room. "Can someone pick her up around ten?"

"Charity and I will be here," Noah said.

I looked over at Levi. I'd hoped he would pick me up, but he shook his head.

"Sorry, Callie," he said. "But as you pointed out, I think it's best if we're not alone together right now. I'm trying to be wise. For both of us."

I understood but was still disappointed. "That's okay. Thanks, Noah. I really appreciate it."

"Someone will meet you at the house," Lizzie said. "I'd be there if I could, but we've got to get the restaurant going again. We can't afford to lose any more business."

"I understand," I said. "That's no problem."

We visited for a while longer, and then they all left. Levi kissed me good-bye and told me he loved me. I was happy to see joy back in his expression. It seemed we were both finding our way out of the dark places we'd been in for a while.

After they were gone, I lay in bed and wondered what

waited for me when I got out. Somehow, I knew my life had changed, but I had no idea exactly what that meant. Would Levi and I be okay? Could my mother and I find a way to establish a relationship? Was I really willing to let her leave? To lose her forever?

These questions echoed in my mind like a cacophony of voices all saying something different.

CHAPTER 20

Noah and Charity picked me up the next morning after my doctor came by to check me out and sign the release papers. Ellery was on duty, and I got the chance to thank her for her excellent care. I asked about Lynne, but she'd gone home. Ellery brought me a note pad and a pen. I wrote a quick note of thanks to the woman who'd impacted me so much.

Ellery insisted I get into a wheelchair for the trip downstairs to Noah's truck, and even though I felt a little silly, I was grateful for the ride. With the pills the hospital sent with me, my pain was manageable. A male attendant pushed my chair. When we got downstairs, he helped Noah get me into the truck. It hurt more than I thought it would. As long as I kept my midsection from twisting, I did pretty well. But any movement that aggravated my broken rib brought about a violent reaction. The doctor had tightly bandaged my chest while warning me that the most important thing was for me to stay as still as possible so the rib could mend.

I was dismayed to see dark clouds in the sky. "Are we supposed to get more snow?" I asked Noah when he got behind the wheel.

"No, thank goodness. It took some time to dig out from the

last storm. Lizzie checked the weather this morning on our radio. Lots of clouds, but no snow predicted. Today anyway."

"It's so dark out. Can't remember the last time I saw the sun."

Noah grinned. "It's still there. At least that's what I've been told."

It was extremely cold, but my cloak kept me warm. I wore the dress I'd come to the hospital in, but I'd tucked my prayer covering in the suitcase Lizzie had packed for me. It wouldn't have provided any protection against the chilly temperatures anyway. I was relieved to find out that Noah had retrieved my suitcase from the wreck so I would have my own clothes when I got to Lizzie's. Noah's old truck warmed up nicely, and the three of us had a pleasant ride home.

When we reached the house, Noah got out and helped me from the truck. I worried about leaning on him too much.

"You're still recovering too," I said when he wrapped his arm around my waist. "I don't want to hurt you."

"Don't worry about it," he said. "I'm doing much better. There's very little pain now."

I wasn't sure if I believed him, but I decided to accept his offer of help since I didn't have much of a choice. There was no way I could make it up the stairs and into the house by myself. When we got up the steps, I was happy and surprised to see Hope holding the door open for us.

"I didn't know you'd be here," I said with a smile. "I'm so glad."

"I am too," she replied. "I closed the quilt store this morning so I could stay with you."

"Oh, Hope. I hate for you to do that."

She laughed. It was a light, uplifting sound. "I'm thrilled

to spend some time with you. I can't think of anything I'd rather do."

"You're so sweet." I could feel myself getting emotional. There'd been a lot of that lately. "Thank you. I owe everyone so much."

Noah got me to the couch. "You don't owe anyone anything," he said. "Like I already told you, we're family, Callie. It's what family does."

"I guess so." I took a sharp intake of breath as Noah helped me take off my coat.

"Did I hurt you?" he asked, concern in his voice.

"It's not you. I'll just have to get used to moving slower until I'm better."

"Here," Hope said. "Let me put some pillows down to support your back." She took two pillows from a nearby chair and positioned them against the arm of the couch. Then she and Noah lowered me gently down onto the cushions. Once I was seated, Noah swung my legs carefully around until I was comfortable. Hope took the quilt off the back of the couch and put it over me. It was a gorgeous Lone Star pattern with deep purples and violets.

"Oh my," I said. "This is one of the most beautiful things I've ever seen. I don't remember Lizzie having a quilt like this." I smiled at Hope. "Purple is my favorite color."

"I know that," Hope said, smoothing the fabric with her hand. "That's why I made it for you."

"What? What are you talking about?"

She grinned. "It was supposed to be for your wedding, but when I heard about the accident I decided to give it to you now. An early wedding gift."

"Oh, Hope." I couldn't hold back my tears.

Noah looked decidedly uncomfortable. "I think I'll get going," he said. "I need to get Charity to school, and Lizzie needs my help at the restaurant. Besides, there's been way too much crying lately. It's starting to get to me."

Hope and I laughed.

"I've seen you pretty misty-eyed," I said. "I'm not sure you have any right to complain."

"That's just it," he said with a grin. "It's time I reestablished my masculinity." He looked at Hope. "Lizzie told you where everything is, didn't she?"

She nodded. "I've got it all figured out."

"Bud will be here sometime around noon to work," Noah said to me. "He's offered to stay until I get home with Charity. Is that okay with you, Callie?"

"Of course, but won't you need to go back to the restaurant tonight?"

Noah shook his head. "Lizzie's mother is going to help her this evening. Anna's worked in the restaurant many times and really enjoys it."

"Do you feel uncomfortable being here alone with Bud?" Hope asked, frowning. "I wish I could stay the rest of the day, but I have a quilting class this afternoon."

"No. I like Bud. But what if I need to . . . you know . . ."

"Go upstairs?" Hope said.

I nodded.

"Why don't I stay until one o'clock?" she said. "My class doesn't start until two. That way, you'll be here with him only a couple of hours. I'll make sure to get you upstairs and back before I leave."

"That sounds great."

"Callie, I want you to know," Noah said in a serious tone,

"that this should be the only time you'll be alone in the house with a man. Lizzie and I have a schedule set up for your care, but we couldn't fill this one short time period. I ran it by the elders and they approved it."

I smiled. "It's fine. I don't think anyone will believe Bud and I were up to anything inappropriate."

He laughed. "No, I think you're safe there. Charity and I will get home as quickly as we can."

"I hate to be a bother," I said.

"We're very glad you're here," he said softly. "We owe you more than we can ever repay, and we intend to make sure you're well taken care of."

"I have no doubt about that. And thank you, Noah, for everything."

He nodded. "I know you and Levi have had a tough time lately, but I know things will work out. Just have faith, Callie."

"I will."

He said good-bye, and he and Charity left. Hope and I heard the truck engine start and listened as he drove away.

"How about something hot to drink?" she asked.

"About what Noah said—"

"You don't need to tell me anything." Hope clasped her hands together. "If anyone understands how difficult relationships can be, it's me. It's a miracle from God that Ebbie and I are together."

I stroked the beautiful quilt. "If anything happens . . . if Levi and I don't get married, I want you to know that I'll give you back the quilt."

"Oh, Callie, don't be silly. The quilt is yours, whether you marry Levi or not." She put her hand under my chin and lifted my face to hers. "You're my friend. Even more, you're my sister. That's not based on whether you get married or never marry. It's because I love you."

"I love you too."

She smiled. "Good. Now, do you want coffee, hot tea, or hot cider?"

I settled on tea, since I'd had a big cup of coffee at the hospital. I snuggled under my new quilt and felt quite comfortable. Within a few minutes, Hope was back with the tea and a glass of water. She set a tray down on the coffee table that included my cup of tea, the water, and some cookies. Then she took something out of the satchel she'd brought with her.

"Here are some magazines. I brought *The Budget*, a wonderful new quilt book, and a cookbook. Oh, and here are some copies of *The Mennonite*. It's a wonderful magazine. Have you ever read it?"

"Lizzie had a copy, and I really enjoyed it. Papa didn't allow magazines in the house, so that's the only time I've seen it."

"Well, here are six issues. I get it every month. If you want, I'll pass them along to you when I'm done."

"Thanks, Hope. I'd love that."

"Okay." She placed the magazines on the table next to me. "And here's a book Lizzie told me to give you." She picked up a large book from the other side of the table and handed it to me. Confused, I looked at the cover and laughed when I saw the title: *The Complete Sherlock Holmes: All 4 Novels and 56 Short Stories*.

"I read some of it before you got here," Hope said. "It's really good!"

"Why, Hope Miller, you really are a rebel."

She grinned, as though I'd said something funny. "You'd be surprised." She looked around the table. "Where are your pills?"

"Oh, they're still in my suitcase." I motioned toward the bag Noah had put on the floor near the stairs.

"Do you mind if I open it?" Hope asked.

I shook my head. "Not at all. Lizzie packed it. To be honest, I'm not sure what's in there."

Hope opened the case and quickly found the bottle of pills. She put it on the tray next to my water. I saw her lift my prayer covering out of the way, but she didn't ask why I wasn't wearing it or why my hair was down. She simply put it back with the rest of the clothes.

"What else can I do for you?" she asked.

I smiled at her. "Nothing. Thank you." The tea was delicious, and I drank almost half of the cup before putting it back on the tray.

She stood up, went to the fireplace, and added another log. "Are you sleepy?" she asked.

I shook my head. "I've done so much sleeping I should be able to stay awake for a week. I'd rather talk. How did you and Ebbie fare during the storm?"

She pulled a nearby chair next to the couch and sat down. Then she filled me in on the problems they'd faced, as well as news of others in the community. Aaron Metcalf lost his electricity and had to move some of his food to a back room to keep it frozen. Ruth Fisher's daughter, Myra, had picked her mother up from her house so she wouldn't be alone, but Myra's car had skidded off the road. Thankfully, they weren't hurt and were rescued by Roger Carson, who had been in town visiting Mary's parents.

"How are the Yoders?" I asked.

Hope shook her head. "Oh, Callie. I'm so sad for them. When Mary left Kingdom, they felt they'd lost her forever.

But then she began reaching out to them, thanks in no small part to Roger. It wasn't easy at first, but they were on their way to mending their relationship. Now this." She sighed. "We must pray for them."

"Losing a parent is very difficult," I said. "But losing a child . . . I can't imagine it."

"Nor I." Hope paused and looked down at the floor. "If I tell you something, will you keep it to yourself?"

"Of course, I will. What is it, Hope?"

When she looked up, I could see the happiness beaming in her face. "Ebbie and I are expecting. We haven't told everyone yet, so I must ask you to keep it to yourself."

I clapped my hands together. "Oh, Hope. How wonderful. I'm so happy for you!"

She nodded, but the look on her face didn't match her previous expression.

"What's wrong?"

"Nothing. I . . . I'm just concerned about these murders."

"You mean you feel vulnerable?"

"I guess that's it. Kingdom should be safe, but so much has happened here. I'm not sure I believe we're as insulated from the world as we should be."

"Believe me, you're not the only person who feels that way," I said. Suddenly a picture of the light I saw the night of the storm flashed in my mind. "You know, Hope, we shouldn't depend so much on a place to keep us safe. Isn't God our protection? No matter where we are or what's going on around us?"

She didn't say anything for a moment. Then she smiled again. "You're right. Thank you. I guess I forgot that Kingdom isn't the answer. God is. I was raised to trust Him. To believe that He's good and that He will protect us." She shook her head, a look of contemplation on her face. "Why do I forget that sometimes?"

"I don't know, but I did the same thing. And not just when it came to Kingdom. In a lot of other areas in my life as well. I'm beginning to see that we can't substitute God for certain clothes, rules, churches, or even towns. I'm not saying any of those things are bad, but I'm realizing that things and places don't make us holy or safe. And they certainly don't define us."

Hope frowned. "Sounds like you've been searching for answers, Callie."

Taking a deep breath, I filled her in on everything that had been happening. Remembering the truth about my father and finding out that Margaret Harper was really my mother. Her expression registered surprise at the latter revelation.

"Margaret Harper is your mother?"

I sighed. "Yes, she came to the hospital and told me who she was. Then she explained why she left us all those years ago."

"So will you be able to reconcile?"

I sighed. "I don't know. I hope so. At least now I know she didn't leave because she didn't love me. It's hard, Hope. I spent years trying to forget her. Now here she is. My feelings are all jumbled up."

"One thing I don't understand," Hope said, her forehead furrowed in thought. "Why didn't you recognize her? I mean, you were a child when she left but old enough to remember her. Is it the scar?"

"Not just the scar. She's changed drastically in other ways too. No one except Ruth recognized her." I shook my head. "The truth is, somewhere inside I knew. Right after she came to town, I started feeling anxious. Even angry. I'm sure it was because I figured out who she was and couldn't face it."

"Oh."

Hope drew out the word as if what I'd said had explained something.

"You noticed too?"

She gave me a small smile. "Well, yes. I could see you weren't yourself, but I couldn't figure out why."

I shook my head. "Actually, I think I was finally becoming myself." I cleared my throat. "The problem is, I still don't know how I'll end up."

Hope reached over and put her hand on mine. "Oh, Callie. There might be some changes in the way you think, but in your heart, you'll always be the same warm, caring, and kind person who is my dear friend."

"Thank you. That means the world to me."

Hope nodded. "Well, I hope you two work out your differences. Wouldn't it be lovely to have a mother again?"

I took a moment to answer. "Maybe," I said slowly. "We'll have to see. When Levi and I get married, I won't let her interfere or cause problems between us."

"I understand, and I think that's wise, but I'll pray that you and your mother can find a way back to each other. Her coming to Kingdom shows she cares for you. She took a big chance."

"I guess, but I wish she'd come to me immediately instead of hiding out and pretending to be someone else."

Hope picked up her cup of hot tea and stared into it. "Sometimes it's hard to live by what we know we should do. Human beings are often led by their own fears. I imagine your mother was afraid of rejection. Afraid you would tell her to go away."

"Maybe so. I guess if anyone should understand that, I should." I smiled at her. "You're always so stable and calm, Hope. How do you do it?"

Her eyebrows shot up in surprise. "Oh my. You don't see me all the time. I've had moments when I thought I was coming apart at the seams. The only thing that held me together was believing that God truly has a purpose for my life. That I matter to Him. All of us need to know we're here for a reason. What's that Scripture verse? 'Where there is no vision, the people perish.' We're not wandering generalities, Callie. Each and every one of us has a high calling. A race set before us and gifts specifically given to us so we can cross our own finish line. I believe that with all my heart."

We talked a bit more, and even though I had no desire to sleep, my eyes began to feel heavy. The pain pills were having more of an effect on me than I'd anticipated. I dozed for a while and woke up just as Hope was carrying in my lunch.

After eating, she helped me upstairs to the bathroom. About halfway up the stairs, I was convinced I couldn't make it. Hope is small and not very strong. It took us a while to complete the task and get back downstairs. By the time Hope had me settled back on the couch, it was almost one o'clock.

"I thought Bud was supposed to be here around noon," she said, looking at the clock. As soon as the words left her mouth, we heard a car door slam. Hope went to the window to see who it was.

"It's Bud," she announced. She waited a moment and then opened the front door to greet him.

"Why, hello there!" he announced jovially as he entered the living room. "I hear someone hasn't been feeling up to par." He walked around to my side of the couch. "How are you doing, young lady?"

I smiled at him. "Getting better little by little. Sorry to make you babysit me."

"Oh, *pshaw*," he said. "I'm happy I can help. I was going to be here anyway."

"I know. But I'm still grateful."

"Well, to be honest, bein' around people right now is good for me. Makes me get my mind off my troubles." With a grin, he pulled out a large fluffy teddy bear from behind his back. "Wanted to get you somethin'. Stopped by a flower store, but everything looked a little puny, it bein' winter and all. Then I saw this. Thought you might like it."

"Oh, Bud," I said. "You shouldn't have."

"I just wanted to make you feel better."

"Thank you so much. It's wonderful."

I took it from his hands and set it next to me on the couch. "Now I'll never be alone."

He laughed and nodded. "Guess I better get to work. Lots to do today. I'm gonna pull my van around back so my tools will be closer to the kitchen. Saves me from havin' to make so many trips back and forth. Don't wanna bother you."

The sound of another vehicle came from outside the house. It had to be Noah coming to pick up Hope. Sure enough, he opened the door and came inside. I was surprised to see Roger with him. Feeling a little self-conscious, I pulled the quilt up a little higher and patted my hair to make sure it was still in place. I'd tied it back with a ribbon. It looked okay when I checked it in the bathroom mirror while Hope and I were upstairs, but I had no idea what I looked like now. Not used to wearing my hair in any style other than a bun, I felt self-conscious.

Roger walked over to the couch. I could see the grief in his expression, and I felt bad for him.

"How are you doing, Callie?" he asked.

"I'm fine, Roger. How are you?"

"Doing better. Thanks for asking."

"I'm so sorry about Mary," I said. "If I can do anything . . ."

"There's really nothing anyone can do," he said sadly. "I just have to get through it. But thank you. I appreciate it."

I wanted to say something else. Something encouraging, but I couldn't find the right words. Thankfully, Noah filled in the silence.

"Roger was at the restaurant, and when he heard I was coming to see you, he wanted to ride along."

"That's so sweet," I said. "Thank you."

"You're welcome." He smiled, but the unhappiness in his eyes remained.

"Been praying for you, Deputy," Bud said. "You probably know I lost my wife a while back. I can't say I know how you feel, 'cause we're all so different. But I have an inkling. I'm sure sorry for your loss."

"Thank you, Bud," Roger said. "I'm sorry for yours as well."

"Roger, are you any closer to catching the man who did this?" Hope asked.

Roger sighed and crossed his arms across his chest. "We did get a tip about a possible suspect, but we haven't been able to prove anything. In fact, we haven't been able to find him. When we come across him, we plan to question him. See if we can make any connection to the murders. All we have to do is match the DNA, and we'll have him for the recent murders—and the deaths twenty years ago."

Was he talking about John Lapp? Had John really disappeared? Could he possibly be a serial killer?

"I hope you catch him soon, Deputy," Bud said. "All them poor ladies. It's just too much to bear. Did you ever find out who the woman was they found in them red cedar trees?"

Roger nodded. "Her name's Montrose. Carol Montrose. She lived in Junction City. Was on her way to see a friend in Marysville but never arrived. We've notified her family."

"I'll pray for them," Hope said. "I can't imagine what they're going through."

"Well, I can," Roger said grimly.

Hope's already pale face turned even whiter. "Oh, Roger. I'm so sorry. I didn't mean . . ."

He waved his hand at her. "Don't be silly. Can't have folks walking on eggshells around me forever. This whole situation is just terrible. I can't believe something like this started up right after I signed on with the department."

"You don't think it had anything to do with you, do you?" Noah asked. "I mean, Mary wasn't targeted because of your job with the sheriff?"

Roger shook his head. "No. We wondered about that at the beginning, but it looks like Mary was just in the wrong place at the wrong time." His freckled face flushed red, almost competing with his light red hair. "I asked her to stay home that night, but she left anyway."

"Do you know why?" I asked. Frankly, I couldn't imagine the wife of a sheriff's deputy making such a careless decision. Didn't she know better than to go out alone?

Roger took off his hat and scratched his head. "I honestly don't know where she was headed, but my best guess is the store. She kept talking about chuck roast being on sale. I told her I'd swing by and pick it up on my way home, but it looks like she decided not to wait on me. Her car, with her purse on the front seat, was found on the road between Washington and Kingdom. Obviously someone forced her to drive out of town."

Roger put his hat back on. I noticed his torn pocket had been repaired, but the stitches were amateurish and ragged. Obviously, he'd done the job himself. Somehow it made Mary's loss clear in an even more tangible way.

"Well, we'd better get Hope back to the quilt shop," Noah said. "Thanks for keeping an eye on Callie, Bud. I won't be gone too long. Should be back here around three-thirty at the latest."

"No problem at all. I'll just be workin' in the kitchen."

"Callie, if you need anything, Bud can call us. The phone's working now."

I nodded. "Thank you, but I'll be fine."

Hope came over and kissed my forehead. "I'll be back tomorrow. You be good. Take your pills and rest."

"I will. And thank you."

Bud waited in the living room until the three of them left. "I feel so bad for that young man," he said. "Losin' Thelma wasn't the same as what he's been through. Thelma had been sickly for a while. Hope he didn't think I was speakin' out of turn."

"I'm sure he didn't. It's so hard to know what to say."

He nodded. "Can't even allow myself to think about those poor women bein' wrapped up like trash and thrown away. Most awful thing I ever heard of."

"It is," I agreed.

"Well, I need to let you get some rest. You want anything before I move the van?"

"No, and thanks again, Bud. I really appreciate it."

He waved my thanks away with a smile and went outside. I could hear the van pull around back. A few minutes later, I heard Bud open and close the kitchen door. Then came the sound of his tools clanking as he started to work.

Muffin jumped up on the couch and found a comfortable place to snuggle up next to me. I was happy to have his company. Ignoring the magazines, I picked up the Sherlock Holmes book and opened it to the first story. I'd never read anything like it before and was soon entrenched in the stories of Holmes, Doctor Watson, and the evil Professor Moriarty.

About forty-five minutes later, I heard a faint knock on the front door. Bud was doing some drilling in the kitchen, and I knew he couldn't hear it. I gingerly swung my legs around until I could stand up. Each step I took was painful. It only took a few steps before I could see who was at the door by looking through the front window.

A tall figure dressed in black stood on the front porch. John Lapp.

CHAPTER /21

I turned too quickly, trying to get away from the window before he saw me. My socks slid on the wooden floor, and I felt myself falling. Although I tried to put out my arms for protection, I hit the floor hard. Excruciating pain shot through me in waves. I heard the drilling noise stop, and I tried to call out for Bud, but I could barely get a squeak out.

Behind me, I heard the doorknob rattling. John was trying to get in. Had he come after me? Not knowing that Bud was here? I tried again to call Bud's name, but unless he'd been a few inches from me, there was no way for him to hear me. Racked with pain and out of desperation, I did the only thing I could think of. I wriggled over to the tray Hope had set on the edge of the coffee table, grabbed the edge, and pulled it off. The water glass hit the floor and shattered. I had to put my hand over my eyes to protect them. Thankfully, it worked. I could hear Bud coming down the hall.

"Oh, my goodness, Callie," he said when he came in. "What happened?"

Gasping for breath, I tried to explain about John Lapp.

"Let's get you back on the couch, then I'll have a look," Bud said.

I tried to tell him to leave me there and call the police, but the pain was so bad, I couldn't get the words out.

Bud's boots crunched on the broken glass. Then he knelt down next to me. "Honey, I'm gonna pick you up. I'm gonna try not to hurt you. Can you put your arms around my neck?"

All I could do was shake my head. I was certain that if I lifted my arms, the pain would be too much.

Gently, he slid his hands under me and began raising me off the floor. True to his word, he kept my body steady, protecting me from the agony that crouched, waiting for me to make a wrong move. Slowly he lowered me down to the couch. I sighed with relief once I was back in a comfortable position.

"You . . . you've got to call the police," I whispered. "That man. He's the one the police are looking for."

"What?" Bud said. "Are you sure?"

I nodded.

"You okay now?"

I nodded again. "Muffin . . . the glass," I croaked out. Although Muffin was still on the couch, I was afraid he'd jump down and cut his paws.

"I'll put him where he'll be safe until I can get this cleaned up," Bud said. He scooped up the small dog and took him upstairs. I heard a door close.

Bud came down the stairs. "Muffin's in the bedroom, Callie. He's fine." He walked over to the front door. I could hear him turn the doorknob, and I tried to call out to him. To tell him not to open the door. If John had the strength to overpower and choke several women, maybe he could overpower Bud. It was true that Bud was strong, but he was also older and out of shape. He was probably no match for John. I attempted to get his attention again. This time, my voice was stronger, but Bud didn't seem to be listening. I could hear the door open slowly. Although I wanted to pull myself up so I could see what was happening, I couldn't bring myself to try it. The pain was too great.

I closed my eyes as the door opened, and I felt the cold air rush in. I heard Bud say something, but then the door closed. There was silence for quite a while. Finally, I heard the door open again.

"What's going on?" I asked. I sounded weak and frightened—which I was. "Where are you, Bud?"

"I'm right here, honey," he said, walking over to where I lay. "There ain't no one out there, Callie. Maybe you was dreamin' about the man at the door."

I shook my head as frustrated tears rolled down my cheeks. "He was there. I saw him. You've got to call the sheriff, Bud. I mean it. You've got to phone him right now."

"Okay, Callie. If you want me to, I'll get ahold of him."

I sobbed, happy he was going to get us some help.

"I'll go call him, then come back and clean up this mess. Everything will be all right. Don't you worry, okay?"

"Thank you. Thank you so much, Bud."

I breathed a sigh of relief, which was a mistake because it hurt. Just breathing hurt. I hoped I hadn't done any further damage when I fell. I spotted the bottle of pain pills on the table. But now I didn't have anything to swallow them with. At that moment, relief from the pain seemed more important than worrying about water so I tossed two pills into my mouth, chewed, and swallowed them. The bitter taste made me shiver and gag. I rested in the knowledge that in a few minutes, I'd feel better. Right now, though, knowing where John was seemed much more important. Was he gone or was he trying to get in another way? Maybe he'd realized I wasn't alone and left. But what if he hadn't? What if he was still out there? I wished the sky wasn't so dark. It was like night outside. Much easier for him to hide in the dark.

I waited patiently for Bud to return. What was taking so long? The room seemed to be growing colder, but the fire in the fireplace was still going strong. Suddenly, a thought struck me that took my breath away. The cold air was coming from the kitchen. Was the back door open? What did that mean? Fear gripped me with tight fingers. Why would Bud go outside on a day like this? And why would he leave the door open?

"Oh, God," I whispered. "Help me. Please help me."

I knew I had to get up and go to the kitchen. The phone was there, and I had to have help. Had John lured Bud outside? Was Bud still alive? Not trusting my feet, I rolled off the couch and onto the floor. I would have to crawl to the kitchen. There was no other choice. I brushed the broken glass out of the way. The last thing I needed was to cut myself again. My knees were still healing from the last time I'd crawled on shards of glass.

Praying softly, I slowly made my way to the kitchen. Sure enough, the back door was wide open. Bud was nowhere to be seen. First, I crawled to the door and shut it. Then I pulled myself up with the doorknob and pushed the lock shut. At least now no one could get in. I dragged myself along the counter, using it to support most of my weight. When I reached the phone, I cried with relief, but my joy was short-lived. I put the receiver to my ear and discovered it wasn't working. I hung it up and tried again. Silence. It was obvious I wasn't going to get any help from the dead instrument.

What could I do? I looked out the kitchen window and saw Noah's damaged truck sitting next to Bud's van. It still looked wrecked, but I remembered Noah saying he'd gotten it running. I'd noticed a basket on the counter with keys in it, so I looked inside and found a ring with a large key. Could that be for the truck? I'd never driven a motor vehicle, but I'd watched Lizzie and Noah several times. Surely it couldn't be that hard.

I grabbed the key and made it to the back door. Even though the truck wasn't that far from the house, I had no idea how to get to it. I was standing next to the broom closet, so I opened it and found a push broom. Although it was a little long, I was able to put the broom end under my arm and use the handle like a crutch. Going outside in my stocking feet, without a coat, would be uncomfortable, but I had no other choice. John could show up at any moment.

I unlocked the door and pulled it open. Then I grabbed the side of the door and turned backward, putting my feet on the steps while holding myself up. The pain was there, but thanks to the pills, it was dull and manageable. I held on to the doorframe as long as I could, but I finally had to let go and use the crutch. Thankfully, I stayed on my feet. I began moving across the snow-covered ground as quickly as I could, trying to reach the mangled truck before John could find me. I noticed a long cord lying on the snow. The phone line. It had obviously been cut. My feet felt like blocks of ice, and my body shivered from the cold and the wind.

I finally reached the truck with no sign of John, but the heavy cloud cover made it hard to see more than a few yards. Maybe he was lurking in the shadows, getting ready to pounce. I grabbed the handle and pulled the door open. My plan was to lock the doors as soon as I got inside so that John couldn't get to me. Once I was locked in, out of the elements, I would be safe. But as I took hold of the steering wheel in an attempt to pull myself inside, I felt hands on my shoulders. I screamed and tried to wrestle away. The twisting hurt so much I felt myself go down. Strong arms grabbed me and kept me from falling.

"Callie. Callie, it's me. What are you doin' out here?"

I looked up to see Bud's concerned face staring down at me.

"Oh, Bud. I . . . I thought . . ."

"You thought I was that man you're afraid of. But it's just me." He took off his coat and wrapped it around me, taking away the broom and picking me up in one fell swoop. He carried me back into the house and put me back on the couch.

"Why in the world would you go outside in the snow like that, Callie?" he asked. "You could have really injured yourself."

"You . . . you disappeared. I thought John Lapp had attacked you."

"So you planned to drive and get help?"

I nodded.

"Don't look like you would have gotten too far. That truck is a mess."

I jumped as a twinge of pain rushed through me. "Noah got it running," I said breathlessly.

"You ever driven a truck?"

"No."

"That's what I thought." He leaned down and helped me take off his coat. "You get yourself under this quilt and warm up."

I allowed him to pull off my wet socks and cover me with the quilt. Then he went over and added another log to the fire. The rush of warmth felt wonderful.

"D-did you find John?"

"No. No one there."

I frowned at him. "But I *did* see him. He was standing right there on the front porch."

"Well, he ain't out there now."

"But the phone line . . ."

Bud turned around to stare at me. "What about the phone line?"

"Someone pulled it out. It's lying on the ground out back. Didn't you see it?"

He shook his head slowly. "No. Maybe you imagined that too."

I shook my head slowly. Could the pills really be affecting me that much? I didn't have much experience with narcotics. My eyes fell on the Sherlock Holmes book still lying on the table. For some reason, the story I was reading when I'd heard the knock on the door jumped into my mind. Something about a suspect saying something he shouldn't have known. His comment had given him away. Suddenly, I remembered something Bud had said, and I looked at him in horror.

"The red cedar trees," I said, almost in a whisper. "No one knew about that. Or that the victims were wrapped in plastic. You mentioned the trees earlier, and a while ago you made a comment about the women being wrapped up like trash."

Bud lowered himself down slowly to the hearth and sat there, staring at me.

"You. It's you . . ."

Bud raised an eyebrow as he studied me. "I don't know what you're thinkin', Callie. Maybe you're just in a drug-induced haze. Don't know what's real and what isn't."

"Where's John?" I asked. My voice sounded like it was coming from far away, and my heart pounded so hard I could feel it.

He took a deep breath and blew it out slowly through pursed lips. "I took care of him. You don't have to worry about him no more."

I blinked back tears, determined to maintain my composure. "Is . . . is he dead?"

Bud shrugged. "If he ain't, he will be before long. Nice how he showed up. I didn't know the police suspected him. I appreciate you tellin' me."

"You killed those women."

"Now, why in the world would you say that?" The blaze from the fire highlighted his face, making him look demonic. As the flames danced, the light shifted across Bud's broad face.

A voice inside screamed at me to shut up, but I knew it was too late for that. Maybe it was the pills, but I couldn't seem to control my thoughts—or my mouth. "Why would you kill John? He's no threat to you."

"I had no intention of doin' anything to him until you told me the police thought he might be the murderer. Then an idea just kind of presented itself. The way I got it figured, your friend, Mr. Lapp, broke in while I was workin' in the kitchen. He snuck up behind me and knocked me out. Then he killed you. I woke up and chased him outside. He tried

302

to kill me, and I defended myself. Sadly, he died. By the time I could get help, it was too late for you and Brother Lapp."

"But why, Bud?"

He shrugged. "Things are gettin' a little too hot. This gives me some time. At least until they figure out John couldn't have done it."

"The DNA won't match."

"Nah, it won't. I'm sure other facts won't line up as well. But I'll be gone by then. Already decided to move on. Things got . . . messed up here. Someone's puttin' their fingers in the pot and stirrin' up trouble." He gave me a morose smile. "I didn't have any intention of hurtin' you, Callie. But after I went outside to move my van, I realized what I'd said. About the plastic and all. I realized it was only a matter of time before you realized it."

"But you mentioned the red cedar trees in front of Roger and Noah. They'll remember and you'll be caught."

"Can't believe I slipped up like that. Must be outta practice." He shook his head slowly. "That's why I gotta misdirect them for a while so I can get away. I'm sorry. I really am, but this is the only chance I got."

It was clear to me that Bud Gruber was insane. It was that simple and that complicated, all at the same time. Unless God himself decided to save me, I wasn't going to make it out of this house alive.

"I . . . I just don't understand," I said, hoping to stall him for a while. A quick look at the clock revealed it was way too early for Noah to return, but he was my only chance. I had to try.

"I could give you lots of reasons, but you wouldn't understand them," Bud said softly. "If you don't mind, I won't give you a laundry list of what made me take what they call *the road less traveled*. I just wait until I see someone who appeals to me. Nothin' I can put my finger on." He laughed, but there was no humor in it. "It ain't because my mama didn't love me or nothin' like that. Them psychologists think they got it all figured out, but they don't know what they're talkin' about." He frowned and seemed almost puzzled. "I tried for years to understand my compulsion, but I never did.

"When I met Thelma, I didn't want to do it no more. Somethin' about the woman made me want to be good. But when she died . . . Well, there was nothin' to stop me anymore." He swiped his eyes with the back of his hand. I was shocked to see tears in his eyes. "She was an angel. Too good for this world. Can't figure out why God took her from me. He knew what was gonna happen. What I was gonna do."

"It's not up to you to decide who lives or who dies."

"Maybe not, but I'm doin' it anyway." He shook his head. "I don't want you to think I enjoy killin'. I don't. After I do it, I feel real bad. Bein' honest about it, I just can't help myself. It's somethin' I gotta do. Like breathin'."

I was trying to keep him talking, but it was still more than an hour before Noah was due home. There was no way I could keep him going that long.

"What about Mary Carson? She was my friend. You had no right—"

My comment about Mary seemed to infuriate him. Bud stood up and started for the couch, his face a mask of anger, his hands reaching for me. "About Mary Carson. She—"

Before he had a chance to finish his sentence, I heard a loud bang and Bud crumpled to the floor in front of the fireplace. I screamed and tried to get off the couch, but I just fell back again.

"Callie, are you okay?" Roger Carson came around the side of the couch, a gun in his hand.

"Oh, Roger!" was all I could manage to get out before darkness overwhelmed me.

CHAPTER 22

I regained consciousness to find Roger sitting beside me on the couch, wiping my face with a damp rag.

"Feeling better?" he asked.

For some reason, I couldn't catch my breath. I struggled to inhale, but every time I tried, it hurt.

"Just calm down, Callie," Roger said. "You're having a panic attack. You've got to slow down your breathing and relax. Bud can't hurt you now. I called the sheriff from my car, and he's on the way."

I grabbed Roger's hand, not caring about protocol or decorum. "Thank you," I said breathlessly. "Thank you so much."

"Shh. You've got to settle down."

I nodded and let go of his hand. As I focused on my breathing, it began to slow down. Roger kept wiping my face, and I realized I was covered with sweat. After a few minutes, I felt better.

"I-I'd like to sit up," I said.

Roger helped me readjust myself on the couch. At least now I was upright and didn't feel quite so vulnerable. He handed me a glass of water, which I drank gratefully.

"I'm really tired of passing out," I said, my voice shaking. "It's getting very inconvenient."

Roger smiled. "If it helps, I almost fainted myself when I saw Bud through the window."

"Why did you come back?"

He shook his head. "I was on my way back to the office when it hit me. The red cedar trees. We kept that quiet. Only the murderer would have known about it."

"But why did you shoot him?" I asked after I handed him back the glass.

"He was going to kill you," he replied, frowning. "I didn't think reasoning with him was going to work."

"But he didn't have a gun."

"Bud didn't shoot those women, Callie. He strangled them, and he was getting ready to do the same to you."

I nodded, but it still bothered me. If Roger had warned him, maybe Bud would have stopped. Even though he was an evil man, leaving him alive would have given him a chance to change. To repent and get right with God. At first, I was just grateful to be alive, but now I felt the weight of Bud's death on my heart. And suddenly I remembered John.

"Oh, Roger!" I cried. "Bud did something to John Lapp. I don't know if he's still alive."

Roger frowned. "I saw the buggy tied up on the side of the house, but I assumed it was Noah's."

I shook my head. "Lizzie and Noah don't drive a buggy anymore. And their horses are in the barn."

"Do you have any idea where John might be?"

"No, but Bud said if he wasn't dead already, he would be soon. Oh, Roger. Please find him."

He stood up. "You keep still. I'll look and be right back."

I nodded. As he walked away, I prayed for John. Prayed that he would be all right. As I spoke to God, I couldn't get the look of surprise on Bud's face out of my mind. And I couldn't look at his crumpled body lying by the fireplace. Somehow I knew it would haunt me the rest of my life.

After a few minutes, I heard the back door to the kitchen open. And then the door to the bedroom where I'd slept. Had he found John? Was he alive? It seemed like forever before Roger came back into the room. He looked worried.

"I brought him in, but he's in bad shape. I put him in the back bedroom. I've got to get on the radio and call for an ambulance. He's—"

Before Roger had a chance to say anything else, the front door flew open. Sheriff Timmons stood there with his gun drawn.

"It's okay, Brodie," Roger said. "Bud's dead. He tried to kill Callie, and I had to shoot him."

I expected the sheriff to put his gun away, but he didn't. In fact, he didn't move. Just kept his gun trained on Roger.

"Sheriff," I said, "everything's okay. You can put your gun away."

Two people came in the door behind Sheriff Timmons. Noah and Levi. Their expressions frightened me.

"Take your gun out of its holster, Roger," the sheriff said grimly. "Hold it by the barrel with your index finger and thumb, put it on the floor, and kick it toward me."

"But, Sheriff—"

"Now, Roger."

The sheriff's authoritative tone made me jump. "I don't understand," I said. "What's—"

"The coroner's report came back. Mary wasn't killed by

strangulation. It was a blow to the head. She was strangled after she was already dead. Her death was made to look similar to the other killings. You did it, Roger. You killed her."

Roger's face went slack, and he started to say something, but the sheriff interrupted him.

"There's no use denying it. I talked to your neighbor about an hour ago. She was outside with her dog the night Mary died. She heard the fight, and she saw you leave early the next morning. After you put something large in the trunk of your car. I'm sure a good forensics investigation will turn up the evidence we need."

I swung around to gaze at Roger, shocked by what the sheriff had said. "Roger, what is he talking about? I don't understand." Suddenly, I remembered Roger's torn pocket. "Your pocket. Mary didn't fix it because she was already dead. She never would have let you out of the house like that."

"I . . . I didn't—"

"Yes, you did," Timmons said. "It's over, Roger. Just give me your gun."

Roger slowly slid his gun out of its holster, but instead of obeying the sheriff's instructions, he raised the barrel until it was pointed straight at me.

"What . . . what are you doing?" My voice was barely a squeak. Could this really be happening? I'd thought I was finally safe.

Although Roger's gun was pointed at me, his gaze was trained on the sheriff. "It was an accident. Mary didn't want me to work for you. Mennonite tradition reared its ugly head again. She said it wasn't right. Carrying a gun meant I might have to shoot someone, which was a sin. I tried to reason with her, but I lost my temper. I didn't mean to do it." Tears began streaming down his face. "She just kept going on and on about how she wanted me to quit. She was fine when I went through training, but after I became a deputy, she went crazy. Started spouting all these Scriptures about nonviolence. I've wanted to be in law enforcement all my life, and I couldn't let her stop me. She . . . she grabbed me. Tore my pocket." He stopped to wipe his face.

"So then what happened, Roger?" Levi's voice was soft and soothing. I looked back at him and saw him staring at me.

"I hit her. I didn't mean to, and I don't know why I did it. My . . . my dad used to hit me when I was a kid, and I hated it. It made me angry. It wasn't until I met Mary that I got my anger under control." His voice broke.

"Everyone loses their temper sometimes," Levi said, taking a step closer toward us. "No one's perfect."

"But . . . she fell," Roger said, as if he hadn't even heard Levi. "She fell," he repeated in a whisper.

"It was an accident, then?" Sheriff Timmons seemed to be trying to match Levi's gentle approach, but his revolver stayed trained on Roger. It was obvious they were trying to calm him before something terrible happened. I realized I was caught between two guns. A sob of fear caught in my throat.

"She hit her head on the edge of the coffee table when she fell." He shuddered. "I heard the crack. I tried to save her. I really did, but I couldn't."

"I understand," the sheriff said. "It's not murder, Roger. Turn yourself in now, and I'll help you. We'll go through this together."

Roger slowly shook his head from side to side. "They'll say I should have called an ambulance. That it might have saved her. But that wasn't true. I would have called if there was a chance—"

"But she was already dead," I said, trying to help the sheriff get Roger to put down his gun. "An ambulance wouldn't have helped her."

He appeared to be thinking about this, turning my words over in his mind. Suddenly his expression hardened, and he waved the gun back and forth. I heard Levi's voice from behind me.

"No."

I turned slowly and saw that the sheriff had lifted his gun higher and was looking down the barrel. Was he about to shoot Roger?

"Wait, Sheriff." Levi took another step closer. "We'll work this out, Roger. You haven't purposely killed anyone yet, and I don't believe you're going to. I've known you a long time. Ever since we were kids. You're not a murderer, and you're not going to shoot us. I'm sure of that."

Roger lowered his gun and sobbed. "You're right, Levi. I can't shoot you, but I can end this now." In an instant, he turned the gun around and put it under his chin.

"No!" I cried. "Roger, stop!"

He looked at me over the barrel of his gun. "I'm sorry, Callie. I really am. I wouldn't have hurt you. I hope you believe that."

Forgetting the pain in my chest and my side, I pulled myself up and looked him in the face. "Murder is murder, Roger. If you kill yourself, it's still murder."

"I . . . I can't go on. Don't ask me to."

"I am asking you to. God loves you, Roger. He'll help you through this. We all will. You can still have a life." I saw his finger move on the trigger. "What would Mary want you to do?" I said quickly. "Wouldn't she want you to live? Wouldn't she want you to face what's happened?"

He lowered the gun just a little. As I looked into his eyes, I was shocked by the anguish I saw there. I was also surprised that the sheriff hadn't made a move. Maybe he wasn't convinced that Roger meant it when he said he wouldn't shoot me. For whatever reason, I was thankful for a chance to talk to him. To try to change his mind.

"God tells us not to kill, Roger. If you do this, you're saying that God can't turn this situation around. That He can't bring good out of it. But He can. Remember King David? He had a man killed, and it wasn't an accident. Yet God forgave David and blessed him. He called David a man after His own heart. If God can love David and bless Him, why can't He do the same for you?"

The gun barrel was lowered a few more inches.

"But I'll go to prison."

"Yes, you will," the sheriff said from behind me. "But not for as long as you would have for willful first-degree murder."

"But what if they don't believe me?" I could tell by the tone of his voice that we were getting through to him.

"People around here will testify to the kind of man you are," I said. I looked deeply into his eyes and held out my hand, trying to ignore the stabbing pain that racked my body. "Please, Roger. Don't do this to yourself and don't do it to us. Do you know how much it would hurt us to watch you die? It's something I would never forget. Never get over. You have the chance to make a good decision after several bad ones. Do the right thing now."

Slowly Roger placed the gun into my hand. I gripped it

313

tightly, pulled it away, and carefully placed it onto the couch behind me. Instantly, Levi scooped me up into his arms while Sheriff Timmons retrieved the gun and moved it away from us. Then he took hold of Roger, pulled his arms back, and placed handcuffs on him.

"Callie," Levi said, tears in his eyes, "if anything had happened to you, I don't know what I would have done." He kept me sheltered in his arms until the sheriff led Roger out of the house. Three or four black cars with sirens blaring pulled up into the yard all at the same time. Men ran into the house, looked at Bud's body, and then ran to the back of the house to check on John. In the midst of all the commotion, Levi and I just clung to each other and cried.

CHAPTER 23

"How are you feeling this evening?"

After staying with Lizzie and Noah for almost three weeks, I finally moved back to my own apartment. My mother came to stay with me until I was ready to be on my own. After another two weeks with Mother, I was getting around pretty well.

"Much better now that I've stopped taking those pain pills. Aspirin seems to be doing the trick, and I'm not so jumpy."

"I'm glad."

We were working on our relationship, but there was still a measure of forced politeness between us. We'd talked several times, and things were improving. Realistically, we had to face the fact that we were strangers. There was no way to go back and reestablish a bond that was long gone. All we could do was try to build a new one.

Mother and I ate dinner, but instead of taking our dishes downstairs the way she usually did, she sat at the table, looking nervous, and drumming her fingers on the tabletop.

"Is something wrong, Mother?" I asked finally.

She blinked rapidly, took a deep breath, and started to say something when heavy steps on the stairs stopped her. I looked over and saw Levi come into the living room.

"Have you told her?" he asked my mother.

She shook her head.

"Told me what?"

Levi came over and sat down in a chair across from us. The past few weeks had been rough. After talking through many issues, Levi and I had reached a conclusion about our lives together. Finally, we'd come to a very painful decision. One we hadn't told our friends yet. Or my mother. A choice we weren't sure they would understand.

"Your mother has something to tell you," Levi said solemnly. "I've been waiting quite a while for her to share this. She's been afraid, but she's ready tonight, aren't you Esther?"

Mother didn't look as confident as Levi sounded.

"Wait a minute. Does this have anything to do with what was said during counseling that had to do with the murders?" To be honest, with everything that had happened, I'd forgotten all about Levi's odd assertion.

"That's exactly what I'm talking about. You know, the reason you and Lizzie initially focused on poor John Lapp as a serial killer." Levi shook his head. "Poor John. He only came by to complain about a couple of the hymns we selected the Sunday before. They were too progressive for him."

I smiled. "That sounds like John. You know, Lizzie almost had Sheriff Timmons convinced he might be the killer. Then John went to visit his cousin who lives near Topeka for a few days. That really made him look guilty." I shook my head. "Well, it made sense at the time." I frowned at my mother. "So what is it you want to tell me?" I was surprised to see a look of fear on her face. "What in the world is it, Mother?"

She put her hands over her face for a moment and took a deep breath. Then she lowered her hands and stared at me with tears in her eyes. "Callie, when I got here, I found out about your engagement. I knew you'd never come back to Missouri with me unless I could find a way to break up you and Levi. I hadn't yet learned what a good man Levi is."

"Break us up? I don't understand."

"I . . . I found Levi's book in a pew at the church. You know, the one about the Anabaptist martyrs. For some reason I took it. At first I planned to return it to him, but then . . . I don't know. I guess I kept it out of spite. On Monday morning I was on my way into town when I spotted something odd in the trees by the road. I got out to see what it was and realized it was a body. I was horrified and got back in my buggy, planning to ride into town and get help. But before I drove away, something came over me, and I grabbed that book from under my seat and put it in that poor girl's hands. I guess I thought if Levi was suspected of having something to do with her death, it would ruin your chances of being together. You'd gladly leave town with me when I told you who I was." She sobbed and shook her head. "I can't explain what I was thinking. It was so wrong.

"Once I got to town, I was so ashamed of what I'd done, I wanted to go back and fix it. But Mercy Eberly found the body before I could make things right. The only thing I could think to do was to talk to Levi. So I went to him and confessed." She dabbed at her wet eyes with her fingertips. "He was so kind. So understanding. I realized what a wonderful man he is, and how lucky you are to have him in your life. I was terrified that if you knew what I'd done, we'd never be reconciled. I begged Levi to wait until things settled down, until I could find the courage to tell you the truth."

"So you let him come under suspicion?" I couldn't keep the

anger out of my voice. "I thought you said you were a Christian. What kind of Christian would do something like that?"

"Wait a minute, Callie," Levi said. "She could have stayed silent, but she didn't. And by then, I knew that the authorities didn't actually suspect me. I told your mother it was okay to wait. As long as it didn't put anyone else in danger."

"But what about the investigation?" I asked. "The KBI needs to know the truth." I glared at my mother. "You need to go to the authorities and tell them what you've done."

"Esther and I already met with the sheriff," Levi said. "The KBI believes Bud got the book at some point when he was in town and put it with the body for an unknown reason. Maybe to divert suspicion from himself. Brodie suggested we just leave things alone. Now that the KBI knows Bud was the man they were looking for, they're not concerned about the book anyway. As far as they're concerned, their serial-killer case is closed."

I frowned at him. "I don't know . . ."

Levi looked over at my mother, whose head was down. She wouldn't look at me. "Brodie told your mother that if the question ever came up, he'd be forced to tell the truth. She accepted that. He also asked her to stay in the area until everything was finally settled with Roger. Just in case."

Roger had been charged with negligent homicide in Mary's death. Authorities were also looking into Bud's shooting, not convinced he was killed to protect me. Instead, they believed Roger shot Bud to keep him from telling anyone he wasn't responsible for Mary's death. I had no idea what the truth was, and to be honest, I didn't want to know.

Roger was in jail, awaiting trial and possible further charges. Levi had been to visit him several times. Even Mary's parents went to see him, letting him know they'd forgiven him. It was the Mennonite way to return good for evil. However, it would take me some time to face him—if I ever did.

"If I need to admit to what I did in court, I will," Mother said tearfully. "I'm so sorry. I've been wrong. About everything. I don't know how many times I can ask you to forgive me."

Having endured my father's manipulation and verbal abuse by creating a fantasy world, I could understand a lot of the reasons my mother had acted out of her fear. Even though I was still angry about her actions, I reached for her hand.

"It's okay," I said. "We'll find a way to work through this."

"Th-thank you, Callie," she said. "I'm trying hard to be the mother you should have had for all these years."

"Mother, I've already forgiven you. But no more lies. No more hiding the truth from me. We need to be honest with each other if we're ever going to let go of what's behind and cherish what we have now."

She nodded, and for the first time since we'd sat down, she smiled. "I know it may take us some time, but I believe we can become friends. Maybe more."

"You're my mother, and you always will be. But we'll work on the friendship part too."

We could hear someone coming up the stairs. Noah stuck his head in the room and nodded at his brother. "The regular customers are gone, and everyone you invited is here."

Levi nodded at him. "Okay. We're on the way down."

Mother looked confused. "I'm sorry. I didn't know you were planning something."

"You're part of it, Mother," I said. "Why don't you come with us, and we'll explain."

Although she looked puzzled, she got up and followed us down the stairs. As we entered the dining room, we found friends and family seated around the tables. Lizzie had served everyone coffee and tea.

As I looked around the room, I realized how much Kingdom had been altered by recent events. It seemed as if every life had been touched in some way by the evil committed by two men.

I caught Lizzie's eye and smiled at her. Lizzie and Noah had come to me after the incident at their house, expressing remorse for leaving me alone with Bud. They'd felt guilty for not realizing he was dangerous and asked for my forgiveness. But Bud had fooled all of us. And so had Roger. There was nothing to forgive, and I told them so. In truth, they'd saved my life in more ways than one. I was so grateful for them.

Ruby Wittenbauer sat at their table, she and Charity giggling together. Lizzie and Noah had taken Ruby in to live with them after the church told Elmer and Dorcas they had to give her up or they'd lose any future assistance. They couldn't get Ruby out of the house fast enough. It comforted me to know that Ruby would have a wonderful life and Charity would have a sister.

All the people we'd asked to attend were there, except John Lapp. He was still recovering from his injuries. The day Bud died, John had simply stopped by to check on me after hearing I'd been in the hospital. A nice gesture that went horribly wrong. I hoped his being beaten and left for dead wouldn't curb his desire to be neighborly in the future. We never told him he'd been suspected of being a serial killer, and we had no intention of doing so. There are some things that are better left unsaid.

John's near-death experience did produce one good result. He took his copy of the Mennonite martyrs book to the school and donated it. Seems he originally denied he had it because he didn't want to turn loose of it. His actions had made us suspect him of something much worse than stinginess.

I looked over at Levi. In the past week, his whole demeanor had changed. The carefree young man I'd fallen in love with was back. "I've been so frustrated," he'd told me after Bud was arrested. "I'm sorry I wasn't more open with you from the beginning. I wasn't completely certain what I wanted to do. Now I know I just want to minister to people, but without being surrounded by rules and people telling me every move to make."

His confession freed me to tell him some things that I found difficult to say. An honest look into my heart had brought me to some painful conclusions. Tonight, those conclusions were coming to a head.

I led Mother over to a table and sat her down next to Hope, Ebbie, and Samuel. Hope's look of encouragement fortified me, and I prayed she'd still feel positive after Levi and I made our announcement.

Looking around the room, I saw other people who meant a great deal to me. Dottie Hostettler smiled at me. Levi's parents were the only people who knew what we were getting ready to say. Ruth Fisher and her daughter sat with Matthew and Anna Engel. Anna's sweet smile made me feel braver. Aaron and the elders were together at another table. Lizzie sat down next to Noah, Leah, and Brodie Timmons. Levi and I knew that what we had to tell our friends and family would be difficult for them to receive. I took a seat at an empty table, since Levi would be the one addressing them first. He walked to the center of the room.

"Thank you all for coming here tonight," he said.

I could hear the nervousness in his voice and prayed silently that God would give him courage.

"The past few weeks have been very difficult for all of us. Seeing Kingdom under a shadow of evil made us feel vulnerable. Dealing with death was hard, but enduring the death of someone we cared for was particularly difficult. I pray you all will surround Mary's parents with love and see to their needs." He cleared his throat and stared down at the floor. "I'm also going to ask you to keep Roger Carson in your prayers. Roger is a fellow believer who made a terrible mistake." He looked up and met my mother's eyes. "Sometimes Christians make mistakes. Bad ones. But we have an Intercessor in heaven who defends us when the devil comes before the throne to accuse us of sin. That Intercessor loves Roger and has already forgiven him. I pray you will do the same. And if any of you want to know how to send him a letter or if you'd like to visit him, please see me or Callie after we're done here. We'll give you the information."

I noticed several people nodding at Levi's pronouncement. I was particularly surprised to see Matthew's head bobbing up and down.

Levi cleared his throat again and looked my way. I gave him an encouraging smile, wishing I could make what was coming easier for him. But there was no way I could.

"Callie and I have invited you all here tonight because you are important in our lives. What I'm getting ready to tell you will be repeated in church this Sunday, but we felt we should tell you first, rather than letting you find out with everyone else." He paused for a moment, struggling with his emotions. "After searching our hearts and praying fervently, Callie and I have decided . . ." He paused and took a deep breath. I could

322

feel my heart beat so hard I wondered if others could hear it. "Callie and I have decided to leave Kingdom."

Several gasps erupted around the room.

Lizzie's was one of them. "Leave Kingdom?" she said. "I . . . I don't understand."

Levi shook his head. "Please understand that we love you all. It has nothing to do with you. Any of you. But for personal reasons, we feel we must make this decision. I've accepted the position of assistant pastor at a small church in Newton, Kansas. I'll be living in an apartment at the church, and Callie will be living with the pastor and his wife until we're married. The church has a small house we'll move into after the wedding."

"That doesn't explain why you're leaving," Noah said.

It had been particularly hard for Levi to keep our plans from his brother, and I'd had an awful time not blurting out the truth to Lizzie. But in the end, we'd decided to wait and tell everyone at once.

"For me," Levi said slowly, "it's something that's been building for a long time. I've had a growing desire to minister to people in a . . . a different way. Don't misunderstand me, please. I love our church, and I love our traditions. Well, most of them. But I want to find out what else is out there. What it would be like to serve God with a little more freedom than we have now."

"Are you saying you don't agree with the tenets of our church?" Matthew asked.

"I agree with most of them, Matthew," he said. "The problem is, I'm not sure in my heart I agree with all of them. Maybe after working in another environment for a while, I'll decide we're doing everything right. But I have to find out.

My beliefs should be mine. Not formed because it's the only thing I've ever been taught." He looked at his mother. "Mom, you've brought me up in the nurture and admonition of the Lord. I love Him because of what you taught me and how you've lived. But you made the decision, along with Dad, to come here and live this life in Kingdom. I've never had the chance to make the same choice, and I want to do it now. I pray you'll understand."

Dottie nodded at him. "I do, Son. I will miss you, but I want you to be happy. You and Callie. Your stepfather and I believe you're making the right decision."

"My mother and Marvin knew about this before tonight," Levi explained to the small crowd. "Marvin is the one who contacted his pastor friend in Newton about the pastoral position."

"To be honest, I was afraid you were going to tell us that you weren't getting married," Leah said.

Levi smiled at her. "For a while, we weren't sure about that either. But only briefly. Callie and I love each other very much. We plan to spend the rest of our lives together."

"What about Callie?" Lizzie said. "Is she leaving just because you are?"

I stood up. "No, Lizzie. You know better than almost anyone that I've been living my life in the shadow of my father for a long time." I shook my head. "Maybe that's not fair. I guess it's more accurate to say that I've been living in the shadows I created myself." I smiled at her. "You're the one who helped me to see the truth. You spent time out in the world, and you told me you're glad you did because it made you who you are today. You *chose* Kingdom, and you're at peace with that decision. But I've never chosen anything in my life. Except to marry Levi. Living in the world will help me figure out who I am and what I want out of life." I smiled at Levi. "Right now, I only know for certain that I love God and I love Levi. With all my heart. I just need time to figure out what else I believe."

"I hope the church you are joining is Mennonite," Matthew said in a somber voice.

"Yes, it is," Levi said. "But not as conservative as ours."

Matthew scowled at him but didn't say anything else.

"I know that you think I'm too liberal already in my beliefs, Brother Matthew," Levi said with a quick grin. "I'm sure you're not surprised by this announcement."

Matthew silently studied Levi for a moment. "Pastor, you're a good man. A very good man. I believe you will be a blessing at your new church, and I hope you will come back to see us when you can."

Levi looked surprised, but he quickly recovered himself. "Why, thank you, Matthew. That means more to me than I can say."

"My dear wife and daughter remind me frequently that I am not always right in my opinions. As much as it pains me, I know they are right. I hope you will forgive me if I made things difficult for you. Please understand that I still think you are too young to pastor this church. My belief is not based on your character or spiritual integrity."

"Thank you, Brother Matthew. I appreciate that."

"When will you leave?" Ebbie asked.

"After I announce my decision at church this Sunday. I know this doesn't give you much time to find a replacement, but the elders can lead the services until you find a new pastor."

"That's so soon," Lizzie said. "Can't you wait awhile so we can get used to this? I'll need to find a new helper."

"I'm sorry, Lizzie," I said. "I really am. But the church in Newton needs Levi to start next week."

Lizzie sighed. "I don't mean to sound negative, Callie. Honestly, I know you're doing the right thing. I'm just going to miss you so much."

Several people in the room mumbled their agreement.

"And we'll miss all of you too," I said, my voice breaking. "We couldn't ask for better friends—or family. I'm particularly sad to be away from my mother after finding her again."

"It's all right," Mother said with a tremulous smile. "I totally understand." She shrugged. "I came to Kingdom to take you away. Now you're going, and I'm staying. And not because I have to."

"I don't understand. You mean you're staying here because you want to?"

She gave a short laugh. "I know you find some things in Kingdom restrictive. But if you only knew what this town was like when I lived here. It's very different now. Full of kind and forgiving people. I love it here and intend to stay . . . if it's all right with everyone."

"Esther and I plan to spend lots of time together," Ruth said with a smile. "We used to be good friends. Now we will be great friends. Ja, Esther?"

My mother nodded. "That's right. Thank you, Ruth."

"This is your home as long as you want it to be," Noah said. "We're all here for you."

"Thank you, Noah," Mother said. "But I have a question, Callie. What about your wedding? Will it be here or in Newton?"

"I honestly don't know, but wherever it is, everyone in this room is invited."

That seemed to satisfy Mother.

"Are you finished, or do you intend to drop any other bombshells on us?" Lizzie asked.

Levi and I looked at each other, and I shook my head.

"That seems to be it for now," he told Lizzie.

"Then let's break out some pie," she said with a smile. "I can't say I'm overjoyed with your decision, but I support it, so I think a little celebration is in order."

As Lizzie stood up, conversation broke out. I said a few words to Levi and went back to the kitchen. Lizzie was taking pies out of the refrigerator and putting them into the oven.

"I'm here to help," I said.

She nodded and handed me a cherry pie, which I slid into the warm oven.

"I'm sorry to surprise you tonight. I wanted to tell you from the beginning, but Levi and I decided it was best to do it this way, so no one's feelings would be hurt."

"I understand." She put the pie down on the counter and came over to me. Then she put her arms around me. "I love you, Callie. Like my own sister. If this is what's best for you, it's what I want too."

"You helped me see clearly for the first time in my life," I said. "I don't know what I would have done without your friendship. God used you to break the cloud of unreality from my life. I will never be able to repay you for that."

"Seems I outsmarted myself," Lizzie said. "I never realized I'd lose you. Maybe Noah and I will drive down to Newton for a visit after you get settled."

"You'd better. It's not that far. A little over three hours."

She sighed dramatically. "I suppose we can make the sacrifice."

I laughed. "Oh, thanks." I grabbed her arm as she started to turn away. "I know you'll find someone for my job. Maybe Ruby can help out until you do."

"You know what? That's a great idea. It will help her feel more like a part of the family. She can work with me as long as she gets her schoolwork done first."

"I know you'll change her life," I said, smiling at my dearest friend in the world. "You know, like you did with me."

The tears Lizzie had been holding back fell down her cheeks, and she hugged me again.

Levi and I spent the rest of the evening eating pie, drinking coffee, and talking to the people we loved the most.

———

The next day, after Sunday service and the second announcement of our plans, we finished packing. I'd left my dresses and my prayer covering hanging in the closet, choosing to wear the jeans and sweater Lizzie had already given me, along with quite a few other clothes she insisted I take along. But at the last second, before going down the stairs to meet Levi, I turned back and took my prayer covering from the closet. I opened my suitcase, and laid it on top of my other clothes. My fingers lingered on it for several seconds. I couldn't be sure I would ever wear it again. But then again, I wasn't certain I wouldn't. Time would tell.

I quickly checked my image in the mirror over the dresser. I liked my new shorter hairstyle. Cutting my long hair until it barely touched my shoulders helped me feel like a different person. The woman who stared back at me was a stranger, but with God's help, I would finally get to know her. I smiled at her and went downstairs to meet Levi.

The restaurant was closed and no one waited to tell us good-bye. This was what we'd requested, having already said everything we could.

"I love you," Levi said.

"I know," I replied with a smile. "It took me some time, but I have no doubts anymore."

"Good." He leaned down and gently kissed my lips. Then he picked up my suitcase and carried it out to Noah's extra truck. He'd given it to us as a gift, and we were grateful to get it.

I took a moment and stood alone inside the restaurant, looking around. So much had happened here. Good and bad. It seemed surreal to be leaving.

Prince and Dora sat near the kitchen door, as if they knew I was going away. Lizzie had promised to bring them to Newton after Levi and I were married, so my departure from them was only temporary. For a moment, the realization that I was really leaving Kingdom hit me, and I took a deep breath. But I had a profound peace about my decision. God had a path for me, and I was determined to find it.

"Good-bye," I whispered into the silence.

With that, I walked out the door of the old restaurant, took the hand of the man I loved, and together we took our first steps toward the brand-new life God had waiting for us.

Acknowledgments

To my incredible family. Thank you for your constant encouragement and support. My husband, Norman, who still makes me laugh after all these years. To my son, Danny, my daughter-in-love, Shaen, and the smartest, cutest, and most amazing baby ever born: Aidan Jackson Mehl. I love you all more than tongue can tell.

Thanks to Judy Unruh, Alexanderwohl Church Historian in Goessel, Kansas, for fielding all my dumb questions with grace and understanding. Don't know what I'd do without you!

To Doctor Andy (Dr. Andrea McCarty) for teaching me what happens when you break a rib. Glad our conversation was about a fictional situation! LOL!

To Raela Schoenherr and Sharon Asmus: Thank you for helping me through this process. You always make it better.

To the rest of the staff at Bethany House: Noelle and Debra, the wonderful design department, and all the folks at Baker, thank you. I love being a part of this incredible publishing company.

An important shout-out to all my awesome readers. Throughout the years, many of you have become dear friends. Thank you for taking me into your hearts. You encourage me, lift me up, and make me smile. And a special thank you to my "Inner Circle." You know who you are.

As always, I want to thank the most important Person in my life. Thank you, Father. I will always believe.

Nancy Mehl is the author of fifteen books and received the ACFW Mystery Book of the Year Award in 2009. She has a background in social work and is a member of ACFW. She writes from her home in Wichita, Kansas, where she lives with her husband, Norman, and their Puggle, Watson.

Don't Miss the Rest of the Road to Kingdom Series!

To learn more about Nancy Mehl and her books, visit nancymehl.com.

Lizzie Engel left her Mennonite hometown, her family, and her faith, vowing never to return. But false accusations, a stalker, and a string of anonymous threatening letters have left her with no other option but to run again—back to Kingdom, her hometown.

Inescapable
Road to Kingdom #1

Hope Kauffman has never been one to doubt her Mennonite beliefs—until now. Threatened by a mysterious outsider, the people of Kingdom find themselves divided as some inhabitants begin to question their tradition of nonviolence.

Unbreakable
Road to Kingdom #2